THE PROTECTORATE WARS:
Born Hero

S.A. Shaffer, Esq.

The Protectorate Wars : Born Hero

Cover Art by Austin Reddington
(AustinReddington.com)

Edited by Jennifer Avina

2nd edition

ISBN 9781074025434

Map Of The Fertile Plains

CONTENTS

PROLOGUE

Once, there was a land of vast wealth and power, towering mountains, and lush plains. It was a bastion of hope between the sweltering deserts and the raging ocean. Many peoples lived there and thrived in peace and prosperity, for there was plenty for all.

Berg lay to the north between the Rorand Mountains and the Central Ridge. The Bergs were a strong, proud people, famous for their iron mines and mineral wells. The People's Republic of Viörn, a great realm of rolling grasslands, lay south of the Central Ridge, north of the Southern Spires, and east of the High Peaks. Their land was immense and rich with factories and manufacturers filled with intricate, calculating people always weighing profit and loss. To the west were the Thirteen Houses of Alönia. They were a fringe people living in perpetual rain on the edge of the Fertile Plains, isolated by oceans and mountains.

For thousands of cycles these three countries lived in harmony, trading through the passage that joined the realms. In time Armstad, City of the Five Paths, filled in the pass amidst the trade and prosperity. Peoples from all three countries lived there, and they grew in wealth and sophistication.

However, greed and pride are powerful motivators. The cunning Viörns sought to extract the wealth of the proud Bergs by raising the price of their products. Berg raged, as all Viörn products were made from Bergish resources. War ensued.

Rather than be caught in the middle of two warring countries, Armstad closed the pass and announced its independence as a free nation. While anger between Viörn and Berg remained, the mountains of the Fertile Plains were too high to cross. Their tops overlooked the clouds, and the air was too thin to breathe. The war ceased for a time, but peace is short where hearts and minds are inclined toward battle. And where war strikes, it kills the hostile and the innocent alike.

Armstad was small, yet sophisticated. They possessed the finest airships in the Fertile Plains. Not long after Armstad's independence, excavators began building fortifications in the mountain cliffs. There they discovered a vast deposit of ebony iron, the rarest, and strongest of the minerals. The nation now possessed a great treasure that was as much a burden as a boon.

Viörn and Berg rejected Armstad's independence, and each claimed the city as their protectorate and Armstadi resources as their own. The defenses of Armstad, though valiant, could not resist the forces of the two great realms. Thus began The Protectorate War. The Bergish fleet—

slow and sturdy, each ship a fortress—moved in through the White-cliff Pass while the Viörn fleet, quick and agile, pushed from the Haishan Split. A great battle ensued above the helpless city of Armstad, or so was the belief of the Bergs and Viörns.

Alönia, though a peaceful people opposed to war, valued freedom and independence above all else. Armstad called for aid, and the young men of Alönia answered. The Assembly voted, the armada gathered, brave men volunteered, and Admiral David Ike was tasked with confronting Berg and Viörn, peaceably if possible, violently if necessary.

As his airship, the Intrepid, soared through the mists, Admiral Ike stood at its prow, hands clasped behind his back. His aeronauts bustled about him, loading guns and preparing the airship for war. All were silent as the morning breeze.

The Intrepid steamed away at three thousand feet, leading the airships of a few dozen fleet groups through the gulf pass in a cloud bank—as much of the Alönian might as could be mustered in three days' time. It was little more than half of the Bergish fleet population, let alone the Viörn gunships swarming thick as tuber flies in harvest. Here, Admiral Ike struggled with a question as he watched the clouds pass around his airship. Should he make an attempt at peace before firing on the enemy? If he did, and peace was not possible, he would give up his greatest advantage...surprise.

Nobody knew the Alönians had joined the war, and if they could surprise their enemies, they might even be able to best them.

Admiral Ike knew this. Already his airships arrayed themselves to maximize their effectiveness. If he was going to fight a war, he was going to win, and Almighty forgive him, he wasn't about to fight fair. As they drew closer to Armstad, Admiral Ike could hear the sounds of battle penetrating the cloud bank. His dark mustache twitched in expectation of action. His boatswain called the Intrepid to action; his gunners took their chairs, swiveling the airdestroyer's great revolvers in one last check. Aeronauts manned flak cannons and carousels across all the airships' decks.

Timing was everything, and the time was drawing near. Admiral Ike sniffed the air as his lieutenant calmed the men with boasting words. It smelled of ash. Indeed, the white cloud looked tainted and glowed with whatever fire lay on the other side of the haze. Admiral Ike would give them one chance to surrender—one shot across the bow before he let loose the fires of Hades—but that was all the surprise he was willing to forfeit.

The Intrepid burst from the mists and soared into the ashy skies of Armstad. The beautiful city burned, and the sight of it made Admiral Ike sick. He wasn't sure which side had done the deed. Even to this day it is still unknown who firebombed Armstad, but it did not matter to Admiral Ike.

He looked upon the inferno, his eyes aglow with flame and rage, fueled by the burning homes of the innocent. He nodded at his lieutenant, and the unspoken command passed between them, then the lad gave the order for a full attack. There would be no warning shot. The Intrepid lurched forward to attack speed, leading the charge of the other airdestroyers.

The Viörn airships were completely surprised, never suspecting an attack at their rear where their supply orbitals lay unprotected. Bergish airships were slow and ponderous, and there was no way their flying fortresses could slip behind the Viörn picket unnoticed. But these were not Bergish airships, nor were they Bergish guns that blasted away at their unprotected flank.

The Viörn armada only had two types of craft: gunship and supply orbital. The diamond-shaped gunships were more massive than the Alönian skiff, carrying a crew of ten. They would dive-bomb their opponents, peppering them with carousel and chain-gun fire, before loosing torpedoes and clearing the field for the next wave of their compatriots. Supply orbitals, or mother ships, boasted crews of thousands scurrying about on half a dozen docking rings all orbiting one central balloon. Each orbital could resupply an entire wave of gunships in a matter of minutes. The Viörn attack plan was predictable. Wave upon wave of the agile gunships race ahead of their mother ships, pouring fire into the enemy, only to return and refuel in perfect synchronization. Perfect, predictable, and exploitable by any such admiral as cunning as David Ike.

Admiral Ike gritted his teeth as he watched the first volley of unchallenged fire smash into the rear orbitals. He'd tasked his airships to target those in the middle of resupply first, and they had done well. Two succumbed before the Intrepid's revolvers could even empty their chambered rounds. Each downed orbital meant no resupply for an entire wave of gunships, and once those had spent their torpedoes, it was only a matter of time before they exhausted their fuel and small arms doing little more than scratching the paint on Admiral Ike's heavy warships.

The Alönian destroyers were at knife range now, blasting massive orbital chunks into the air with each shot. The lightly armed orbitals could only absorb the fire and rain ash and aeronauts on the city below. As the guns reloaded and fired for the third time, the Intrepid's boatswain pointed out an orbital in the middle of resupply.

Admiral Ike motioned to his lieutenant, and the Intrepid flashed signal lights. The airship veered to the right, charging the resupplying orbital, trailed by six of its sister ships. They had but a matter of seconds before the mother ship resupplied and released its unruly brood— enough torpedoes to pulverize a full quarter of his airdestroyers. The Intrepid rumbled as its revolvers did their work, firing incendiary rounds in between the mother ship's docking rings at the vulnerable orbital balloon. But as the orbital's decking groaned, two dozen gunships released and raced toward the seven attacking vessels. Thus far, the Alönians had dealt considerable damage to the Viörns while taking few, if any, casualties. But Admiral Ike knew that before the day was through, bodies of friend and foe would litter the streets of Armstad below.

Admiral Ike's lieutenant gave the order, and the warships' small arms readied to do their part. He had prepared for this eventuality. During the harried flight across the gulf, the Admiral had issued an order to all his airships to arm and secure every chain-gun and small arm to their airships. If his airdestroyers had to fight gunships without close support from their skiff-carriers, they needed to fill the air with as many bullets as possible.

Chain-guns howled, and carousels barked as the Viörn gunships flew closer. Some fell in flames, some didn't. But as they neared torpedo range, not a single torpedo launched. There hadn't been time to arm them. This… was a Viörn suicide run.

The collision bell rang as eight of the original twenty-four gunships charged Admiral Ike and his escort ships. Six got through, smashing into the Reliant and Voxil and sending them plummeting to the ground as burning wrecks. Admiral Ike said a silent prayer for the aeronauts, but their sacrifice was not in vain. All the while, true to their orders, the revolver gunners pounded away at the Viörn orbital, ignoring all else around them. Seconds later, the balloon roiled in flames and broke apart in a hiss, dragging man and gunship to the ground. The orbitals were gone, all twenty-two and the tens of thousands of men that had manned them.

Admiral Ike wasn't without loss, though. A handful of airdestroyers, with all hands lost, littered the countryside, and as many more heeling at the outskirts of the battle. But they weren't done yet. More than twelve waves of gunships lay between the Alönians and the entire Bergish fleet, still duking it out with the flying fortresses. The bill from the butcher had yet to arrive.

The lieutenant sounded a few bells and flashed signals to the other airships. The mass of airdestroyers assembled into a double-layered, half-moon formation and advanced. The remaining Viörn gunships, caught between the Alönian line and the Bergish super-fortresses, whirled around in chaos. Some tried for suicide runs, some tried to escape, few found success. With no chance for resupply and no torpedoes, the gunships lit up the early-morning sky as fire from two sides ripped them to pieces.

Then one of the airdestroyers beside the Intrepid burst into flames and dove toward the still-burning city below. The Bergs, now finished with the Viörns, turned their cursed focus-lens on the Alönians, and silent death struck as airships spontaneously combusted. Admiral Ike held up a few fingers, and as if a part of some airshow, the Alönian line split into sporadic maneuvers.

The Bergish airships and tactics were as different from the Viörns as their culture. The mass of Bergish super-fortresses carried immense firepower, both long and short-range, yet they were slow and cumbersome. Each boasted thick armor that surrounded balloon and ship alike. Few of the super-fortresses carried the focus-lens array, but those that did were formidable. Only the Bergish armada knew the secret of the weapon, though rumor had it that the device projects its silent death from some rare crystal discovered deep in the Bergish mines.

As Admiral Ike neared the Bergish blockade, his brave airships rained fire down upon them, but they were no match for the super-fortresses, brave airships or not. Each Bergish ship could shrug off an attack from ten destroyers firing in unison, which is why Admiral Ike had divided his forces before the battle ever began. He separated his skiff-carriers from the fleet groups and left them hiding in the cloud bank. At this very moment, they floated unseen just behind the Bergish picket. A maelstrom of skiffs, each armed with a single torpedo, poured from the clouds like rain in a Southern Ocean storm.

Alönian skiffs are a novelty in the Fertile Plains. A single pilot defends himself with duel stationary chain-guns. While they carry less firepower than Viörn gunships—and are far less armored—nothing in the skies can match their speed. The brunt of the Bergish firepower and focus faced the wrong direction, much as the Viörns had in the first engagement. Half of the Bergish fortresses fell from the sky as Alönian pilots released well-aimed torpedoes at point-blank range, bursting the fortress boilers and melting the structures from the inside out. The remaining fortresses clustered together, trapped amid the resupplying skiffs, the relentless airdestroyer guns, and the Rorand Mountains.

Admiral Ike sighed as he ordered his airships to advance. He knew the Bergish commander—Admiral Vojh Nović. They had met once before, and he was as Bergish as they came—proud and unrelenting. There would be no surrender.

As in the past, so it was on this day that Bergish pride proved their downfall. Admiral Ike removed his hat as he watched. Admiral Nović, rather than admit defeat, superheated his flying fortresses and attempted to cross the Rorand Mountains. Even as he watched it happen, Admiral Ike knew that the remaining super-fortresses would not be seen or heard from again. Their wreckage and the countless souls they carried would be lost along the mountain peaks. When Admiral Ike looked back at his men, every single aeronaut gazed in wonder at him and at the great victory they had just witnessed. His face grim, the Admiral said words that would echo through Alönian history.

"A fine job, my fellow Alönians, as fine as ever there was. Make safe the city. Assist in any way you can. Collect our wounded … and the dead."

The aeronauts set to their tasks, and Admiral Ike looked back across the Armstad valley, and the massacre he had wrought, grateful his men had forgone the usual cheering. A single tear carved a furrow on his dusty cheek. So much death—would it ever wash off?

Against all odds Alönia proved victorious in the Protectorate War, establishing themselves as the supreme power in the fertile plains. Armstad was free to profit from their unearthed treasures, not as a protectorate, but as an independent country. Trade resumed between the realms as peace settled upon the Fertile Plains. For so long as the fleets of Alönia remained strong, Berg and Viörn would remain passive.

"This is the end of the Protectorate War program. Up next, the history of the Outland Syndicates. Stay tuned for—"

A woman stopped the program, and the steam projector issued one last puff before its lights flickered out.

"No, Mommy. Play the next program," said a little boy from under his covers. He pushed out his lower lip, but after the mother glanced at him, he quickly sucked it back in.

"One program is quite enough before bed," the mother said while brushing her hair. "No complaints."

The boy nodded sheepishly and twisted the tassels on the edge of his blanket. "Mommy," he asked.

"Yes, dear?" she replied, finishing her combing and resting her hand in her lap.

"Why did the Berg and Viörn want to take the ebony iron from Armstad?" The boy pinched his brow in contemplation. "Why couldn't they leave them alone? Armstad is nice. They would have shared."

His mother fixed deep brown eyes on the boy as she thought. "Greed is a powerful force that can make people envious of others. Berg and Viörn didn't want to share the ebony iron, they wanted it all for themselves."

"They hurt a lot of people, didn't they?" the boy said.

"Many, many people," the mother replied, running a hand through the boy's hair.

"Is that why father fights them?" the boy asked.

The mother smiled. "Father doesn't fight them, he… watches them and makes sure they aren't trying to start another Protectorate War."

"If they do, I want to fight with Father!" the boy exclaimed.

The mother smiled, but it did not reach her eyes. A moment later, the expression was gone and replaced with a mischievous smile. The boy squirmed, knowing what was coming, but he could not escape the confines of his covers in time.

He squealed with laughter as his mother tickled him. Such was his state that he hardly had time to inhale between his shrieks.

"Who's making all this racket?" a tall gentleman asked with mock irritation as he strode into the room. He wore an unbuttoned military uniform, and his boot heels thumped the floor with every step.

"Father! You're home!" the boy yelled as he jumped from the bed into the man's outstretched arms.

The man laughed and spun in a circle.

"I had to come back. Mommy needs me," the father said conspiratorially.

"That she does," the mother said. She stood and kissed her husband. "Welcome home, darling."

"You missed it, Father," cried the boy. "We just finished a program on the Protectorate War."

"Oh, and did you see Admiral Ike fly his airships and save the Fertile Plains?"

The man lifted the boy to his shoulders, racing around the room as an airship in flight. The boy cried with delight at every twist and turn. The mother raised her hands twice, a concerned look on her face, but restrained herself. Finally, the man guided the boy back onto the bed with all the gentleness of a loving parent.

"Alright, then, time for bed," he said, as he pulled

back the covers. The boy climbed in, and his father kissed his forehead and stood, waiting for his wife. The young mother fished a toy from under the covers and tucked the boy in.

"When I grow up," the boy said softly, "I want to be just like Admiral Ike."

"I have no doubt that you will, Son," the father said. "You have a hero's name, and the heart to back it up."

The mother bent over the boy and kissed him several times before she nuzzled his nose. "Sleep well, my little David," she whispered. Then she joined her husband.

Together they switched off the light and closed the bedroom door. The boy shut his eyes and drifted off to sleep, likely dreaming of a daring young aeronaut fighting to defend the Houselands.

Chapter One

THE SURPRISE MOTION

David hobbled for all he was worth. It was the first day of the rest of his life, the fifty-second day of Úoi Season, and he was not about to be late. He limped through the mugginess of the dark cobbled streets, mechanical arm slanting his shoulders and weak leg slowing his progress. Stone and steel structures shadowed the alley as he sloshed through the myriad of puddles. Steam fluttered his sandy hair as it puffed out from different exhaust ports while the under-city factories yawned, welcoming the start of the workday. He rounded the last building in the industrial district of Capital City, and the bright morning sunlight prickled his eyes in a rare display of Alönian blue sky—a good omen. He squinted up toward the Capital Orbital and smiled.

The orbital filled a good portion of the small blue patch. Rainbows and sunbeams accented the construct as it hung motionless. Four massive balloons held it aloft, each emblazoned with a thirteen-pointed golden star, the symbol of the Thirteen Houses of Alönia, though David couldn't make out the points from so far away. The rest of the orbital's structure looked like glittering crystal in the sunlight, with polished brass and glass windows catching the light.

A variety of airships dipped in and out of the clouds. Old galleons drifted along at a lazy pace, looking like ancient seafaring ships of war. Some of these vessels were upwards of a hundred cycles old, with real wooden hulls and oversized balloons. There were others too: great construction blimps, their hulking bulk looking small next to the Capital Orbital while carrying massive chunks of the new tower being built on the opposite side of the city. Warships glided along in guard patrol around the Houselands' capital, swaying beneath their armored balloons, mounted revolvers and chemical throwers pointing out of their decks at odd angles. Tiny skiffs zoomed in the larger ships' wakes, ferrying people to and from ship, orbital, and city. The sky hissed with activity.

David let out a long sigh. Four cycles had passed since he'd been in the sky. Four long cycles of shoveling sludge, cleaning muck, and eating gruel. Finally! He had finally made it. Finally he could live in comfort. Finally he could provide for his mother the way she deserved. Finally he could leave the commons and frequent the clouds. If only his father could see him now, Jeshua rest his soul.

"I'm doing it, Father," David whispered as he walked out from the buildings amidst the bustling people. "I'm finally honoring your memory. I'll do you proud."

David had been awake for three hours, two of them in the dark. From his apartment he'd boarded the nearest public train to the only steam transportation hub in all of House Braxton. He had then traveled by airship across the Easterly River to the outskirts of Capital City. He couldn't afford to go any farther by airship, at least not right now, but that was all about to change. From the city outskirts, he took another public train to the industrial district. Now, finally, he could board a public sky-liner direct to Capital Orbital, free of cost.

David moved through the crowds to the transportation tower. Together they bunched into lines and packed into steam shafts that rocketed them to the top of the facility. Massive sky-liners with rotating turbofans affixed to their sides sat anchored at the tower's sides. They were the newer model, cockpit and cargo hold built directly into the balloon instead of cabled beneath. Portholes dotted the lower portion of the balloon, and a windscreen gleamed at the bow. As David waited on the roof of the facility, one of the massive ships weighed anchor and drifted away from the tower. After a few seconds the turbofans whirled to life, and the ship's lazy drift transformed into a controlled ascent.

David gaped at the spectacle. *What it must be like to captain those behemoths in defiance of gravity …*

But as he dawdled, he let a gap form in the line, and another wayfarer prodded him in the back. "Move on now. We don't got all day."

"Right, sorry," David apologized, putting on his most earnest smile.

But the other traveler only grunted as he checked his pocket watch.

As David neared the front of the line to board his airship, another sky-liner drifted in and filled the space left by the departing one. The ship slid into dock without so much as bumping the tower, lowering four cargo doors like ramps for its passengers.

"Well done," David said in a quiet voice.

But then he noticed he'd let a gap form again, and he hurried forward. No one else seemed to even notice the pilot's skill anyway, let alone care.

As he stepped into the sky-liner, he felt the floor beneath him sway ever so slightly as more people crowded into the open bays and filtered toward various seats. David marveled at the number of people the ship could hold as hundreds packed in, filling the seats and then the spaces in between. His stomach tingled with excitement. How he'd dreamt of this day. He took a seat next to an elegant-looking lady and across from an old man who appeared to be very crotchety. Neither one seemed interested in conversation. The old man's face looked more accustomed to frowning than breathing. One young lady looked interested in talking, but when she hid her smile behind a hand, David realized she was smiling at his manner of dress and not his friendly disposition. No doubt she believed him another tramp attempting to sneak onto the orbital for a little sightseeing, only to soon be thrown out by the capital guards. David let his head hang as his cheeks flushed. He knew his suit was old, but was it really that bad?

They had been his father's clothes, one of the last things David had to remember him by. The shoulders drooped and the sleeves hung too long, ill fitting to be sure. David the father had been tall and broad shouldered. David the son—well, half of him was the same: the nonmechanical half. He had his father's face too: handsome and naturally gruff. It suited his father just fine, but on David a strong face with a broken frame looked awkward. He unconsciously flexed his mechanical hand and listened to the fingers click.

The ships swayed a little as the dockmaster cut her loose from the tower. A voice crackled over the intercom: "This is the captain. We are underway. Please remain seated for the remainder of the voyage."

David looked up in expectation as the boiler heated and the rhythmic hiss of the engine pumped away from deep inside the ship, the great beast coming alive. He wasn't near a window, but he could feel the ship list and sway as it rose into the air. As they gained altitude, David felt his ears pop. He clutched his satchel to his chest—he alone knowing its value.

The trip was shorter than he expected, and within ten minutes they slid up against the orbital dock. The travelers climbed to their feet and made their way to the bay doors. David neared the doors, and he felt his pulse quicken as bright, pure sunbeams radiated through the opening. He stepped off the sky-liner and gasped. He'd seen the orbital before from the ground, but being on it was so much more than he had imagined. What he could see of it was enormous: a golden polymer dock stretched out next to the airship and funneled everyone into a glass atrium, shaped like a half-moon. The Alönian Houselands colors of royal blue and gold trimmed the floor, railing, and ceiling. The sky-liner docked on the side of the orbital at the second level, looking like a skiff next to a man-of-war. Pure, crisp air filled David's lungs and was then exhaled in steam—not cold enough to bring a chill, but enough to redden his nose. A twenty-five-degree difference separated the ground and the orbital.

There were three levels to the orbital's structure, each winding between and around the four behemoth-class balloons. From what David could see, glass paneled every surface of the orbital, everything save the massive balloon on the right side of the dock. How much glass could there be on such a massive structure before it broke apart? Rumor had it that even some of the floors were glass, though David doubted it. What kind of idiot would stand on glass nearly a grandfathom in the air?

From here David could count every point of the Alönian star. The center of the orbital represented the Alönian Assembly Room, the place where the representatives of the Houselands gathered and conferred, proposing and striking laws.

"Come on now, move along," said the same man David had held up back at the transportation tower.

"So sorry, it's just so many new things to see," David said.

But when he looked back, the man was lost in the crowd.

David walked with the rest of the day workers to the

glass atrium at the end of the dock. The throng broke into several lines that filtered through security checkpoints. Large capital guards stood at attention and wore unfriendly expressions as they eyed the passersby. A wide bandoleer betrayed the repeaters resting on their backs, and the bulges in their doublets spoke of hand cannons resting against their hips. One of them cradled an impressive chain-gun, his thumb idly rotating the many barrels. David was so preoccupied admiring the weapon that he failed to notice the guard glaring at him. The guard's eyebrow twitched, and he nudged one of his companions. David saw the movement and put his head down, making his way to the checkpoint with purpose.

"Name," a checkpoint agent asked in a curt tone.

"David Ike."

"Of course you are," she said, rolling her eyes. "Let me have your authentication, then. Come on now. We don't—"

"I know, I know," David said as he presented his papers. "We don't have all day. So I've heard."

"Quite right," said the checkpoint agent as she squinted and held the capital pass out a good distance from her face. "Well, well, another David Ike. What a surprise. Unlike the others you might actually get noticed, in that suit anyway." She handed his papers back and motioned him along.

David sighed as he returned his papers to his satchel. It wasn't his fault that *Ike* was such a popular last name and that practically every Ike within the last sixty cycles had named their sons *David*. However, David was different than all the other lads named David Ike because he was not named after the Alönian war hero. David was named after his father. It was his father who had been named after the admiral of the Protectorate War. So in reality it wasn't so different at all. But to him it was.

After asking a young woman in a bustled dress for directions, getting lost, and asking two other gentlemen, David found his way through vibrant halls of more blue and gold and down a steam lift to the lower level. Everything looked like brass, but the weight would surely be too much for an orbital. David rapped his mechanical knuckles against a golden wall and listened to the hollow thump—polymer.

Eventually David reached a small, out-of-the-way office with a sign above the door in gold lettering: *The Offices of House Braxton—Third District Representative.*

David paused in front of the door for a moment, heart racing. He drew a few long, calming breaths.

This is it, he thought. *Here goes nothing.*

He knocked on the door three times and stepped back. As he heard footsteps moving toward the door, he attempted to straighten his ill-fitting jacket. His mechanical arm was seeping fluids again. Luckily the stain faded against his royal-blue coat. As the door rattled open, he stiffened and assumed his best posture.

An elegant brunette woman with hazel eyes opened the door. She looked tall and proper in her navy-blue dress and satin teardrop hat, feather poking from the top. A silver pendant hung at her neckline. She seemed deceptively young, her natural beauty slowing the touch of time, perhaps middle-aged, or not—impossible to tell.

"Good morning," she said in a round, silky voice. "May I help you?"

"Hello, I'm David Ike here to see Mr. Blythe. I'm his new aide."

"Yes, we've been expecting you. Won't you come in? Ms. Paula Carbone, secretary for the Third," she said with a curtsy.

"Pleased to meet you, Ms. Paula," David replied, entering the office.

It was a huge room, at least to David—though if he'd visited any of the other political offices, he might have known it was actually rather small. One circular main office space conjoined two other rooms. A few benches lined the wall next to the entry door. Five desks spread out to the right. Closed double doors stood opposite the entry door, and on the far left side of the room a solitary couch sprawled beside a tall, narrow door. A long blue-and-gold carpet ran from the entry to the double doors opposite.

"Mr. Blythe is having a meeting in his office right now but will be with you shortly. How about I show you around?" Paula asked as she took David's arm—his real right one—and led him to a desk second closest to the double doors. "Here's your new home. We get to be neighbors!" She squeezed his arm as she pointed to the desk next to the doors. "Mr. Blythe's through the double doors, obviously."

David could see shadows shifting back and forth along the crack at the bottom of the door.

"As of now these other desks have no occupants," Paula continued, a smile on her face. "But of course we are expecting big things in the future. Typically when visitors, constituents, or, heavens forbid, lobbyists call on us, we seat them on the benches or the couch until Mr. Blythe is available to see them. And over here ..." Paula walked across the office toward the tall door opposite David's desk. "... we have the file room. It's where we keep our records and such."

She opened the door, and David looked down a long, narrow closet with floor-to-ceiling file cabinets on both sides and a rolling ladder in the middle. "Campaign contributions, proposed legislation, one or two documents on rival politicians, true or otherwise. I don't venture in there too often given that I'm just the secretary. Politics have always been a bit too dramatic for my tastes."

She rolled her eyes as she shut the door and led David back to the middle of the room. "I'm afraid Mr. Blythe has the only window throughout all the rooms. Sometimes it can get claustrophobic in here, but he does share on occasion ... if you ask nicely." She rolled her eyes at David. "So what do you think? Will you be comfortable here?"

"It's perfect," David said.

He set his satchel on his desk and looked around. His eyes returned to his desk, and he ran a hand along the polished wood surface in appreciation. His desk ... his very own desk.

"Well, we are very glad to have you, Mr. David."

"Oh, David will do. I'm just David."

"In that case call me Paula." She smiled and her eyes crinkled in the corners.

Just then Blythe's office doors opened and a short, porky man exited, clad in a green double-breasted suit with a long gold chain dangling from a side pocket, but behind him walked the man himself: William Jefferson Blythe IV. Tall, regal, handsome, well-built, he was everything a man should be, and nothing he shouldn't. He wore a spectacular blue suit with gold piping, his silver hair betraying his middle age but crowning him in wisdom rather than frailty.

"Ah, and whom do we have here, Paula?" Blythe asked with a voice to match his persona.

"This is David Ike, our new aide," Paula said.

Blythe turned toward David and extended a hand, which David shook. "David Ike," Blythe said, "it is a pleasure to finally meet you in person. I'm sorry to have kept you waiting. I had a meeting with Mr. Lloyd Bentsen here. Lloyd, meet my new aide, David Ike."

"Another David Ike?" Bentsen said as he stuck out his hand. "Wasn't that the name of your last aide?"

"No, that was Benedict's old aide," said Blythe, pulling on an earlobe.

Bentsen nodded and silently mouthed "Oh."

"Actually I'm the grandson of the actual David Ike," David said.

Everyone froze, wide-eyed, for a split second until David sighed and looked at the ceiling.

"It was a joke," he said.

Then everyone laughed.

"I think we will get along fine, lad," said Blythe. "Won't you come in and we will have a chat about your duties. Lloyd, thanks for stopping by. I'll see you for dinner at the end of the week."

Bentsen waved as he walked toward the exit. "Good to meet you, David."

"And you, Mr. Bentsen."

Blythe turned toward his office once Bentsen had left. "Come on in."

David hurried after Blythe's long strides. When he stepped into Blythe's office, he discovered that it did indeed have a window—*on the floor*. One large piece of glass covered most of the circular office floor. David stumbled as he stepped over the expanse. He held his arms out to steady a sudden bout of vertigo. Air traffic bustled beneath them, and the city buildings below appeared as a mess of children's building blocks on the island they inhabited. David could see the whole of Capital Island through the hazy clouds in the span of the window.

Blythe laughed. "I did the same thing the first time I stepped into this office. It is a bit disturbing, but you get used to it."

David nodded, but still stepped gingerly over the glass.

"Not to worry, it's quite safe," Blythe said as he hopped up and down a few times on the window.

Every impact made David wince. "It's ... um, fascinating."

Blythe chuckled and took a seat in a leather chair

behind a wooden desk. "Well, David, why don't you sit down and tell me about yourself. Do you have any family?"

"Just a mother, sir," David said, sitting in the chair opposite, "but she's been sick for quite some time. This new position will help me provide for her."

"She must be quite proud of you. You're rather young for an Alönian aide, yet you achieved the highest score on the PLAEE in history."

David smiled. The Political and Legal Aide Entrance Exam was the test all aides took before entering politics, an exam that had consumed the past four cycles of his life. "She is proud, sir, and very grateful for your kindness in giving me a chance to prove myself."

"Oh, it was no kindness at all. It was pure selfishness." Now Blythe smiled as well. "I was not about to let one of my political opponents hire you and take all that intelligence for themselves. Besides, you are a part of House Braxton's Third. You belong here."

David felt himself blush a little at the compliment.

"I think we have a mutual opportunity," Blythe went on. "The harder you work, the more I rise. And if I rise, you rise. I think it will be a very profitable relationship for both of us."

David gave a small nod. "I am eager to prove myself, sir."

"Good, good. And now—"

But the whistle of a clock on the wall interrupted Blythe.

"Ah, that would be the call to Assembly," Blythe said.

"Fancy a walk?"

David furrowed his brow. "To the Assembly?"

"Well, I didn't hire you to make tea. Don't you want to come?"

"Yes, sir," David said.

He jumped to his feet and then wobbled on the glass floor, but steadied himself and followed Blythe out. Blythe led David through the halls of the Capital Orbital. David would casually maneuver around the window-floors—and the thoughts of falling, screaming, and death that accompanied them. It happened much more often than David would have preferred.

"Good morning, Mr. Blythe," said a young lady, catching David off guard as he sidestepped another window-floor.

"Good morning, Susan."

David twisted around as he walked, trying to nod politely at all the faces that looked at him. Eventually Blythe led them into a grand foyer, a good ten fathoms high and twice as many wide. An enormous bay window stretched across the wall, capturing the rising sun within an enormous frame that almost stretched across the entire room. David had a hard time removing his eyes from the gilded Alönian mountains in the distance. They stood as brothers with the Capital Orbital, equal in height and grandeur. He gaped, right up until he stumbled into the back of someone who uttered a short yelp.

David spun and caught a young woman before she fell to the floor, but not before she dropped an armload of books. She regarded him with narrowed green eyes, peering out of her now messy hair—beautiful hair. Deep auburn tresses billowed around her shoulders like rolling red waves.

As he helped steady her on her feet, David stammered out an apology, then bent to pick up her books. "I'm … I'm so very … very sorry. I'm an idiot. I've just never seen so many things and …"

Everything else David planned on saying dribbled away as he proffered her books and looked into her eyes. They sparkled green in the sunlight.

"Um … new … here," David finished.

She reached for the books with pursed lips and just the hint of a smile. "It's quite alright," she said. "It's not the first time someone bowled me over in these halls, but it is the first time someone has refused to give me back my books."

David jerked his head back upon noticing that he indeed still did clutch her books while she tried to accept them.

He let go of them, and she chuckled as she tucked the books under her arm. "First time on the orbital?"

David hung his head a bit and nodded.

"Don't feel embarrassed. If it was the first time I'd seen this view, I probably wouldn't have noticed plain, little me either." She flashed an exquisite smile at him before walking away, a red sash billowing behind her as she disappeared into the crowd.

"Are you going to flirt all day?" came Blythe's voice from an uncomfortable distance, giving David a start. How long had he been there?

David hurried after Blythe as the man crossed the foyer, but looked back twice at where the beautiful girl had been. Once at the opposite end of the room, they walked through a grand arch. David stepped through and froze when he realized where he was: the Assembly Room of the Thirteen Houses of Alönia. The auditorium thrummed as people filtered in from every side of the circular room. The domed ceiling and tiered floor gave it an egg shape, with a glass skylight at the top and a glass floor at the base.

"Up here, David."

David looked to the right and saw Blythe climbing a flight of stairs to a box. Some gold lettering marked it as *Braxton Third District*. Once David had climbed up the stairs and entered the box, he gazed around in openmouthed astonishment. The circular room divided into thirteen different sections, each labeled on a giant banner that hung down over its section: *Hancock, Barlett, Thornton, Hopkins, Ellery, Huntington, Floyd, Livingston, Stockton, Franklyn, Stone, Nelson,* and *Braxton.* Each house possessed between four and ten districts, depending on its size. Braxton held seven.

"William, my boy, how have you been?" a representative called from a neighboring booth.

"Edward, how are you?" Blythe said. "You haven't been back since … well, since that little incident at the lake," he added in a subdued voice.

At this David perked up, realizing to whom Blythe was speaking. He leaned toward the conversation. After twenty cycles of being a representative, Edward Moore had taken House Braxton's center stage, but not via his political career. After a financial banquet Moore, a married man, had given a woman named Josephine a ride home in his racing skiff. Officially, there were no romantic inclinations between the two, and the skiff malfunctioned and crashed into Opal Lake. Moore had attempted several times to resuscitate Josephine before leaving and seeing to his own injuries. He'd also failed to report the incident until the next day. Given that Josephine was already dead, there was little need.

"Yes, dreadful business," said Moore. "Haven't been able to sleep since, what with all the accusations flying around. The *Voxil* actually mentioned murder and adultery in their last printing."

"The *Voxil* always accuses us of murder and adultery." Blythe said with a snort. "Sorry to hear it, old boy. Probably for the best you've been hanging low. Good to see you back, though. Oh, Edward, this is my new aide, David Ike."

"Really? I used to have an aide named David Ike," said Moore, a twinkle in his eye. "A relative of yours, perhaps?"

"I think we all have a relative named David Ike, sir," David replied to the merriment of the others.

"Yes … yes, I suppose that is true," Moore said. "And, William, I presume you remember my aide, Eric Himpton."

Blythe nodded. "Yes, how are you Eric?" Then, turning to David, he added, "This is my new aide, David."

Eric stood as tall as Blythe, with tan skin and slicked-back charcoal hair. He stuck out a hand and presented David with a wide, handsome smile.

"It's a pleasure, David," Eric said.

"Likewise," David replied as the two shook hands.

However, when Blythe turned back to Moore, David winced as Eric squeezed his hand with considerable force. When he pulled away, the tan aide made a show of wiping his hand on his trousers.

"Good to see you, Edward," Blythe said as he and David moved on to their box.

Blythe stopped and leaned toward David. "So what did you think of Eric, David?" Blythe asked under his breath.

"Um … well, he has quite a grip," David said as he massaged his hand.

Blythe gave a sly smile. "He does have some cause not to like you. You knocked him off his pedestal."

"How so?" David asked.

"He was the previous record holder for the highest score on the PLAEE."

"Oh," David said. He chanced a glance up at Eric, who stared stone-faced at the central dais.

"Hello, Representative Blythe," came a female voice.

David turned and saw a young brunette with short-cropped hair walking up the stairs next to their box.

"Hello, Cynthia," Blythe said, smiling at her.

"How do you remember all their names, sir?" David asked. "There are so many."

Blythe paused to wave at two additional aides coming

up the steps. "Sarah, Mary … good to see you both." He looked back at David and smiled. "Remembering names has always been a gift of mine. … Oh, hello, Representative Hilton. How is your son doing, Amy?"

But before she could answer, there was some commotion as the speaker of the houses took his seat at the central dais. David noticed a bit of a frown wrinkle Blythe's face as they sat and the room stilled.

"You disapprove of Speaker Walker, sir?" David whispered. "I thought same-house representatives were close?"

"Tell me how one becomes speaker of the houses of Alönia, David," Blythe whispered as the echoes dissipated and the room grew silent.

Sensing this was a test, David chose to give a detailed reply to a question that every schoolboy would know how to answer: "Every three cycles there is a house census. The district representative with the largest population represented becomes speaker. For the past eleven cycles, it's been Representative Walker, from the Sixth District of House Braxton."

"Quite right," Blythe said. "And despite being one of the only Pragmatics in an otherwise entire Assembly of Equalists, he manages to snag the most coveted position—and despite being from a geographically ordinary district, without any beaches or impressive mountains to speak of. … Tell me, how?"

"Well …" David said, pausing.

"Take your time," Blythe said as the speaker called the Assembly to order.

An enormous puff of steam shot from the center of the auditorium and resolved into the bored shape of Speaker Walker rising from his seat.

"Comes now this 9th Assembly of the 3241st cycle," Walker said. "We shall now hear all motions, starting with the representative from the Fourth District of House Floyd—Representative Albert Arnold."

Another puff of steam resolved into Representative Arnold's form as he enthusiastically rose to his feet.

"Mr. Speaker, the House Floyd representatives are unified in their motion to ban all uses of aerosol polymers as quick sealant for airship balloons. We are convinced that releasing such aerosols into the atmosphere could cause lasting damage to all air-breathing inhabitants."

"You are convinced that they *could*?" Walker asked. "If they could or could not, how are you convinced?"

David heard some general rumbling in the Assembly as Representative Arnold sputtered before saying, "We are convinced that our house is unified in this motion and that it has the support of representatives from many other houses. Will the speaker not recognize the overwhelming support of the representatives and, by extension, the people?"

"Well, when you put it that way," said Walker, "I really have no choice, now do I? If you would submit your scientific proof of recorded damages caused by aerosol polymers, I will begin the banning process immediately."

"Thank you, Mr. Speaker," Arnold said. "You will find our scientific proof of theoretical damages inside our motion. It very clearly points out that if any organism breathes such polymer, there would be—"

"I'm sorry," Walker interrupted. "You said *theoretical damages.*" His steam projection picked up Representative Arnold's motion and thumbed through the pages. "There is not a single recorded incident to any type of organism resulting from aerosol polymers. As I understand it, these particular aerosol polymers harden and become harmless once they reach temperatures below 180 degrees. Therefore the aerosols are harmless once they exit the balloons. Unless you know of any organism that lives inside of airship balloons where the temperatures are in excess of 250 degrees, I fail to see how your theoretical propositions have any practical merit."

The auditorium rumbled with jeers and boos.

When the noise died down, Arnold said, "You would risk so much in the face of probable harm? What if one of these airships crashed in a schoolyard? Will you swear, here and now, that any children involved in such an accident will not have their lungs filled with aerosol polymers? There is enough support in this motion to push it forward with or without your consent."

"Interesting," Walker replied. "Your theoretical situation requires a ship to crash in order to create the possibility, which is exactly what would happen if you took away that airship's aerosol polymers and it was not able to seal a ruptured balloon."

The auditorium rumbled again, sounding to David like a zoo during feeding time.

"In addition," Walker said, "you are wrong about my authority. Every Alönian warship in the armada uses aerosol polymers, and the speaker has the right to veto any motion that affects the military if that motion does not have direct and applicable evidence to credit it. Your motion is vetoed."

As the speaker called for the next motion, David's eyes grew wider when an idea struck him. He leaned close to Blythe and didn't bother hiding the surly tone in his voice when he whispered, "Isn't a massive aerosol polymer company incorporated in Speaker Walker's district? If I'm correct, they held a fundraiser for him in the recent past."

A faint smirk appeared on Blythe's face as he nodded slowly. "You are on the right track."

"Mr. Speaker," said House Stockton Representative Delano. "House Stockton is unanimous in its decision to grant psychologists the power to prescribe antipsychotics to minors without parental consent. A certain sect of individuals has refused to allow their children to partake in vital antipsychotics despite the insistence of qualified physicians. House Stockton feels that such ignorance …"

As Representative Delano droned on, David whispered, "How many of the mass employers reside in the speaker's district? If my memory is correct, five of the ten largest companies in Alönia dwell in the Sixth."

"Very good," Blythe said. "Five is correct, but you haven't told me how that has made him speaker?"

David pursed his lips and thought for a moment. "Well … his district has the lowest taxes of all the districts in all the houses of Alönia. This tempts greedy business owners to relocate to his district, bringing with them a vast amount of jobs. And where the jobs go, the people follow with little choice in the matter. This would swell his population and give him a windfall in the census."

"I think I picked the right aide." Blythe gave a reassuring nod. "However, elections happen every three cycles and the general public would have an opportunity to voice their opinion through their vote. How has the speaker managed to maintain the popular vote in his district for over a decade? If a majority of the population in the most populous district approves of his representation, perhaps he deserves to be speaker? What do you say to that?"

David furrowed his brow, unable to come up with a viable solution off the top of his head.

"But … But, Mr. Speaker!" Delano almost shouted. "Recent studies show that the latest antipsychotics may improve focus and decrease impulsivity and hyperactive behavior in minors. These results are crucial to the development—"

"Representative Delano," Walker cut in, "your motion is denied."

David continued thinking while the rest of the Assembly grumbled its disapproval.

"So …" David whispered, leaning closer to Blythe, "if that were true, why are 85 percent of all the other district representatives in Alönia Equalists?" he asked, thinking aloud. "If I'm correct, the businesses in the speaker's district are given an additional tax credit for providing private education to their workers. These private schools are well known for their Pragmatic approach to politics and economics." David could hear himself talking faster now as the answer unraveled itself in his mind. "Speaker Walker brings companies into his district, and then uses district funds, donated by the same companies, to fund his very own indoctrination program."

As the rest of the representatives booed the speaker's veto on yet a third motion, Blythe slow-clapped and smiled at David. "You are a natural at politics, my boy," he said. "I have a prodigy protégé."

David smiled and blushed at the compliments but frowned inwardly. *Natural* had nothing to do with it. If Blythe only knew how many hours he had spent in study the past four cycles to prepare for this day.

Speaker Walker denied three more motions, including one to cut government spending for the manufacturing of new warships—warships that just so happened to be crafted by a company residing in the speaker's district.

"I find it unwise to constrict our military funding any further given the threat of Outlanders," the speaker said.

Of course, there hadn't been any Outlander activity in five cycles.

As the Assembly wound down and the representatives shuffled in eager anticipation, Speaker Walker made one more announcement, surprising everyone: "Before we conclude today, I wish to raise my own motion."

The entire auditorium hushed, as this was the first motion the speaker had made in several cycles.

"I have been in conference with Don Hezekiah Johnson, manager of Alönian Public Pharmaceuticals. As Public Pharmaceuticals has grown substantially with the rise of psychological diagnoses in the general public, they have decided to build a new facility and move their headquarters to the Sixth District of Braxton. As this motion requires speaker approval before an Assembly, I hereby approve the relocation and the acquisition of land from the Sixth District."

The auditorium gasped like a rush of wind as every participating member sucked in a breath. Then, like a roar of thunder after the silent flash of lightning, representatives jumped to their feet and shouted their outrage.

David knew what this meant, and he swallowed hard as he looked over at his new boss, wondering how Blythe would react to the surprise motion.

Chapter Two

THE BURDENED LOCAL POPULACE

David looked on and Blythe said nothing while the rest of the representatives raged in the Assembly Room. Blythe simply steepled his fingers and tapped his lips. After several minutes he rose and walked out of the box. David had to scramble just to keep up with him. Blythe remained silent—hands folded behind his back the entire way back to their offices.

"With me, David," Blythe said as he entered his private office.

They walked into the unsettling, window-floored room and took their respective seats.

Blythe rested his hands on the bridge of his nose for a few moments before he took a deep breath and spoke. "You're having an interesting first day. I'm assuming you know that Speaker Walker rarely makes motions, and never without particular purpose. You know the ramifications of this one?"

"Yes, sir. Public Pharmaceuticals is the largest organization in Alönia. Larger than the top three Alönian companies put together. This would cement Representative Walker's speakership indefinitely."

Blythe nodded. "*Indefinitely* is correct. However, there can never be difficulty without opportunity. Can you guess what that opportunity might be?"

David looked at Blythe for a few seconds until it hit him. His eyes widened, and he sucked in a sharp breath. "Public Pharmaceuticals is moving. You mean to bring them here—I mean, to the Third District."

Blythe nodded slowly.

"But how?"

"That's why I hired you, my boy. We have a problem. We need a solution. I know it is your first day, but are you up for a little challenge?"

"Yes, sir," David said, unable to keep himself from smiling.

"Good lad. Now we need to find a way to tempt Don Johnson into changing his mind about the Sixth District. I was thinking—"

"Um," David interrupted. "Begging your pardon, sir, but that might not be necessary."

"Oh?" Blythe said with nearly concealed condescension. "Why is that?"

David swallowed, then began, "Well, sir, Public Pharmaceuticals is just that—public. They are a hybrid organization that is just as much a government entity as a private corporation. Even if you could convince Don Johnson to move the proposed site to the Third District,

Speaker Walker would probably still hold veto power over the transfer."

Blythe's countenance darkened a little as he got to his feet and walked over his window away from his desk a bit. "So you are telling me that the site is permanent and there is nothing we can do about it?" He shook his head. "We need a solution, David. This will effectively make George Walker a monarch."

"Yes, sir," David said. "But … there may be another option. There is nothing we can do, but there is something the entire Assembly could do."

Blythe turned and looked at David, lips pursed and brow furrowed. "Go on."

"Well, granted, this is a particularly old section of House Rules. But the Assembly can assert authority over a project in which it has an interest if there is a financially more tenable option available, there is a strong public interest in Assembly interference, and the current project situation is a burden to the local populace. True, the speaker would still have veto authority on the transfer, but in this particular situation a simple majority vote of the Assembly would overrule his veto."

Blythe paced across the window-floor a few times before returning to his chair. "Show me the law."

David scrambled out to his desk and retrieved a worn book, *House Law*, from his tattered satchel. Once back, he turned to the appropriate page and showed Blythe to which section of House Rules he was referring.

After reading it over, Blythe gave a heavy sigh. "This rule hasn't been used in over a century," he said. "Are you sure it is still a good ruling?"

David gave a firm nod. "It has never been challenged or overruled."

Blythe nodded in return as he looked over the rule again, rubbing his jaw. "Yes … this might work. It just might work. Could be difficult convincing the other houses to vote with us, though."

"Why? Would the other houses prefer that Speaker Walker veto their motions indefinitely?"

Blythe laughed. "Never use a sledgehammer when a scalpel is all that's necessary. There's another reason Walker is still speaker. It isn't that all the other representatives wouldn't love to see him go; it's that they all want to be the one who fills his shoes."

"Well, they needn't worry about that. Even if we acquire Public Pharmaceuticals, we would still be a far cry from unseating Speaker Walker." David chuckled … until he noticed that Blythe was not laughing with him. "Wouldn't we?"

"David, I assume you remember the portion in your contract that designates everything said in this office as confidential," Blythe said, his tone still pleasant but his eyes firm. "I don't need to remind you of the consequences of violating that confidentiality."

David swallowed again. "Absolutely not, sir."

"Good. Because I'm about to tell you something that only a handful of people know. For the past three censuses I've concealed certain portions of our house population."

David felt his mouth fall open as a thousand questions

filled his mind: *How does one hide population? ... Is it illegal to mislead a census? ... Sure, it's illegal to inflate your house numbers, but has anyone ever deflated their numbers? ... Why would they want to?*

When David said nothing, Blythe went on, "I noticed as a first-term politician that after every census, neighboring representatives pilfered population from any district that was experiencing growth. So for the past nine cycles or so, I've limited our population growth in each census, despite the popularity of my social assistance programs. The truth is, if we acquire Public Pharmaceuticals, our population will become a very close second to the Sixth District."

"How close?"

"Very close. By my estimates, between a one and two percent difference. The question is, if we reveal our hand at the up-and-coming census in four months, what will we gain? Walker will still be speaker, and even if I maintain my charade, the wolves will come to call. How long will it be before they realize our true population?"

David thought for a moment, then asked, "Do we have any alternative?"

"No, we do not," Blythe said as he clasped his hands behind his back. "This just means we have until the census to acquire both Public Pharmaceuticals and an additional two percent of the population. The time to strike is now. We will never get another opportunity like this. But we must proceed very carefully, because if our actions are discovered before we make the motion next week, another district could make the same proposal and ruin our prospects. Understood?"

"Yes, sir."

"Excellent. In the meantime I would like you to think of why the Sixth District site is counter to the public interest and why our district isn't. I will handle the 'financially more tenable' element of the rule. I know of a particular piece of property that should do the trick."

"Very good, sir. Will that be all for now?"

"Yes, I think so. You can go and get settled in. It's going to be a busy first week for you."

David smiled and then nodded as he got up. He tried to tiptoe inconspicuously across the window ... floor ... thing, giving a little wave to Paula as he exited Blythe's office. She winked at him and continued filing her light-pink nails.

After sitting down at his desk, he noticed that his left arm was growing sluggish. He glanced over at Paula, who was still busy at her nails, before rolling up his sleeve and swapping out a finger-sized power-pack with a fresh one from his satchel. The silvery digits of his hand twitched with the fresh power, and he spun the wrist a few revolutions before pulling his sodden sleeve down over the awkward metallic appendage. It dangled a little lower than his natural arm because it weighed more, forcing him to hunch. He might have been above average height if the clumsy thing didn't pull him forward, but it was still better than no arm at all. It wouldn't have been so bad if he didn't also have a limp. The combined hunch and limp gave him a damaged appearance.

After shoving the spent power-pack into his satchel,

David pulled open one of his desk drawers to start figuring out what he'd need. He blinked upon finding that it was already filled with supplies. He looked up in surprise at Paula.

"I took the liberty of stocking your desk while you were out," she said, smiling as she blew dust from a nail. "Hope you don't mind."

"Thank you, Ms. Paul—um, thank you, Paula." It was a simple act, but probably the first nice thing anyone had done for him since … well, since a long time.

Paula smiled and went back to her nails.

David rested his copy of *House Law* on his desk and stared at the title. They had until next census, the twenty-first day of Prumuveour Season. He puffed out his cheeks and counted off the days in his mind—117. That was not a lot of time to install a massive facility and scrounge up an additional few percent of population, and it would come at a price. Partnering their district with a don could be dangerous.

The thought made David cringe, and he considered the ruthless history of the dons. Centuries earlier the Houses of Alönia were still made up of family houses with tentative alliances. The original thirteen family lines held all the power in the land—almost. A number of merchant families, while without lands, gained vast amounts of wealth through monopolies over different products. In time they granted themselves titles and became the "Dons of Alönia." Over the centuries their power grew to rival that of the Alönian houses. Now the old family houses existed in name only, but three dons still stood.

Don Hezekiah Johnson managed all pharmaceutical production and distribution across the entire Houselands. His management, so to speak, was more of a cover, as all profits from the government-funded entity flowed directly into his pocket.

Next, Don Rafael Hephnaire owned several resorts, though his true source of power came from his stronghold over the Alönian labor unions.

Finally, Don Alphonse Gabriel remained the most elusive of the bunch. Nobody really knew how he collected his exorbitant amount of wealth, though a majority of the Alönian dance clubs sent him massive distributions every cycle. David had also heard the rumors that Gabriel ran a blackmail organization through the dance clubs, as well as an illegal drug distribution system, though no one had ever proved it.

David sighed. Yes, working with a don could be dangerous, but as Blythe said, they really didn't have a choice. David opened up his *House Law* book and started reading, searching for a modern answer to an ancient bit of law. A few hours later he was knee-deep in magistrate decisions, Assembly rules, and governmental projects, pulling from his own books and some of the extensive resources in the file room. He paused his pensive thoughts when Blythe exited his office and walked over to David's desk. Paula jumped up and retrieved Blythe's coat from the rack.

"Any luck?" Blythe asked.

"Some, sir. Still looking," David said.

"Tell me what you got," Blythe said as Paula helped him into his coat.

"Well … I have identified many public interests that would qualify under the rule, but the issue is that each one is just as strong in the Sixth District as it is in the Third. For instance the Assembly can interfere in the interests of providing jobs to an underemployed populace. But the Sixth District can show a need for jobs just as easily as we can and our greater need is irrelevant." David let out a frustrated sigh.

"Keep at it. I'm heading to the Third to see about a piece of land, and I'm taking Paula with me."

"Oh, wonderful, I'm *so* glad I finished my nails," Paula said. "Now I can go and get them dirty at some construction site."

"It's not so much that I need you, Paula; it's that I don't want you not there." He winked at David. "I find that my negotiations are far more effective when Paula accompanies me. We will see you tomorrow, then," Blythe said. "Oh, and take this." He flipped David a silver coin. "Buy yourself some dinner on the way home. Call it a first-day bonus."

"Thank you, sir!" David said after he'd caught the coin from the air and realized it was a full sterling.

He watched as Blythe walked with Paula on his arm over to the wall behind David's desk. He was about to say something, but the odd sight of the two of them just standing in front of the wall robbed the words from his mouth. Paula held her hat tight against her head. Then, Blythe reached out and pulled a lever that David hadn't noticed before. Chilled wind burst through an opening, blowing all the papers off David's desk as the wall opened into a tiny garage docking a sleek, two-seater skiff—and not just any skiff: a Cloud Cutter 71. Skiffs were named after their seafaring counterparts, a holdover from the far past. From where David sat, he could see the little airship's sleek pontoons cradling the wooden hull and the single, internal turbofan, a thing of beauty and craftsmanship as much as functionality and sport. He gaped as Blythe and Paula climbed in and buckled themselves.

"Oh, and David," Blythe almost shouted over the whistle of the wind. "Welcome to the Third District family!"

At the pull of another lever, the wall snapped shut and David heard the sound of the Cloud Cutter's burner engage and then dissipate into the distance.

He stared for a few more moments before scooting his chair away from the false wall. If it opened while he leaned against it, he'd have plenty of time to scream before he hit the ground.

The Third District family … he mused. It had been a while since somebody had called him *family*. He stood and walked around his desk to pick up the papers when he had a thought.

"It's not so much that I need you; it's that I don't want you not there." Blythe's wordplay gave David an idea. He didn't need to prove that their district was a better option than the Sixth District; he just needed to prove that there was a good reason to have the facility at the Third and a good

reason not to have the facility at the Sixth. Those two reasons did not have to be connected. That meant providing jobs to the people of the Third District would qualify as a "strong Assembly interest" in the Third District. It didn't matter that the Sixth District had the same interest.

So now he just needed a reason why the Sixth District project situation was a burden to the local populace. David slumped back in his chair. He was right back where he had started. Letting out a deep sigh—he'd been doing that a lot recently—he stood to his feet. It was 5:00, his brain was dead, and he still had a long way to go before he could rest it. As he walked out of the office toward the sky-liner dock, he mumbled the same question over and over in his head: *Why is it a burden to the local population?*

* * * * *

David had a window seat on the sky-liner trip back to the Capital City. He watched as the ship dipped beneath the cloud cover and into Úoi Season's light rain. Once the sky-liner had landed, David walked through the grimy streets toward the train. As he walked, he marked the difference in people on the lanes as compared with those on the Capital Orbital. Down here his suit stood out as high class compared to the drab brown vests and leather overcoats everyone else wore. Many of the passersby had bionic appendages like David's fake arm. They whirled and hissed with movement as the owners bustled about. Here and there, a prosthetic eye bulged on the side of a pedestrian's face. David always wondered if that kind of eye squeaked something awful inside the wearer's head as it swiveled about. A deliveryman wheeled by, calling everyone to stand to one side, which of course they did not. The man's legs were gone at the calf, and he'd affixed permanent rollers. David hoped he had his delivery job for a good long while, as those upgrades wouldn't be much use in any other job. However, the most significant difference at the ground level was that nobody smiled— all glares, scowls, or vacant expressions, many with creased foreheads. A majority kept themselves to themselves, rarely looking up and never looking anyone in the eye. Many meandered aimlessly without any apparent duties. Every corner David turned, he saw users exhaling unnatural clouds of drug infused vapor—whether they were prescribed or of the so-called *recreational* sort, he didn't know. These days, what difference was there?

He turned off Durbin Street and took an alley toward the train station. As he walked, he thought of Blythe and how exciting it would be to work with him in service of Alönia. His thoughts were such that he didn't notice the rancid stench of the alley or the shadows lurking on either side. He limped along, fingering Blyth's sterling in his pocket and considering how he would spend it.

Sweet buns filled with cream? Or perhaps some mountain lamb to go with dinner? It had been a while since he'd had that. Or maybe he should save it for this month's rent. He barely had enough as it was.

Suddenly, something caught his foot and he sprawled forward onto his hands and knees. The cobbles felt wet and sticky, and not from the day's rain.

David rolled over and saw what, or rather who, had tripped him. Two men in bowler hats with half-lidded eyes and scruffy faces grinned down at him.

"What's in your pocket, lad?" the smaller of the two asked.

"Nothing—" David said, but before he could say any more, the larger man put one dirty boot on his chest and the other on his mechanical arm and pinned him to the ground.

"It don't look like nothin." The larger man said. He slipped a hand in David's pocket and drew out the silver coin. Then he smiled and held the coin up between his dirty fingers.

David reached for the coin with his free hand, but the big fellow was too fast. The coin vanished, and a revolver appeared in its place.

David cautiously moved his hand away in a gesture of peace. "Well, nothing worth dying for at least," he added.

"If that's nothin, then we'll be taking nothin from you." The smaller said and the other chuckled.

"Yeah, you got anymore nothins on you?" the larger asked. He pawed through David's clothes with his pudgy fingers.

David grunted under the larger man's weight. "I don't know which is worse, being robbed, or being assaulted by your terrible sense of humor."

The large man put a little more weight on David's chest, and his breath rushed out.

The smaller man upended his satchel and kicked the

contents around on the cobbles.

"Well, well," he said when he kicked David's copy of *House Law* over. "It appears we have a student of the law on our hands."

"We don't like the law." said the larger man.

"True enough," said the smaller man. "But this is an excellent opportunity to ask a legal question, given we have ourselves a captive audience." He wiggled his eyebrows at David and the larger man guffawed. "Is it against the law to steal... nothin?"

The larger man laughed even harder, finally removing his foot from David's chest and stepping back. He flipped Blythe's sterling to the smaller man who caught it and held it out between a thumb and forefinger.

"We thank you for this generous contribution to our evening's entertainment."

David raised himself to his elbows and looked at the coin. "What contribution? I see nothing."

Both men pinched their eyebrows and looked at each other and then broke out laughing.

"He's got a point," the smaller one said. "Technically it cost him nothin!"

They tipped their hats to David, and chuckles echoed off the dirty cobblestones as they turned to go.

"He's a good sort to mug."

"Aye, why can't they all be like him? No fuss, good coin..."

Their voices dissipated into the distance, and David climbed to his feet. He tried brushing himself off, but he only succeeded in smearing the slime into his jacket. He groaned and picked up his satchel and replaced its contents.

"Great job David!" he said as he stomped down the alley. "Why don't you give all the vagabonds your money."

He was still sulking as he climbed the stairs to the train station. He waited on the platform until a massive steam engine hissed into the atrium, its triple steam stacks filling the room with pungent humidity. It looked like a long, slate-colored snake as the seamless length of its body curved with the track and jerked to a stop with a hiss. The sides of the compartments opened outward, creating a ramp downward and a cover from the elements for times when the train stopped at an outdoor station. Fresh rainwater ran down the side of the caboose, sending up puffs every time drips hit the exhaust valve.

David followed the other commuters as they packed into the train, filling every available seat and then some. As the sides sealed shut, David looked out a narrow window at a few latecomers racing down the platform toward the uncaring train. It rolled forward without them. Watching from his window, he saw the atrium columns flash by faster and faster as the train gained speed. Within a few seconds they were outside the station and speeding along a sky track two dozen fathoms from the ground. All of a sudden the ground fell away and waves replaced streets. They'd left Capital Island and were crossing the bay. A dozen other tracks stretched like strings across the bay at a few other points along the island, interlacing the small Capital Island with the larger island portion of

Alönia and the Capital City Transportation Facility on its shores.

Within twenty minutes David hobbled down the train ramp and across the street to the transportation facility. He missed the first flight back to House Braxton's only transportation facility by a few dozen passengers. But once the second had landed and he settled into a seat for a long flight, exhaustion smothered him like a wet blanket. He might have nodded off, but this particular airship captain was very different from those on the Capital City sky-liners. Several of the passengers looked a little green by the end of the trip. The idiot couldn't even keep a consistent lift in his balloon, and this flight cost money.

As the flight drifted down for a landing at the Seventh District, he looked at the towering mountains surrounding them, tops capped with snow. A stab of pain shot through his heart as guilt washed over him adding to his already sour mood. He hated those mountains. He kept his head down as he walked through the streets and caught the Braxton train on the final leg of his journey. Once back at House Braxton, he paused to check his mail at the post office next to the transportation facility. He purposefully had all mail sent there. Most employers would feel squeamish if they knew where he actually lived. Probably think he'd rob them.

"Bills ... Why are they always bills?" David mumbled to himself as he walked between the city power plant and Linden Airsail Limited toward a dingy apartment facility. A half-lit sign designated it as *"Linden Lodgings."* Most of the residents referred to it as *"Lousy Lodgings."*

He stepped into his apartment steam lift and caught a strong whiff of mildew. The tube was leaking again. Sure enough, after he'd selected the top floor, the lift moved sluggishly. Water dripped on his head, but he didn't move. *Why bother?*

He fumbled with his keys for a moment until he managed to unlock his apartment door. His apartment was just as worn as the rest of the facility, but much cleaner. Everything that could be maintained with clean living and a little elbow grease, was. His *palatial* abode encompassed three rooms: a kitchen, a living room, and his mother's room.

David dropped his keys into a jar on the counter and shuffled toward his mom's room.

"Mom, I'm back," he said as he pushed the door open.

Inside sat his mother on a torn, old easy chair, wrapped in blankets. She didn't answer. He knew she never would, but he couldn't bear to stop talking to her. Beside his mom, on a stool, sat Ms. Ella, an elderly lady from down the hall who'd agreed to look after his mother during the day in exchange for some help with her rent.

"I'm so sorry I'm late, Ms. Ella," David said. "I got mugged by a couple of—"

"That's quite alright, dear," Ella said as she stood, clearly missing what he had said. "She's already had dinner and a wash. There are some leftovers in the preserver if you're feeling hungry." She patted David on the cheek as she walked by him. "Go on now. I'm sure you want to tell her all about your big day."

David gave a little smile and said, "thanks again."

Ella left the apartment, and David turned back to his mother, looking as motionless and lifeless as ever. He leaned in and kissed her on the forehead. Pulling up Ella's stool, he sat down and picked up a comb from the table. He shoved all his fatigue aside, doing his best to put on an energetic tone as he brushed his mom's thin, graying locks.

"Well, I'm back, and it was fantastic. I got to ride a sky-liner. I walked through the Capital Orbital and even sat in on an Assembly. Can you believe it—an Assembly on my first day? And Blythe—blimey, he's fantastic. Just as kind and considerate as I thought he'd be. Paula—that's his secretary—she's really sweet. She set up my entire desk without me even asking."

David sat there, brushing his mother's hair and telling her about his entire day, every detail, from what Paula wore to the motion Speaker Walker had personally made, though he left out the part about his run in with thieves. All the while his mother said nothing—no nodding, no speaking, not even blinking, and barely even breathing. The doctors had said there was nothing they could do. She would remain like this until either her organs gave out or old age took her, eating from a tube and reliant on David and Ella to clean her. It had been like this for four cycles. Time allowed David to recognize a few subtle responses. She could still cry—though whether they were tears of joy or sorrow, he did not know. Sorrow, probably, since there wasn't much to be joyful about in her situation. But every rare once in a while, David could swear he saw a twinkle in her eye, like when he told her his score on his PLAEE, or when he got his position with Representative Blythe. Tonight, however, their conversation ended with tears running down his mother's cheeks. He didn't know why, and she couldn't tell him.

David hugged his mom. It was all he knew to do when the tears came. He hugged her until he thought she might be asleep. Then he lifted her emaciated frame from the chair, carried her to the bed, and tucked her in.

After slipping out of the room and closing the door with the deftness of a cat, David walked to the kitchen and spooned some of the leftovers onto a plate. He slid it into the steamer for a few minutes, infusing some appeal back into the lumpy Charra gruel. When the steamer chimed a moment later, David took the plate and walked to his bedroom, which also functioned as the living room, his study, and his exercise room. Some might complain, but in David's opinion he thought it quite convenient. Everything he needed was at his fingertips. His bed—or couch, depending on the time of day—was only a step away from his bookshelf ... or wardrobe—again, it depended on the time.

This apartment sat amidst the top floor of *Lousy Lodgings'* seven stories. The air-conditioning had never worked, and the heat only worked in the warm seasons. At first David filed work orders with the landlord, but when several additional charges showed up on his rent bill for *Apartment Modification*, David got the hint. All in all, the rooms were hot and humid in Swollock and Prumuveour Seasons, and cold and drafty in Derecho and

Taumore Seasons. Úoi Season alone presented a comfortable temperature. All this for the modest cost of seventy-five sterling a month. Nobody cared about the poor—at least nobody but William Jefferson Blythe IV.

"You're a good man, Mr. Blythe," David said as he stepped over to an enormous pinboard that covered one entire wall of the apartment. It was his method of study. A few months ago hundreds of PLAEE questions had plastered the surface. Now a picture of Blythe hung in the middle of the wall, surrounded by Blythe's wife, every known associate, and his proposed motions—even details as simple as favorite foods.

"Your social assistance programs are helping individuals all over the district," David said. Just the other day he'd read a testimonial from a hopeless citizen who could not live a decent life. David had tried to enter the program for his mom's sake, but they were not yet eligible. It was underfunded, given the number of applicants. If the district manufacturers paid just a little more, there would be enough funding for all.

David spooned a bit of gruel into his mouth, then he picked up a new card and scribbled down a new name.

"Lloyd Bentsen," David said as he wrote. "Who are you? Investor? Accountant?"

He pinned the card next to some of Blythe's other known associates. Sometimes David felt a bit creepy by his in-depth study of Blythe, but in order to please the representative, he needed to know what Blythe wanted even before he asked. All the same, he had to be careful to feign ignorance in the face of things he already knew.

David looked at the card with Paula's name on it. He added *Hides her intelligence* under the Notes section. David decided against adding a card about the district population distortion, given Blythe's stern words.

"But we have new questions to ask, don't we?" he whispered, moving to a blank section of the board, where he pinned up *Alönia Public Pharmaceuticals* and *Don Hezekiah Johnson,* and to another section of the board, *What is a burden to the local population?*

David swallowed a few more mouthfuls of gruel as he pondered the new additions and walked to the window. His apartment, despite all its shortcomings, had one wonder. It was situated on the top corner of the building, and his room had windows on two sides. This provided him, on the rare occasion that the clouds parted, an excellent view of the sunrise and sunset.

It was setting now. Golden rays sparkled as they passed through the evening rain. Oranges, pinks, and purples cascaded across the undersides of clouds. Steam from the city power plant swirled with colors, and David's entire room glowed with light. Jeshua's creation was truly wondrous. That thought brought a pang of guilt. It had been seasons since he'd been to Sanctuary, or had it been cycles? He'd had a hard time making himself go ever since the accident, partly because he didn't have time with all the extra work … and partly because he didn't want to. Jeshua was out there, somewhere, but in the past few cycles he hadn't been looking after the Ike home, and if he had, he certainly wasn't smiling upon it.

David sighed. In the distance dozens of private yachts

and skiffs glided into the city and docked at different towers in the residential sector.

"Must be nice," David whispered. "No burden of commute. No muggings. No worry. Just off to dinner and then back home on your own private yacht." He shook his head. "Talking to myself … again."

David closed his eyes and let the day's last light play across his face. When he opened his eyes, it was dark. He turned around and flicked on the only working electric light. He had to go to bed soon if he wanted a reasonable amount of sleep before he got up for his own commute. Why was it that House Braxton only had one air transportation facility servicing all seven districts?

How are the local peoples supposed to get any sleep if they spend six hours out of every day traveling to and from … work …

His thoughts trailing off, David whirled around and looked back at his pinboard. *Burden to the local population.* What if a commute was a burden to the local population? Or better yet, surely an overworked, public train network was a burden on the local population. It certainly was for him. He pulled a book from one of the nearby shelves and flipped through the well-known pages.

"*Braxton v. Collin, Braxton v. Collin, Braxton v. Collin Manufacturing* … Ah, there you are," David mumbled to the empty room. He ran his finger along the page until he came to a case summary. House Braxton had ratified an immediate tax increase on the Sixth District manufacturing companies in order to assist the train transportation system. The reason being: *"It is overly burdensome on the local population to have to travel on trains packed with workers commuting from different houses to the manufacturing facilities.*" David let the book fall to the floor. He had an idea, and it was brilliant!

Chapter Three

CONDEMNATION

The next morning David crashed through the double doors right into Blythe's office, not even noticing the window-floor this time. His abrupt entrance startled Paula so much, she squeaked and jumped up from the chair where she was taking notes for Blythe, knocking her cup of tea over in the process.

"I figured … it out," David said between gasps. "I know how to show … an undue burden … on the local population."

"Have you really?" Blythe said from his desk chair, his face morphing through an entire host of expressions: first shock, then curiosity, and then bemusement.

"Transportation!" David exclaimed, nodding at Blythe like he had just solved the Alönian power crisis.

"Mm-hm. That's, um, very interesting, David, but why don't you start from the beginning?" Blythe smiled at Paula and handed her his kerchief to clean up the tea she'd spilled on her dress.

David stepped forward and dumped his armload of documents onto Blythe's desk, oblivious to his rude interruption and haggard appearance.

"How many airship transportation facilities are there in all of House Braxton?" David asked.

Blythe opened his mouth to answer, but David cut him off: "One! One facility to service all the public air traffic in the entire house." He spread a House Braxton map across the desk. "It's located on the far end of the Seventh District, predominantly servicing vacationers to the Seventh's mountain resorts. All commuters to the other districts have to ride steam trains to and from that transportation facility. The Sixth District has the highest population by far, but a good portion of workers still commute from out of district via the transportation facility. They haven't bothered building their own airship transportation facility since they are relatively close to the Seventh District. Rather they built additional trains to facilitate the commuter traffic."

David paused and laid another map down on the table, this one showing all the train lines out of the Sixth District. "Given all of the work inside the Sixth District, these train lines are packed to capacity. Anyone wishing to travel in or out of the Sixth District waits upwards of four hours. Adding Public Pharmaceuticals would probably crush their local transportation system. According to *Braxton v. Collin Manufacturing* …" now David stopped to pull out his copy of *House Magistrate Opinions*, then continued, "… it is 'overly burdensome on the local population to have to travel on trains packed with workers commuting from different houses.'"

David looked up after his hasty presentation. Paula still wiped at a large brown stain on her light-pink dress. Blythe, on the other hand, tapped his folded hands on his lips, searching David with pensive eyes.

"How much sleep did you get last night?" Blythe asked after a moment.

David shook his head. "I didn't. No time."

"Paula, would you get David some Jorgan tea?" Blythe smiled at her. "I think he'd benefit from a cup."

"Sure, and I'll get myself a second, since I'm wearing my first." She walked off after a few more dabs with the handkerchief.

"But don't you see what I'm saying?" David asked. "It means we have the power to move the project to our district."

"I see your point, but I'm not sure if I'm more impressed at your result or the fact that you are this excited after missing an entire night's sleep."

Paula returned and handed a cup of tea to David with a forced smile. "I'll let you boys work. If you need me, I'll be in the ladies' room washing my dress in the sink."

"Very good, Paula. Thanks for the tea," David said before he took a sip.

"Now," Blythe said after Paula walked out the door, "I see one problem with your plan. The Third District does not have an airship transportation facility either. I have a hard time believing the Assembly will transfer Public Pharmaceuticals to our district when we have no airship facility and only one single train line in or out. I would think the Assembly would transfer the facility to the Seventh District before the Third."

"Quite right. But don't forget, all we need to make the motion is proof that it's of public interest, and that the current site is burdensome on the local populace. Keeping the facility in our district is another argument."

"Yes, but what is the point if we can't keep it?"

David handed Blythe another document by way of reply.

"What's this?" Blythe asked.

"Those are plans for a transportation facility proposed by your predecessor. At the time, the Third didn't have a large enough population to justify the project. Now, however, this cycle's house grant should provide enough to start the project, and the prospect of Public Pharmaceutical's arrival should convince a bank to loan the rest. Once the transportation facility is in progress, that is enough to thwart any other district from making the same *burdensome* argument against us." David folded his arms and smiled.

"Wait, wait," Blythe said, shaking his head. "You're telling me that as soon as we start work on an air transportation facility within our district, no one else can claim that the traffic will be burdensome on the local population?"

David nodded with a broad grin. "That's the beauty of it. Anyone else seeking to thwart us will need to come up with a different reason, and for the life of me I can't think of any."

Blythe stared at the plans for a few more seconds until his eyes got very wide. "Ha! David, you are worth every penny of your meager salary."

"Thank you, sir ... I think. But there's more. You asked me yesterday if there was any way we could boost our population another two percent. I've found it. If we can convince the Assembly to interfere and move Public Pharmaceuticals to our district, and if our transportation facility is approved, I propose that we approach one of the medium-sized construction companies—Beldon, perhaps—and convince them to move their headquarters into our district in return for the contract on both projects."

"Hmm ... Beldon Construction is too small," Blythe said, again shaking his head. "Even if they move their entire work force to our district to complete the project, it will only move our population a percent at most. That isn't enough."

"True, but think of it this way..." David took a few gulps of tea, then went on, "Beldon is located in the Sixth District. It is one of many construction companies in Speaker Walker's district and currently struggling for work. Any of the larger companies in that district have strong ties to the speaker and would never move. Beldon needs a change-up, and if they move, that is one percent for us and one percent away from the Sixth, effectively swinging two percent."

Now Blythe laughed. "My boy ... my dear boy, you've done it!"

He rose and clapped David on the back with so much

force that David spit out a whole gulp of tea—thankfully right back into his cup.

Blythe pointed and said, "I have one thing I want to change, though." He picked up a pen from the desk and crossed out a word at the bottom of the plan's abstract. "The residential section has enough air traffic with all of the private yachts. They have no need for a public airship facility." Then he penned in *Industrial District.* "Now, David, tell me, how much do you know about condemnation?"

"Mm, a fair bit. I have the Governmental Notice Form in my desk. In addition to that, we will need to show that we are taking the property for public use with just compensation."

"Quite right. There is just one problem. After we provide land to Public Pharmaceuticals, purchase land for the airship transportation facility, and begin construction on the airship transportation facility, well, we simply don't have the funds for that. I found a piece of land yesterday that I intended to use for Public Pharmaceuticals, but I think it is better suited for an air transportation facility. A few lanes down from that lot is a manufacturing facility. Over the cycles it's lost a lot of its former glory, laying off workers and condensing its workspace. As of now, I should think they only use a quarter of the space within the facility. If we could condemn that land, it would save considerable—"

"You're not thinking of Linden Airsail Limited, are you?" David asked.

"You know the place?"

"That's next to where I live. Their CEO, Linden, used to employ all the workers in my apartment, Linden Lodgings, and owned the apartment itself. Then he up and sold Linden Lodgings, made a killing, and laid off all the workers to save on production costs. Not long after, rent increased and the building fell into disrepair. Rumor has it that he still lives in a penthouse in the residential district."

"Well then, this should be easy. Come on, let's away."

"Away?" David asked. "Away to where?"

"The Third, my boy," Blythe said as he walked out of his office toward the false wall. "We need to pay a visit to one of our constituents. Grab that Governmental Notice Form." He pulled the lever on the office wall, and a gust of icy wind fluttered around as sunlight radiated through the doorway. "Come on now. We don't have …"

The rest was lost as David grabbed his satchel and hurried after Blythe, climbing into the Cloud Cutter's white leather seat. He was not about to miss a ride in this skiff. Blythe switched on the burner, and in a matter of seconds the pontoons heated and the sleek craft rose into the air. David knew every detail of this ship, but then again, he knew every detail of every airship. The 71 two-seater boasted three fathoms of sleek red böaga-wood paneling with a convertible cockpit at the very front of the retro bull-nose vessel. A twin-purpose burner allowed for lift and propulsion without any additional weight. That's why it took no time at all to acquire lift at a cold start. David buckled himself in and put on the goggles Blythe proffered. Blythe squinted his eyes as he set the odometer to chime at 170 grandfathoms.

When the skiff was clear of the private dock, Blythe opened the internal turbofan, which hummed as it drew air into the front of the ship and then rocketed it out the back. The acceleration squished David into his plush leather seat. They made a wide arc around the orbital until the large central compass on the dash pointed southwest, toward House Braxton and the Third. The sun gleamed on the orbital as the skiff carved a swath through the dense clouds below. The agile craft darted through the rest of the orbital air traffic at an almost reckless pace. In mere moments they were outside the city limits steaming toward the Third.

David could see the Alönian mountains circling the outskirts of ten of the thirteen houses, peeking up over the cloud cover and fading into the distance, their tips sparkling in the sunlight. It looked like a bowl of rocky spires holding a soup of frothy cloud. Most of Alönia lay on an abnormally large island, its north, west, and south shores guarded by high mountain peaks. While providing excellent security from the perpetual Southern Ocean storms, these mountains also acted like an enclosure to any wayward clouds, collecting and condensing them.

Alönia, with the exception of the coastlands, enjoyed five seasons of seventy-four days apiece, each with a varying degree of rain, making up the 370-day cycle. Taumore Season, the first of the cycle, offered mists and chills for sixty straight days—not quite freezing, but that was little help when the endless mists found their way into someone's clothes. Taumore Season ended with the only respite from the five-season rain cycle: the Golden Days. The Golden Days lasted a fortnight, with clear skies and crisp air as the winds transitioned into Úoi Season. Every single Alönian would wait all cycle for the Golden Days—and all the holidays, garden parties, or other celebrations that accompanied this special period, as it was the only time in the cycle anyone could rely on decent weather.

The next season of the cycle, Úoi, presented light rain and moderate temperatures. Most considered it the pleasant season when compared to the interminable humidity and muggy fog of the next season, Swollock. Alönia's hot Swollock Season meant nothing but sweaty shirts and grimy fingers for weeks on end, and it only got worse from there. Prumuveour Season was monsoon season, with constant thunderstorms and flooding for the whole period. However, Prumuveour Season could bear a dangerous kind of beauty in the midst of the squall. Sitting at night and watching lightning split the black expanse in brilliant shocks of blue and white could be soothing, but only if someone watched from a comfortable, dry place. While the stifling humidity would soon end in Derecho Season, the wind and rain would not. The fifth and final Alönian season, Derecho, battered the Houselands with wind gusts and pelting rain and, on rare occasions, hail. By the cycles' end Alönia lay sodden and ready for Taumore Season's mists to start again.

That was why every Alönian dreamed of owning a skiff like the 71 and rising above the clouds to bask in the light of the sun. Inhabitants could only take cloud cover and rain for so long, for everyone yearned for warmth and light. The nice thing about Blythe's 71 was that with a length of less than eight fathoms, it could fly outside the regulated air traffic lanes at whatever altitude the driver preferred.

Blythe stayed above the clouds and flew the most direct line to the Third District. David breathed in the air and closed his eyes as the wind whipped his hair and the sun warmed his face. It had been awhile since he'd felt that—not since … not since the accident. He put a hand up and let the draft whistle through his fingers. How he had missed this. After a little more than an hour of slicing swaths through the tops of clouds, the odometer chimed like a kitchen steamer, and Blythe pulled the altitude control. He raised the skiff's cloth roof before dropping through the clouds, but not before fogging David's goggles. After wiping them, David looked through Úoi Season's light rain at the familiar landscape of the Third District of Braxton. As pleasant as the journey had been, he could only wonder what kind of reception they were in for below.

* * * * *

"Condemn?" Linden said, snorting. "You can't do that." His greasy hair shook as his scruffy faced puckered. The man's squat stature looked out of place with the half dozen grim-faced bodyguards arrayed around him in the middle of his lavish office.

"Linden," Blythe said, "the house has the authority to

take your land if it is for a public use."

Blythe sat opposite Linden and next to David, both in plush armchairs, the *Linden Airsail* logo embroidered on the cushions. The only thing that overshadowed the office's extravagant furnishings was the excess of dust.

David saw Blythe blow a bit off his lapel before continuing, "In this case it is for the use of Public Pharmaceuticals, who will be a mass employer of the unemployed in this district."

"What you want to help those wretches for?" Linden said. "If you ask me, we ought to stop feeding them so they quit being a burden on the responsible populace."

David sat bolt upright and might have pounced on Linden if Blythe hadn't rested a firm hand on his shoulder.

"Well, nobody did ask you, Linden," Blythe said, giving David a stern look before removing his hand. "The point is, we have a public use."

"And you're going to take my business away so Public Pharmaceuticals can make more dope for the children of neglectful parents? The hallucinogen-addicted miscreants? The ... The lazy hypochondriacs? Downright thievery, it is!" Linden shook his head and some greasy strands of hair flopped around. "The government can't just waltz in and steal whatever it wants."

"Nobody is stealing anything," David said, which was exactly four more words than Blythe had authorized him to say. But now that he'd stepped in the muck, he figured he might as well wade through to the other side. "You will be fairly compensated according to the property's value. Besides, just think of all those people you laid off having a job again. But I suppose the only thing you care about is the clink of sterling, you greedy little—"

"Scalpel, David, not the sledgehammer," Blythe whispered between smiling lips as he dusted off an armrest before resting his elbow there.

"Well," Linden said, "if the government is going to take my property, I want double its value. Seems only fair that if everybody else is going to make money out of this deal, I should make the most."

"David, why don't you explain to our friend what the legal definition of *just compensation* is," Blythe said in a tone that made his meaning clear: *"Stick to the script, kid."*

"*Just compensation*, according to long-standing House Rules, is equal to the tax-assessed value. We took the liberty of pulling the property records on our way over here."

David leaned forward and handed Linden the Governmental Notice Form with the stated public use and the proposed compensation already filled in.

"But … But this is half of what it's worth," Linden said with his recessed jaw resting on a palm. "It's only assessed at that value because you've scalped all my profits through your social assistance programs."

"Linden," Blythe said, resting his head on a thumb and forefinger, "let's not play games. You live in an extravagant house in one of the nicest areas in the whole district. You have two yachts, and two mistresses—and a wife who doesn't know of either. I'd say your profits are just fine if you're able to live like that. Wouldn't you agree?"

Linden's hands gripped the arms of his chair, chest heaving and breath hissing between clenched teeth. "I won't let you take my business only to ... to ... to fill it with city scamps making worthless piles of—"

"Fine," David interrupted. "We'll let the courts decide."

A long pause hung in the air like a stench. Linden's face contorted through several versions of rage. For a moment David thought Linden might set his thugs loose and the district police would work overtime the next day looking for all his pieces.

"Take it!" Linden shouted. "But you won't find me in this city any longer. I'm not going to sit back and applaud while a bunch of know-nothing do-nothings ruin my facility. Now get out. GET OUT!"

David and Blythe ignored the rest of Linden's shouts and the glares from his bodyguards and saw themselves to the door.

"I think that went rather well, don't you?" Blythe said as the two stopped at a food cart on their way back to Blythe's Cloud Cutter.

"Agreed," David said before sinking his teeth into half a dumpling. "We would have won condemnation, but the expense might have pushed us over the edge."

"True, true," Blythe said, looking around the street and letting out a deep sigh.

David glanced around. It definitely wasn't the friendliest part of the Third—bars or boards on all the windows, locks on all the doors. The only businesses doing well were those of a sexual or illegal nature. A couple of old, dented steam cars rattled by and splashed water on David's trousers.

"You know…" Blythe began. He used his napkin to brush off David's pants, and then he continued. "I can remember a time when this street was filled with commerce. Happy, laughing people eager to do a good day's work. It wasn't too long ago that all the commercial ships in Alönia were designed and manufactured right here in the Third. Then the Sixth came along and pulled all our jobs away. Look at us now—one measly little airsail company and a whole host of dance clubs. Everybody we walk by is either between jobs, between homes, or between sedatives."

Even as Blythe spoke, a man stumbled out of the nearest dance club and breathed out an unnatural cloud of vapor.

David frowned but then nodded at Blythe. "We can change it, sir. We already are. If we succeed this week, this area will never be the same."

"You are an absolute pleasure to work with, David. You really are." Blythe smiled. "You are going to go far in life, and all the houses will be better for it."

David blushed. He couldn't think of a reply to that, so he just smiled. After stuffing the rest of the dumpling into his mouth and savoring the sweet and salty flavors, he and Blythe walked back to the 71.

The rest of the week flew by like an airship on high burn. The Third District Property Administration approved the condemnation papers without question.

District engineers certified the site plan for the airship transportation facility, agreeing to keep the documents off the public record for two weeks. After a quiet meeting with many winks and nods, Beldon agreed to move their headquarters, contingent on Public Pharmaceutical's relocation. Overall, after the first few sleepless nights, David found himself with very little to do. The only thing left was the Assembly motion, and that was on Blythe. Day after day David watched his mentor's shadow move back and forth across the crack under his office doors as the politician rehearsed his speech. However, in no time at all David sat gazing down at Speaker Walker's bored expression as he announced the 10th Assembly of the 3241st cycle.

Blythe squeezed David's arm and gave him a reassuring nod, reminding David to let out a breath he hadn't realized he was holding. The auditorium quieted as William Jefferson Blythe IV keyed in his motion. He stood and waited as the central steam projector puffed out his form.

Every second that passed felt like an eternity as David's heart ran wild with anxiety.

It will work, he thought. *It has to!*

Chapter Four

THE MAN IN THE SHADOWS

"Mr. Speaker, honored Representatives of this grand Assembly, I make this motion by myself," Blythe said with his baritone voice. "My fellow representatives know nothing of it. Indeed, it is the first time I have spoken of it." Blythe tilted his head and rubbed his jaw with a palm. "I have spent the last nine cycles promoting social fairness, seeking a balance in taxation according to individual capacity. My goal was to impart finances back into the hands of the needy. It has not been enough, and I know in the depths of my soul that I could have done more."

As Blythe paused for effect, David leaned forward in his seat in anticipation.

"My schools are underfunded. My populace is underfed. And each day that I delay making a commitment to my district's children carries a dear cost. Physicians are increasingly diagnosing my people with acute depression. Suicide is on the rise as my people turn to self-help drugs because the availability and funding for antipsychotics is far below demand. We are few, we are feeble, but the benefit of Public Pharmaceuticals would help us more than you know in both jobs and available antipsychotics. I petition this Assembly and make a motion to transfer Public Pharmaceuticals to the Third District of House Braxton. As I am alone, I am in need of a second to present my motion to the speaker."

"I second," said Representative Hilton of House Braxton's First District.

Blythe nodded toward her. "Truly, Representative Hilton, the Third District thanks you."

The entire room held its breath as everyone looked toward Speaker Walker. The speaker's steam projection appeared perplexed, like he suspected a trap but was unsure where to take a step to move forward. "Although your story is … painful," he finally said, "I cannot grant a motion that would take work and resources away from my own district. With regret, Representative Blythe, I must deny your motion."

The Assembly booed and shouted.

"Think of the children!" someone yelled.

"Have you no heart at all, sir?" another called out.

David did his best to put on a face of disgust, but in truth he was smiling on the inside.

Once the voices died down, Blythe asked, "Is that truly the reason, sir? You hide behind the needs of your people, but in your heart you only crave power. Will we allow this?" Blythe said as he turned to speak to the rest of the Assembly. "I come to you today to appeal to your better judgment. For too long we have bickered. Too long we have squabbled over power and ignored the needs of our constituents. When did the representatives of Alönia trade the good of the people for the comforts of wealth? When did the representatives of Alönia prostitute their offices to the highest commercial bidder?"

He shook his head and let his shoulders slump a bit. "I grow tired. ... I grow tired, I say, as my floundering district suffers and nobody lifts a finger. I remember a time when the citizens of the Third were wealthy, prosperous, and content. I remember a time when commerce flowed in and out of our district, as it did in every district of every house ... but no longer. Greed and pride swallowed it up. Companies more interested in helping themselves than their fellow Alönians left for better prospects and deeper pockets. Were we ignorant of their leaving? Are we innocent in their absence? No. It happened because *we* let it happen. It happened because we Equalists were so busy seeking to better ourselves that we lost sight of the betterment of the whole."

Blythe paused and glanced around. "Do we not remember our party's creed? *'Equal in prospects, equal in stance, equal in whole means equally more.'* That is not just some sonnet for the masses. It applies to us too—the representatives of the people. I ask you to stand with me. Stand with me in unity to redress the balance. We Equalists have a common goal and only one hindrance. And, no, it is not Speaker Walker."

Many faces that had been nodding along with the

speech paused and cocked their heads, until Blythe continued, "It is each other. We have spent these past cycles squabbling, and the houses are worse for it. We have an opportunity today ... an opportunity to strike a blow for the common Alönian. Help my district, please."

The speaker, though, simply shook his head and said, "Representative Blythe, I have already denied your motion. What do you think this little tirade will afford you?"

"I ask you, Mr. Speaker, how long will you pursue this reign of terror?" Blythe said, and David now noted a little bit of fire in his voice. "I come to you with a legitimate concern regarding suffering people, and you throw it in my face. Do you deny the needs of my district?"

"I do not," Speaker Walker replied. "But I cannot advance the needs of your district over the needs of my own."

"Your district is fat on finances," Blythe countered. "Do you deny that?"

"I do not deny that my district is where all of your constituents wish to be," Walker said, dropping his empathetic tone. "Perhaps you should consider some of my policies."

David frowned. *Come on, Blythe! Don't let him gain the upper hand. Drop the hammer.*

"I move for an Assembly vote," Blythe said. "I move for a majority vote to transfer Public Pharmaceuticals to the Third District without the approval of the speaker."

Walker's eyes grew wide before he said, "You don't have the authority to attempt such a thing! Sit down,

Blythe, before—"

"Actually I do," Blythe said, interrupting the speaker.

All across the Assembly people hushed and gasped.

"I have here," Blythe pushed on, "a study of your rail-line population usage, dated last week. It shows your local population waiting upwards of four hours due to the burden of the workers commuting in and out of your district. Do you deny this, sir?"

"I deny nothing. My district is the most populated of all the houses, hence the fact that I am speaker. Come to the point, Representative Blythe."

"I would like to read to you a particular portion of *House Law*." Blythe held up a slip of paper as Speaker Walker's steam projection actually rolled its eyes. "'An Assembly can assert authority over a project in which it has an interest, wherefore there is a financially more tenable option available, wherefore there is a strong public interest in Assembly interference, and wherefore the current project situation is a burden to the local populace. If said Assembly has produced such evidence in a valid motion, the Assembly may ratify such authority without speaker approval through simple majority vote.'"

It took a few moments for the words to set in, but slowly Speaker Walker's bored expression transformed as his eyes narrowed and his lips pursed. "Your point, Representative?" he asked.

"Forgive me, Mr. Speaker, I am getting there. A few cycles back there was a magistrate opinion issued to resolve a dispute between House Braxton and Collin Manufacturing. Within that opinion is one line of particular interest: 'It is overly burdensome on the local population to have to travel on trains packed with workers commuting from different houses to the manufacturing facilities.' Therefore I present to this Assembly four undisputed facts: One, as Public Pharmaceuticals is part owned by the Houses of Alönia, this Assembly has an interest in its operations. Two, the Third District has already acquired property suitable for the proposed facility at a substantially reduced cost. Three, the Third District has a strong public interest in the jobs and resources Public Pharmaceuticals would bring. Fourth, as you yourself have admitted, Mr. Speaker, your district steam lines are packed to capacity. Adding Public Pharmaceuticals' population to your district would be overloading your already strained public transportation system, and, according to *House Braxton v. Collin Manufacturing*, that is an undue burden on the local populace. Given these four facts, and in accordance with the *House Law* I quoted earlier, this Assembly has the power through majority vote to move the proposed site of Public Pharmaceuticals from the Sixth District to the Third."

The Assembly was so quiet that David thought he could almost hear the burners hissing several rooms over as the orbital's turbofans worked to keep the facility stationary.

"Generous Maker, he's done it!" exclaimed a representative from a neighboring house.

After allowing time for his words to make the needed impact on the other representatives, Blythe said, "I propose a vote. Do I have a second?"

"Wait!" Speaker Walker said, a sneer on his lips. "If Public Pharmaceuticals would overly burden my district's four transportation lines, how would your single train line ever dream of handling such traffic? I would think there are several other districts more capable than yours to handle such commuter traffic?"

"That indeed may be true, Mr. Speaker, but that can be addressed in a future motion. Perhaps there is a better location. However, for now, we are simply voting to move Public Pharmaceuticals out of your district and into mine. I say again, do I have a second?"

"I second," Representative Hilton said, and David could hear a bit of laughter in her voice.

"Then it is pushed to a vote," Blythe said.

He leaned against his podium as a second puff of steam from the central dais began a live tally, currently projecting the number two. A long pause stretched out as every representative considered what was happening and the possibilities it could bring.

"Come on, people! Take the bait," David whispered to himself.

Then, in an instant, the tally flickered into the number seven, then eight. As the votes came in, the projector had trouble keeping up and the steam clouded. After a few moments the whole Assembly sat still, and the mist resolved into the number sixty-one. That was every single Equalist representative.

David couldn't help himself. He jumped up from his chair and pumped his fist into the air, yelling, "Yes! We did it!"

And then he instantly regretted it. Every eye in the entire Assembly turned to him. Even Blythe turned back toward him with a bemused look.

"Did you want to say something?" Blythe asked.

David didn't answer. Instead he sat down quickly and tried to imagine himself completely invisible. He could hear Eric Himpton say something and then snicker a few rows up. *The little snot.*

"It appears your motion succeeded," Speaker Walker said. "Little good it will do you. Do we have any other motions?"

A dozen representatives stood to their feet, but the Second District representative from House Franklyn was first to key in: "Mr. Speaker, the Second District of House Franklyn makes a motion by itself without the majority of its representatives."

"Let me guess," Walker said, sounding bored again. "You wish to move the proposed site to your district. We are going to be at this all day."

"Mr. Speaker, the Second District of House Franklyn has an airship transportation facility. We make our motion for the same reasons stated by Representative Blythe. Our airship transportation facility will provide the needed passage for all the commuting workers and relieve the Third District's rail lines of their traffic burden."

David smiled. *That trick is only good once, sir.*

"Mr. Speaker," Blythe interjected. "The Third District is fully capable of handling whatever commuter traffic comes with Public Pharmaceuticals."

"Really?" Speaker Walker said, his steam projection looking down his nose. "Enlighten us, Representative Blythe."

"The Third District engineers approved an airship transportation facility last week. It just so happens to be across the street from the Public Pharmaceutical's proposed site," Blythe said. "Construction begins tomorrow, and the facility will be finished before Public Pharmaceuticals can complete their headquarters' transfer. This airship transportation facility will alleviate any burden presented by Public Pharmaceuticals."

One by one the representatives waiting to make their motions sat back down. A couple chuckled at Speaker Walker's stunned look. He had very nearly succeeded in becoming a de facto dictator, only to be thwarted by a representative hardly anyone had ever heard of.

"Three cheers for the Braxton's Third!" Representative Hilton said.

While some grumbled—the Pragmatics, no doubt—most in the auditorium gave applause.

As much as David wanted to join in the jubilation, he took a moment to look around the auditorium and note any potential threats among the other representatives. Speaker Walker, obviously—he looked as angry as a Viörn when his numbers didn't add up. Eric Himpton wore a frown as deep as a Bergish oil well—again, not a surprise. The Second District representative from Franklyn looked none too pleased either; nor did some of the other representatives who had attempted to make the same motion. All the representatives from the few remaining Pragmatic districts wore deep frowns and scowls, the end of their minority hold over the speakership meaning big changes. David noted each on a small pad of paper. Everyone else looked genuinely pleased, but then he had a thought. *Never forget to look where no one else is.*

David turned and looked up toward the citizens' gallery. There were only a handful of people there—Paula, for one—and they were all applauding … all of them except one. A tall man in a triple-caped coat stood in the shadow of a curtain. David would have missed him altogether if the man hadn't placed a hat on his head and then moved from the shadows toward the exit. Right before he vanished through the door, he turned. David could have sworn the man looked right at him from under the brim of his hat, but then he was gone.

"David, my boy, we did it!" Blythe said as David wrote another note in his pad. Then Blythe caught David up in an embrace. "By the way, that was quite some outburst. You might have a future in politics, lad. Never mind that, though. We did it!"

David did his best to keep from blushing as Blythe squeezed him.

"I feel like celebrating," Blythe said. "What do you think?" But Blythe continued before David had a chance to answer: "I know a great spot in the residential area of Braxton's Third District where we could have dinner. Come on, come on, we don't have all day."

Blythe hurried David along back to their offices. Paula had apparently already gone for the day, so the two of them climbed into the Cloud Cutter and sped off toward House Braxton. It was dark by the time they arrived at the most glorious restaurant David had ever seen called The Dancing Skyfish. It sparkled at the top of the Third's central tower, taking up the top three floors. An enormous crystal chandelier dangled in the middle of the foyer, reaching down all three floors. All the guests arrived on the roof, naturally, as all of them had private yachts or skiffs.

After Blythe handed his 71 off to a valet, he and David walked across the roof amid beautiful women and well-dressed men. David gawked at the people around him. He was so enamored that he even forgot to be embarrassed at his manner of dress, which was woefully inadequate. The two of them stepped into an all-glass steam lift. When they exited at the bottom, David looked up in awe. Everything around him glittered.

"Mr. Blythe," a waiter said. "Your usual table, then?"

"Quite right, Mallory," Blythe said. "Lead the way."

"You've been here before?" David asked.

Blythe nodded. "A couple of times. The wait staff here is trained to know the faces of all the local representatives," he said behind his hand as the waiter walked ahead.

The waiter seated them in a quiet corner of the restaurant with a great view of the city lights. It was then that David realized how ridiculous he must look in his father's old suit, mechanical arm dripping lubricant down the sleeve. As they sat, David collapsed into himself and hid behind his menu.

"You know," Blythe said, "I wasn't always a well-to-do representative for the Third District."

David looked up from his menu, eyebrows knit. "What were you before?"

"I was once a poor aide to the representative of the Fourth—a Mr. ... Mr. ... You know, I've quite forgotten his name. I suppose I blocked it out. I only had one suit back then, an old thing I got from a secondhand vendor. No, I had humble beginnings, much like your own. Look at me now, David; I might be the next speaker of the houses of Alönia. I'm not boasting, honestly. Without your help I wouldn't have ever got this far. Point being, I used to hunch like you, hide behind my menu, and hope nobody would notice me. Then one day I decided I didn't give a damn what they thought of me. Why should I? What do I owe them? What have they ever given me but a dirty look? I decided I'd do what I wanted, and I'd stop asking for permission from people with nothing more than a thicker pocketbook. That being said, sit up straight. You're twice as smart as half the people in this building, combined. It's time you started acting like the man you've worked so hard to become."

David blushed and shifted up in his seat, straightening his shoulders. He considered his mechanical arm for a moment before resting it on the table.

"Now tell me, doesn't that feel better?" Blythe asked.

David nodded.

"Good. So what do you see in the next season and a half as we move toward the district census?"

David paused for a moment, absently running a finger

down the menu items. He didn't even know what half of the entrees were. "Well, I don't think Speaker Walker will let us win so easily. He feigned indifference today, but I'll bet he and his aides will work overtime to find a way to thwart us before the census."

"Quite right," Blythe said. "The man puts on an indifferent face, but he is as cunning as a voxil, that one. … Oh, thank you, Sydney," Blythe said as he took a glass of some exotic pink drink before continuing, "So what should we do to protect ourselves?"

David nodded as Sydney handed the same drink to him. They hadn't ordered anything, so perhaps it was a favorite of Blythe's.

"I suggest we remain silent for the next three months," David said. He took a sip of the drink and clenched his jaw as he forced the bitter liquid down his throat. He scratched his face to conceal a twitching eye, before he continued, "No motions, no communication of any kind with any other representatives. It might even be a good idea to close the office and spend the next few months visiting with constituents. Despite the vote today we really have no idea who our friends and enemies are. Anyone could be colluding with Speaker Walker."

Blythe nodded as he took a sip of his own drink. He smacked his lips and sighed in satisfaction. "I agree … in part. We definitely don't want to make any motions or join with any representatives in theirs. However, whether we are at the office or not, Speaker Walker will try to undermine our actions. It makes sense to me to hire new staff and prepare for the office I am about to fill. We did alright in our attack today because we were in the mists all the way until the killing blow. Now we are in the wind without an anchor, and if we are challenged by one—or possibly multiple representatives—we are not going to have the steam to defend ourselves."

"You think it will come to that?" David asked.

Blythe nodded, finishing his drink and holding it up. Sydney appeared out of nowhere and swapped the empty glass for a full one.

"What do you think we should do?" David asked.

"For now, we are going to enjoy this dinner," Blythe said. "We've earned it. Tomorrow show up bright and early as we add to our defense."

David did enjoy the dinner. Roasted sky fish, xyle root salad, fresh bread … It was the best food he'd had in four cycles, but all the while he couldn't help but wonder what Blythe had in mind.

The next day, David stepped into the office and was surprised to see that Paula wasn't in yet. He didn't pay it much mind, as he was a little earlier than usual. He sat at his desk and waited for a few moments before Blythe walked in.

"Morning, David," he said, flashing one of his perfect smiles. "Has Paula made tea yet? I could sure use a cup."

"She hasn't arrived yet, sir."

"Oh, never mind, then. I'll make it. Poor girl could probably use a late start after the past two weeks. Fancy a cup?"

Six cups of tea later Blythe finished laying out his plan. Paula still hadn't arrived, nor did she for the rest of the day. However, David didn't have time to consider her absence. He powered through the day posting employment opportunities and soliciting other political staff. Blythe wanted to pack their office with workers ready to defend the Third, and who better to solicit than qualified personnel from other districts? David left the office a little early hoping to get back to his mother at a more reasonable time, but when he walked into the Lousy Lodgings complex, a work crew nearly knocked him down with the ladder they were carrying.

"Watch it, lad," one of the men said.

"Please excuse me, sir," David said. He flattened himself to the wall as the men carried the ladder through the hall. "What's all this for?"

"Remodel," the same man said. "About time this decrepit old girl got a facelift."

"A remodel …" David said.

He made it to his apartment and shut the door behind him. He smiled … his first genuine one in a while.

"Mom, things are starting to look up!"

Chapter Five

THE GIRL IN THE RED DRESS

"Ms. Samille, could you redo this section here?" David looked over the top of the form at the buxom young lady. If she leaned over his desk any more, she might fall over, but that was probably the point. "You put down your date of birth as this cycle. I presume you are in fact more than a cycle old?"

"Oh," she said, fluttering her eyes. "Much older than a cycle."

David leaned as far back in his chair as he dared and tried to look anywhere else as he handed her the form. "Yes, I should say so."

As she corrected the error, David glanced around at the applicants. Ninety percent women, all of them dressed in some provocative manner or another, accenting different features, none of which were listed in the job requirements. The room buzzed with giggles, whispers, and general conversation. Paula was absent for the third day in a row and didn't answer her phonograph when David called to check on her, so Blythe had David contact the police about her missing. Thus David was pulling double duty, checking in the applicants and sitting with Blythe for some of each interview.

"Thank you, Ms. Samille," David said after she returned the form. "If you will have a seat, I'll call you back in a minute."

He took the latest stack of forms and walked to Blythe's office. As he opened the double doors, the room stilled but then reanimated as he shut them behind him.

"I don't see how we're going to find anything close to what we are looking for in this list of floozies," David said.

"Now, David, that is no way to talk about a group of young women."

David sighed. "I suppose you're right. Even still, I doubt you could find a pair of brain cells among them. If I have to stare down any more cleavage, I'll need a sick day."

Blythe laughed at that. "A few pretty faces in the office will go a long way to boost our popularity, and in the world of politics, popularity is everything."

"Probably," David said with a shrug.

"Who do we have next, then?"

"Ms. Samantha Samille," David said, shuddering.

"Bring her in if you would."

David brought the buxom young woman in and then spent the next fifteen minutes squirming in his seat as she batted her eyes and giggled at everything Blythe said. The problem was, she actually had a pretty impressive résumé. She came with the recommendations of several businessmen and a few politicians.

"Thank you, Ms. Samille," Blythe said. "We will contact you in a couple of days and let you know." He stood and walked around his desk.

She dropped into a low—very low—curtsy and lifted the back of her hand toward Blythe. "Thank you, sir. You have no idea what this job would mean to me. I hope you know, I am your biggest supporter."

You and every other girl in the office, David thought. It really was a shame. She was a fetching girl, but no stranger to the art of seduction.

"Ms. Samille, I am only here to serve," Blythe said as he graciously took her hand and brushed it with his lips.

When she did not rise, David took her arm and dragged her unceremoniously across the floor. Once they'd exited the double doors, she gave David an indignant look and pulled her arm free. She sashayed out of the office, chin held high in a show of propriety, as if the last hour of lewdness had never happened. David sighed and selected the next résumé from the top of his stack.

"Mercedes Eleanor Alexandra Lorraine," David said to the crowd, rolling his eyes at the extravagant name.

Toward the back of the room a tall, slender girl in a vibrant red dress and matching tilt hat stood and then picked her way through the crowd. She walked toward David with all the poise of a monarch, and the closer she got, the more his jaw dropped. She was ... elegant, like his mother used to be. Lush auburn hair cascaded down and curled over one shoulder.

Then it hit him: *It's the same girl!* The same girl he'd bowled over in the grand foyer at his very first Assembly. Still, she was a breath of fresh air in comparison to the other girls, bright-eyed and pleasant.

"You're … Ms. Lorraine?" David asked.

"Good morning, Mr. Ike," she said with a polite smile. "Call me Mercy. My name is a bit too fancy for casual conversation."

"Right, um, Mercy. I'm David." He fumbled with the double doors as he gazed into her emerald eyes. "But you can call me David. I mean, would you like any refreshments?"

Mercy hid her face behind a hand and shook her head, making her auburn locks dance across her shoulders.

David tried to chuckle as he put both hands on the door handle and forced it open. "If you'll come with me, we will begin your interview."

I'm an idiot—a complete idiot! he thought as he held the door for her.

Mercy glided into the room and held back her skirts so she could admire the view of Capital City below her. Her eyes sparkled with something like excitement.

"And whom do we have here?" Blythe asked.

"You can call her Mercy—I mean, um …" David said, blushing to his core. He felt like even his earlobes had to be glowing like beacons.

"Pleased to meet you, sir," Mercy said, offering her hand and a short bob. "I've heard much of you these past few days. Apparently the Third is the new place to be."

Blythe smiled. "We have grown in popularity these past few weeks. Have a seat, Ms. ..."

"Oh, just Mercy, sir, like David said." Her face was impassive, but her eyes were full of laughter.

"Have you two met before?" Blythe asked.

"We bumped into each other once," Mercy said.

David winced as she hinted at his clumsiness a few weeks earlier.

"Well, have a seat, then, Mercy, and we will begin," Blythe said.

Mercy perched on the edge of a chair next to the table and smoothed her red skirt around her legs. Back straight, chin up, her hands clasped in her lap—she looked regal.

"Now, first off," Blythe said, "how did you hear about this job opportunity, and what about it interested you?"

"I was the aide of Representative Herald of the Second District of House Livingston, though no longer. Recent events convinced me to make an employment change."

"Recent events?" Blythe asked.

"Until recently the Second District of House Livingston was famous for being the second largest district by population," Mercy said. "Representative Herald intended to bid for the speaker position this census. Your speech at the last Assembly destroyed all such hopes. In truth I never saw your job offers for this position. I intended to apply here after the completion of the Assembly vote."

Blythe eyed her. "Why is that? What would cause you

to leave such a coveted position?"

"I don't particularly care what district I work for, sir," Mercy said. "As long as I'm working for the district that unseats Speaker Walker."

David smiled even as Blythe did so.

"So it's ambition," Blythe said.

"Ambition? Yes … I suppose that's accurate," Mercy said. "Ambition and anger, sir. Speaker Walker has been in power for as long as I've been old enough to follow politics, despite his unpopularity within 80 percent of the district. No one has had the poise to unseat him, not even my old boss—no one … until you. I know it is not very loyal of me to say it, but I don't care where I work. I will serve whatever district has the best chance of assuming the speakership."

David gulped. This girl certainly didn't mince words.

Blythe observed her for a moment, rubbing his jaw. Then he held out a hand and David passed him her file. Blythe opened the folder and looked over her résumé.

"Mercedes Eleanor Alexandra Lorraine," he said, raising his brow. "You're Armstadi."

"Indeed," Mercy said with a single nod. "My parents were first-generation immigrants to the Houses of Alönia not long after they married. I was born a few cycles later."

"Interesting. Interesting. Oh, and my, my, would you look at that?" Blythe said as he turned the page. "You're in fine company, David. Ms. Lorraine here has a PLAEE score that could rival your own, but she took it when she was sixteen." Blythe leaned toward Mercy and said, "David is the current record holder."

Mercy's eyebrows shot up, and she looked at David as though it were the first time. "That's very impressive. Your family must be proud," she said.

David looked down and nodded. "I thought I was young when I took it, but sixteen? How ever did you manage it?"

"Yes, yes, you are both very smart," Blythe said. "Thank you for rubbing it in. Mercy, you're hired."

"Hired?" Mercy said, eyes widening. "That's it? Don't you want to think about it or something?"

"I just did," said Blythe. "Your résumé is stellar. Your letters of recommendation come from first-class citizens. Your political examination score is outstanding. I would be a fool to let you out of this office without tying you up in several contracts. Not to mention, I know Representative Herald, and he only surrounds himself with the best and brightest."

Mercy smiled and looked at her lap.

David decided he liked it very much when she smiled.

"You're too kind, sir," she said.

"Please." Blythe stood and walked around his desk, taking her hand.

Blythe opened his mouth to say something else, but some commotion in the outer office interrupted him. Three firm knocks rattled the double doors. David stepped over to open the door, clenching his jaw. If it was one of those provocative girls come to see about the wait, he was going to toss her out the false wall. However, as he pulled opened the door, he came face to face with a tall constable of the Capital City Police.

"Oh, good morning, Constable," David said, dropping the scowl from his face. "Is there something I can help you with?"

"Truthfully I hope not," the constable said. "May I come in?"

David let the constable in with a wave of his hand and closed the door on many wide-eyed women.

"Good morning, Mr. Blythe," the constable said. "I am Inspector Kenneth Winston of the Capital City Police. I am terribly sorry to disturb you, sir, but I am in need of a small service from you and your aide, in follow-up to your report of a missing person."

David stiffened and chanced a look at Mercy. She appeared as calm as an anchored airship, but her eyes narrowed at the inspector, looking pensive.

"This is about Paula?" Blythe asked, and the inspector nodded. "Yes, of course, Inspector … anything. Mr. Ike—David here—and I will do whatever we can to assist finding her."

Winston nodded, looking grim. "Thank you, sirs," he said. "And it's okay if I discuss the matter in front of this young lady?"

"Yes yes," Blythe said, leaning forward. "She's a new employee. Please go on, Inspector."

Winston pulled a photograph out of his coat pocket. "I need to know if you can identify this woman."

David leaned forward and looked at the photograph. It was of a woman, middle-aged, deathly pale, with a white sheet covering everything below her shoulders. She was so gaunt that it took David a few moments to recognize her.

"Paula!" David gasped. "Is she—"

"Dead," Winston said, nodding slowly. "The boys found her body in a Capital City alley last night. We estimate she's been dead three days or so."

"No," David whispered, then swallowed. "Paula ... no."

David saw Blythe reach a shaking hand up to the photo, but he stopped just short of touching it. His eyes went wide as his mouth opened and closed, but no sound came out.

"Representative Blythe?" Winston asked. "Is it her?"

Blythe nodded. His hand fell to his side, and he turned and walked over the window, gazing down on the city. He cleared his throat. "How?" he asked, not looking up from the window.

"Ms. Carbone was tortured, sir, best we can tell. If it's all the same to you, I'd rather not go into detail."

Mercy put a hand over her mouth, stifling a gasp.

"Tortured?" Blythe asked. "Maker above."

David saw Blythe swallow hard and shut his eyes.

A moment later Blythe looked up. "I'm sure you have some questions for us, Inspector."

"Yes, Representative," Winston said. "In point of fact I do."

Blythe turned to Mercy, who still sat in her interview chair. "Mercy, I know you have not signed any contract yet, and I do not mean to demean you, but would you mind terribly making some tea for us while the inspector asks his questions? I could do with a good strong cup right about now."

"Of course, Mr. Blythe," Mercy said, rising.

"Thank you, dear. You will find everything in the corner over there. Inspector, please." Blythe turned to Winston and motioned to a chair.

"Much obliged, sir," the inspector said.

David took the chair opposite.

"Let's see here." Winston rummaged through a few pages in a little book and wetted a pen with his tongue. "Can either of you remember the last time you saw Ms. Carbone?"

"For my part it was the morning of the 10th Assembly," Blythe said, his tone somber. "She saw us off from the office and wished me luck before my ... my grand speech."

He held his composure, but David saw a few tears run down his cheek.

"And you, Mr. Ike?" Winston asked as he jotted a few things down in his book.

"Same, sir. I was with Mr. Blythe—No, wait, I did see her after that," David said, mouth falling open as he remembered.

Winston paused and looked up from his book.

David closed his eyes and thought back to the last moment he had seen Paula. "It was at a distance, and only for a moment. The Assembly vote had just concluded. I took notes on any disgruntled representatives in the room. That's when I had a thought to look up in the gallery. Paula was applauding with the other citizens."

"Was there anyone with her, or anyone near her that

you recognized?"

David thought about the man that stood in the shadow of the curtains, but he had absolutely no idea who that individual was. What was he going to say? *Yeah, there was a strange man that didn't clap when he was supposed to. He wore a funny hat, and I think he looked at me.*

David shook his head. "No one I could identify, sir. It was just too far away."

"Was there anyone in particular who looked unhappy after the speech?" Winston asked. "You mentioned you wrote some notes down."

"Nobody out of the ordinary. Speaker Walker was none too pleased, obviously. A few other representatives who sought to steal away Public Pharmaceuticals after the Third got it. Maybe one or two other aides, but none of them looked like they wanted to kill anyone. It was just politics." David gripped his chair to keep his hands from fidgeting. It was one thing to sit in the presence of a gorgeous girl, but to do so while an inspector asked you questions? He clenched his fists so hard his metal fingers scored the wood.

The inspector grunted as he made some more notes. "Politicians never look angry enough to kill anyone, and they never do kill anyone. They simply have someone else do it for them." He breathed out a puff of air. "Do any of you know if Ms. Carbone had any enemies? Anyone who would want to cause her harm?"

"No one," David said. "I only knew her for ten days, but I can't imagine anyone would want to do her harm."

"Same," Blythe said. "She's been my secretary for just

over five cycles. She was the best secretary I've ever had. Knew what I needed even before I did. Kind ... considerate ... and absolutely despised politics." Blythe choked out a half sob, half laugh.

Just as David wondered if Blythe would be able to hold it together, Mercy walked over with a tray of tea, offering a cup to Blythe first, who took it with grateful, teary eyes.

"Thank you, lass," Winston said as he took a cup, adding six spoonsful of sugar before continuing. "Did she have any family you know of? Our records say she lived alone."

"She was an orphan," Blythe said. "She mentioned that her parents died cycles ago. I'm not sure about any other family. I ... I didn't know her before, and she never told me anything about her private life."

Winston took a long sip of his tea. "I admit we don't have much to go on with this case. Everything you've told me here only confirms our fears. Ms. Carbone lived the quiet life. The facts surrounding her death are very random. There is a good deal of crime within the Capital City, especially for well-dressed women like Ms. Carbone. It could, indeed, be a random attack on a vulnerable target, but the manner of the attack gives me pause." Winston took another sip of tea.

"Why is that, sir?" David asked.

Winston looked into his tea. "Nobody tortures a woman like that unless they are extremely depraved. Almighty knows we have our fair share of those these days, but I can't imagine Ms. Carbone frequenting the kinds of areas where people like that roam. That alley we found her in, I doubt she'd ever been a grandfathom from it while she lived. No, somebody killed her grandfathoms from there and dumped the body, separating her from every possible lead."

"Is there any hope, then?" Blythe asked. "Any hope of bringing whatever monster did this to justice?"

"Some, Mr. Blythe," Winston said, offering a small nod. "Some, but not much. We will keep looking, regardless."

"We thank you, Inspector," David said, as he could tell Blythe was in no condition to see the constable out. "Paula was a good woman. If you need anything to help you keep looking for her murderer, remember that."

The inspector finished his tea and set the cup down on the desk. "That I will, Mr. Ike. That I will. I'll leave you to it. It appears you have a lot going on right now."

David got the door for Winston, grimacing at the gawking women before he shut it. As he turned back, he saw Mercy. *What an odd interview this must be for her.*

She stood quietly a fathom behind Blythe, hands clasped behind her back. She really was beautiful, but in a different way than the hussies in the waiting room. How did the woman manage to remain somber and regal at the same time? She looked up and caught David staring at her. He tried to cover it up with a reassuring smile, but he felt pretty sure he looked like an idiot—again.

"Mr. Blythe," David said. "We have people waiting, sir. Would you like me to end the process for the day? We can start afresh in the morning."

Blythe looked up from where he stood. Then he shook his head. "No. Let's keep on and be done with this dreadful business. Ms. Lorraine, are you sure you want to work for us? It's not too late to back out."

"Why would I leave, sir, when I'm needed most?"

Blythe gave a tight smile. "Good girl. I'm appointing you as my second aide. David, add *secretary* to our list of available positions."

David nodded, feeling a swirl of mixed emotions, made all the worse when he opened the office door and saw the crowded room of women.

Chapter Six

THE COST OF LOVE

David took a deep breath and let the cool mountain air wash through his lungs. It smelled of pine and prickled as it flowed through his nose. The mountains of the Seventh District were tall and white capped. Snow glistened, its milky surface broken up by gray stone and green tree. Frozen waterfalls poured out of crevices in the rock, some still flowing beneath the crystal encasing. David's hair whipped in the wind as they rounded a mountain peak at a reckless speed, yet he smiled in defiance of the danger.

"David!" his father called. "This next one's yours. Take the wheel."

"Yes, Father," David said as he took hold of his safety line and ran back to pilot the yacht. Most would stumble if they tried the same trick, but he had practically been born on an airship and his balance was superb.

"Be careful, David," his mother said, chocolate locks

flowing in the wind. "If you break your leg doing something stupid, I swear to the Maker I'll break the other one."

"Don't distract me, Mother," David said as he passed her. "I could break my leg." He ducked as she swatted at him. A moment later, and he reached the wheel.

"Right, now take the wheel," Father said, then, "Do you have control?"

"I have control," David replied.

He was only a few inches shorter than his father now, and still growing. With any luck at all, he might just fill in the family's military jacket.

"Good man," his father said. "I want you to round the peak and dive into the ravine. What are the concerns you need to compensate for?"

"There's a downdraft in the ravine," David said. "I'll have to flicker the altitude control and level off the balloon's temperature as it takes me down."

"And if you want to pass between the mountain and the Gländzend Falls?" his father asked.

"Oh … can I? Please, Father?" David asked, his eyes alight.

"Perhaps, if you can correctly explain how to do it."

David nodded. "I'll need to lower the balloon temperature as I near the falls to compensate for the cooler temperature, and then bank toward the mountain to counteract the backing wind."

"Then set to it," Father said with a devilish smile.

David gripped the wheel with one hand and the balloon temperature control with the other. Then he lined up the front of the yacht, just to the left of the mountain peak, leaving enough room to pull away if there was something unexpected on the other side of the ravine.

This was a forty-four-foot Seeker 17, one of the less expensive pleasure yachts. The Seeker 17 was an older model, which still had a hanging fuselage cabled to the underside of the oblong balloon. The sleek fuselage looked like a miniature seafaring frigate of old—at least it would if someone removed the wind fins that extended off the bottom and sides of the vessel. The Seeker's two decks allowed for a small cabin, though it was of little use after David and his father upgraded the airship's mechanics. The mini-kitchen and single bed had to go in order to fit the new burner and extra engine. While Seekers usually had two engines, this one had three: one for forward thrust, and two for directional thrust. The new burner provided exceptional lift, giving the pilot superb altitude control. All in all, the little airship pulled its weight and then some. Just the other day, David and his father clocked the Seeker doing 130 grandfathoms an hour. Not bad. Not bad at all.

David smiled as he felt the wind picking up behind him, catching the balloon and pitching the ship forward a little. He adjusted his pitch and the ship responded with grace. As the maneuver drew ever closer, David felt sweat dripping down his arms, despite the cold. Then it was upon them. The yacht passed over the mountain and the ground fell away beneath them. For a split second the airship hung in the air and David had an instant to admire the spectacular view of the winter valley, but then David saw his mother's hair shift from flowing with the wind to floating against gravity. He felt a tingle in his stomach and knew they were about to dive.

"Hold fast!" his father said as the yacht dropped with the downdraft.

David braced himself and the ship dipped forward and dove into the ravine, eating away the distance with a ravenous appetite. He had somewhere around a grandfathom between him and the icy valley floor. His hand was slippery on the altitude control, nervous sweat fouling his grip. David shared a moment with fear, but then he saw it: the Gländzend Falls. An enormous jet of water spurted out from the cliff face in a jagged ice encasement—frozen solid in an instant of time. It plunged the entire depth of the valley, melting halfway down into water and filling Diamant Lake. David spun the wheel and leaned as the ship banked toward the mountain. He flickered the altitude control, bringing the balloon's temperature up at a controlled rate, slowing their fall in time with the widening gap between the mountain and the falls. He had to level off the ship at the right altitude, low enough to fit through the gap and high enough to avoid the spray from the melted portion of the waterfall. And then he felt the wind backing.

When wind blew across those mountain peaks, it could do crazy things. Ravines the size of that one could capture portions of the wind and create a wind spiral within their depths. As David drew closer to the mountain, the spiraling wind backed against the mountain and pushed the yacht out, toward the falls. David adjusted some wind fins to try to keep the deck moderately level. Then he placed both hands on the wheel and turned it a few more times, pitting his muscles against the wind. The yacht bucked a few times before complying and angling toward the cliff face. As they drew nearer and nearer, David gritted his teeth. They were right on course. Another couple seconds and they'd spear through the gap. He looked down at his slippery hands and had a terrible thought: both hands were on the wheel. You never kept both hands on the wheel; one always had to be on the altitude control. And what was worse, the frozen falls would chill the air and send them rocketing to their doom if David wasn't ready to lower the balloon temperature.

He tried to take one hand off the wheel, but his hands were too slippery and he almost lost control. As the gap grew ever larger, panic set in. He nearly shouted for his father, until he had a thought. He let one hand slip off the wheel and flip the wheel lock so fast that the ship never even shifted. Then he dried his hands and placed one on the altitude control while the other braced against the wheel. They were almost to the gap now. David used his chin to flip the wheel lock off and gasped when the wheel pulled against his arm, but his grip held. As they passed through the gap, David pulled the altitude control, lowering the balloon temperature as they rounded the falls. As soon as they cleared the falls, David superheated the balloon and let go of the wheel, allowing the wind to push the ship back to the center of the valley. In a matter of seconds the superheated balloon carried them out of the ravine and back into the mountain peaks.

"Well done, lad!" his father said. "Couldn't have done it better myself. Of course, I would expect nothing less from the youngest cadet in Alönian history. What's the lesson to be learned here?"

"Never put both hands on the wheel?" David said, a little embarrassed.

Father nodded. "True. Using your wheel lock more effectively would have allowed for more control. But what's the lesson learned for battle?"

David thought for a moment. "Always keep an eye on the terrain. Just because you are in the air doesn't mean the ground won't mess with your navigation."

"Right you are. Terrain is king," his father said with a clap on David's shoulder. "Backing wind, updrafts, downdrafts, hot drafts, cold drafts—you won't know they're coming unless you keep an eye on the terrain."

"Was that stunt really necessary?" Mother asked, concern on her face.

"Absolutely, Marguerite," his father said. "If I'm to train this boy to fly, I already know he'll attempt something stupid. I might as well show him how to do stupid the smart way. Besides, this is the most difficult place to fly in the Fertile Plains. Where better to practice for the next academy cadet skiff race? If the last one is anything to go by, I'll wager you'll win it the next three cycles."

David's mother hmphed and looked away across the mountains. "You two are one and the same—same voice, same face, and same recklessness."

She looked regal sitting at the front of the yacht, yellow dress flowing in the wind. Many had said and many more believed that she was David's elder sister and not his mother.

"Now now, Marguerite," Father said, a smile on his lips. "That was half as dangerous as the things we did while flying after our wedding."

His mother shot Father a dangerous look, cheeks flushed.

"I hardly see how that's relevant," she said, tossing her head.

"You were conceived while pulling a stunt like that," David's father whispered.

"Oh, Father!" David said. "What makes you think I want to know that? And also, how?"

His father laughed, and his mother pointedly looked away, round cheeks betraying her smile.

"Maybe I'll try the same stunt myself someday," David said.

"You will not!" his mother said, turning around so fast her hair whipped around her shoulders.

"Yes, my boy. Your mother is quite right." His father held out a finger. "Marriage first."

"Oh heavens, David," Mother said. "I don't know why I married you."

"I'm pretty sure it was because of my skill at piloting," Father said, struggling to keep a straight face. "Come now, lad, give me the wheel. I'll dock this tub at the resort and remind your mother why she married me."

David slid across the safety line and started making the

yacht ready to dock. As they neared the resort, he looked out at the magnificent structure carved into the sides of the cliff, inverted buildings fastened to the bottom of overhangs, great docks and hot springs, intermittent between hundreds of frozen falls. David marveled at the beauty of it all, until he heard the worst possible sound in all the Thirteen Houses. An explosion rocked the deck and sent David sprawling. Aerosol countermeasure hissed as David climbed to his feet and puzzled at their shriveled balloon. It was on fire. How on earth was it on fire?

"David!" his father yelled. "Get the life-balloons. I'll get your mother."

David looked at his father for a split second before he comprehended the crisis. The yacht was already falling. They had seconds to abandon ship before they crashed.

"David!" Father shouted again.

The second call spurred him to motion. David ran to a storage cubby and threw open the lid. He felt his stomach drop.

It was empty.

"No! No no, they're not here, Father!"

"Did you put them there like I asked you?" his father asked as he hauled his wife over to David.

"I ... I know I put them here. I know I did!" David said.

"Never mind that now. To the stern, quick now!" Father said.

The ship rocked violently as it pitched back and forth, its glide turning into a plummet. The three of them staggered toward the stern of the little vessel, and David's father tore the lid off a storage cubby where they kept an emergency life-balloon—one emergency life-balloon. His father didn't waste an instant. He spun David around and fastened the restraints to his shoulders. Then he took a length of rope and tied David's mother to the restraints.

"David!" Mother said. "What are you doing? I'm staying here with you. I won't risk our son's life for my own. Stop!"

"It's strong enough to hold you both, Marguerite," Father said as he finished the knot. "We don't have time." David's father wrapped his arms around them both, squeezed them together, and whispered in their ears, "I love you both with all my life." Then he picked them up and threw them off the back of the ship.

Time slowed down as David watched his father grip the railing, shoulders square and silent tears rolling down his cheeks, yet a content purse to his lips. He looked every bit the great man he was—a man unafraid of death and ready to meet his Maker. Pain wrenched David's heart as the doomed airship careened out of control and exploded against the cliff face, disintegrating man and vessel into fire and ash.

David flailed for a moment until his wits returned to him. He could hear his mother's wailing over the top of the air whistling in his ears. He had to inflate their life-balloon. They were falling dangerously close to the cliff, and any one of the many outcroppings could dash them to pieces. He reached for the package dangling on the end of the cable. It wasn't as easy as he remembered in training, especially not with another person tied to the restraints. He checked to make sure the cable wasn't around his neck, and then he pulled the tabs on the package. A small balloon flash-inflated and bobbed above him. At the same time he felt the most excruciating pain shoot down his arm. The cable had wrapped around it in the fall and now constricted his bicep. He cried out in pain and looked up at their life-balloon. It was slowing them down, but not nearly as fast as it should. The combined weight of David and his mother was taxing the capability of the balloon. His mother noticed the problem and began untying herself from the restraints.

"Mother, no!" David yelled, pushing her hand away from the knot.

"Let me go, David," she said. "We aren't slowing fast enough. I won't trade your life for mine."

But David wrapped his legs around his mother and held her close. "I won't lose you too!" he said through gritted teeth. The pain in his arm had subsided some. In fact he wasn't sure he could feel it at all now.

His mother resisted a little, but then gave up and hugged him close. "It's going to be alright, David. I promise."

David looked one last time at the rapidly approaching ground, then he shut his eyes … and all went black.

When he opened them, he was in his apartment, his steam clock whistling beside him. Tears flowed down his face, soaking his pillow. He'd had the dream again—worse than any nightmare, because it was true, and when he awoke, the pain remained.

"I put the life-balloons in the cubby. I know I did,"

David said as still more tears flowed.

He rolled off his couch and forced his complaining limbs to function, his ruined leg buckling and his mechanical arm slouching his shoulders. Switching on the light, he bent down and retrieved a small box from under the couch. He placed it on the covers and opened it with a trembling hand. He pulled out the first item: a photograph of his mother and father. They were kissing in front of a sunset. They were always kissing, back when his father was still alive. David used to hate it, but now he'd give anything to see them kissing again. He set the photo aside with reverence and pulled out the next item: a lump of tattered rag wrapped around a hard object. Unrolling the rag, he grabbed the familiar grip of his father's triple-barreled revolver, still first in its class. David sniffed away some tears as he rubbed the sleek metal and fiddled with one of the cylinders. Then he reached in the box and pulled out a letter with the academy crest emblazoned across the top, the lines burning into his already watery eyes:

Cadet Ike,

Due to your recent and unfortunate accident, we are medically discharging you from the Officers Academy and releasing you from all commitments to the Houselands Armada. Your country thanks you for the service already rendered.

Sincerely,
Commandant Cripton

Everything in him wanted to crumple the letter up into a wad and throw it across the room, but the same burning in his heart also kept him from such action. He folded the letter up and placed it on top of the gun. Then he reached in and pulled the last item out of the box, another photograph.

It was his first event at the academy—the annual academy skiff race. In it he posed in uniform with two others. On one side his father, David Ike II, stood with an arm around David's shoulders. On his other side stood a tall, stately gentleman with white hair and a wide mustache, a man who died of a broken heart not three weeks after David's father. Admiral David Ike, hero of the Protectorate War, smiled with his son and grandson, ushering in the family's third generation of Alönian armada officers.

It was some time before David could calm himself enough to get his mother up and sit her in the living room where she could see the sun, if it dared to make an appearance in the midst of Swollock Season. She looked so different now than she did in his dreams. Her body was failing, slowly. While she used to look barely older than David, now she looked like she could be his grandmother.

Several minutes later David took a deep breath of the humid air as he walked to the train, washing away all his pain. The past was the past, and he had the future to concern himself with. He swung by the post office and picked up the mail, having forgotten it the day before, and caught the train only moments before it left. Things were going to be so much easier when the airship transportation facility was operational.

Construction rumbled along at the site. A little more than two weeks after Blythe's grand speech, Beldon Construction had laid the foundation for the transportation facility, and gutted Linden Airsail in preparation for Public Pharmaceuticals. As they neared five weeks, the transportation facility looked like a steel crossword puzzle. Another six weeks and the first airship ever would make port at the Third District, ferrying in people to the shiny new Public Pharmaceuticals facility.

David glanced through his mail, pausing when he noticed a letter with a *Linden Lodgings* crest. He popped the seal as he stuffed the other letters into his satchel, but choked on his own spit once he'd read the letter's content:

Dear Mr. Ike,

Due to recent developments in the industrial sector, apartment rentals are in high demand. As such, there will be a significant increase in rent beginning next month and continuing indefinitely. Please be informed monthly rent will amount to: 149 sterling.

LL Management
26th Day of Swollock Season

David gawked at the letter. That was double the previous rate. There was no way he could afford that, not even on his new salary. And there certainly was no way he could continue supporting Ella's rent. His mother would be all alone during the day—no one to feed her, no one to wash her. David crinkled the paper in his hand. This wasn't how it was supposed to go. He was an aide to the Third District, but rather than rising to the top, David felt squeezed out of the bottom. He fumed all the way to the office.

He was early, as usual, but Mercy was still there before him. That was four weeks running … four weeks since Paula died … four weeks since they'd hired all new staff.

"Good morning, David," Mercy said with a pleasant smile.

"Morning, Mercy," David answered, doing his best to look at her eyes and not her exquisite dress. It was white this time, with a red sash—always something red with her.

She eyed him. "You look a bit flustered. Is everything alright?"

"You don't miss much," David said. "My rent just doubled. I might have to move, but I don't know where yet."

"David, that's awful. I'm so sorry," Mercy said, eyebrows knit. "If you live in the Third's industrial sector, everything's likely to get more expensive due to the recent commerce."

David pursed his lips and nodded. "I know, but I didn't think it would happen so soon."

At that moment Blythe opened his office doors. "David, Mercy, with me."

David dropped his satchel onto his desk and followed Mercy into the office, shutting the doors behind him.

"We have a long day ahead of us, but first ... some tea," Blythe said as he carried a tray over from the corner, walking across the glass floor and the thick carpet of golden clouds fifty fathoms below it. "How has your morning been, Mercy?"

"Very fine, sir."

"Excellent, and you, David? How's your mom?"

"She's managing, sir, but it appears we'll have to move." David hoped his voice didn't sound too agitated.

"Really? Why on earth would you do that?" Blythe asked. "You're right next to the future transportation facility."

"Precisely. Rent just doubled," David said, trying to keep the venom out of his words.

"Doubled?" Blythe asked, eyes wide.

"Doubled, sir."

Blythe's mouth worked for a moment before he slammed his tea down on the desk, causing a bit of it to slosh over some papers. "Doubled! Those greedy, no-good bastards! Oh ... pardon me, Mercy. But, David, you can't afford that, not with your mother to take care of."

"Quite right, sir," David said. "We'll manage, though. I'll find another apartment."

"You will not," Blythe said. "Not if I have anything to say about it."

"Sir, don't trouble—" David started to say, but Blythe cut him off with a flourish of his right hand as he picked up his phonograph.

"Yes, Operator? Get me the manager of Linden Lodgings."

David glanced over at Mercy, but she appeared as perplexed as he was. A moment later the phonograph's steam projection wavered into the form of a gangly man, his face as narrow as a weasel.

"Are you the manager of Linden Lodgings?" Blythe asked even before the steam projector could finish solidifying.

"I am. Who the devil are you?"

"William Jefferson Blythe IV, Representative of the Third District."

"Oh, do forgive me, sir. I didn't, um, recognize you. My steam projector is getting a bit old, and—"

"Did you just double rent for your apartments?" Blythe interrupted.

"Well, yes, times being what they are …" The manager uttered a nervous chuckle. "Big things are happening here in the Third—"

"My aide lives in your apartment," Blythe said, interrupting him yet again. "Did you know that?"

"Um … uh, well, no, sir. I had no idea. The owner—"

"Well he does, and I didn't spend all this time and effort to make big things happen in the Third so sniveling apartment managers could starve my employees right out of their homes. Is that clear?"

"Yes, sir, of course, sir, but the owner—"

"Good. I want you to stop this foolishness. David Ike's rent will be reduced at once."

"Absolutely, sir," the manager said, practically slobbering out the words. "But, sir, I do not mean to be obstinate, but we in fact have three David Ikes in residence here. To which one are you referring?"

David groaned and rested his head in his hands. "The one on the seventh floor," he said.

"Did you hear that?" Blythe asked the manager. "The one on the seventh floor."

"Yes, sir, I see him here in my records. His rent will be reduced at once. We are so terribly sorry for this inconvenience and we want you to know that we have nothing but the greatest possible respe—"

"Good, see that it gets done," Blythe said before closing the line.

"Mr. Blythe," David said, looking up from his hands with a wide smile, "I don't know what to say."

"Nothing, David. You don't have to say anything, because I'm not done yet. What is the current state of your mother?"

"She's … immobile, sir," David said, puzzling at the question. "Airship accident a few cycles back."

Blythe nodded as he wrote something down on a slip of paper. "I want you to file this today with the house clerk," he said as he finished writing and then handed the slip to David. "It's an application for a nonprofit to support victims of airship accidents. I have a fundraiser tomorrow night. I'll introduce the nonprofit and see if we can't get some donations to help pay for your mother's medical bills."

"Sir," David said as he took the paper, eyes watering. "I … I don't know what to say. It's more than I could ever ask for."

He glanced over at Mercy again. She favored him with

a warm smile. Then he hid his face in shame as a few tears lined his cheeks.

"David, again, you don't have to say anything," Blythe said. "I require nothing for my friendship. Part of friendship is love, and part of love is caring for the needs of others. I don't want anything from you but a smile."

David wiped a sleeve across his face and nodded.

"Now," Blythe said, "I have a task for you two. Next week we are dining with Don Johnson, manager of Public Pharmaceuticals. Both of you are coming, as well as my wife and one of Johnson's assistants. I want it to be at the nicest restaurant in Capital City. I want them to serve Johnson's favorite food, which, you will soon discover, is a big deal to him. Technically speaking, we do not need Johnson's cooperation with us in order to move Public Pharmaceuticals, but it would sure make the transition smoother if we had it. This dinner must be a hit. Do you understand what I'm asking?"

"Yes, sir," David and Mercy said in unison.

As the two of them walked out of the office, David felt energetic, eager to start a hard day's work, but when he saw Samantha sitting primly at her desk in her latest seductive outfit, he struggled to hold back a frown. How she had managed to fill Paula's secretarial position, David did not know. Apparently, on top of her first-class letters of recommendation, her father was also a prominent admiral in the Houseland's armada, a valuable ally.

The new staff wasn't all bad news, though. In addition to Samantha, Blythe had hired assistant aides, one each for David and Mercy. David's assistant, Bethany, was as brainless as an overripe gourd and wholly smitten with Blythe, though nowhere near as sensual as Samantha. When Blythe asked David which applicant he would prefer working with, David picked Bethany, as she was one of the only applicants not exposing herself in some fashion—and she was too stupid to be a political spy. She would be next to no help at all—after two weeks she still couldn't figure out how to make tea—but David preferred to work alone anyway.

"Samantha," Blythe called through the still open doors, "I need you in my office, if you would."

"Right away, sir," Samantha said primly, standing with a haughty look and stepping into the office.

Mercy's assistant, on the other hand, was quite the opposite of Bethany. Francisco Martin Duran was in his thirties and silent as a lamb. He had a very odd mechanical eye that swiveled on its own accord and rarely in time with his good eye. David could never really tell where he was looking. The man seemed perfectly content to do as he was told. Thus far the only words David had heard Francisco say were "Yes, mum." It did seem strange that a man his age was still an assistant aide, working for a girl half his age, but Mercy was an intelligent, powerful woman, and David didn't judge. And besides, Francisco did flawless work. Blythe had selected him personally, as Francisco used to work for one of his old friends.

"Francisco," Mercy said. "I want you to go down to the city. Visit all the top-tier restaurants in the gold sector. Find out which ones Don Johnson frequents."

"Yes, mum," Francisco said, jumping up from his desk and walking toward the door.

"Oh, and Francisco," Mercy called after him, "see if you can't find out what he prefers to eat."

"Yes, mum," Francisco said again, looking at the door with his good eye, and her with the other one.

David glanced at Bethany, feeling as though he should give her something to do as well.

She looked at him with pursed lips and a vacant expression.

"Bethany, would you ... um ..."

"Yes?" Bethany said, nodding along with every word.

"Would you mind making me a cup of tea?"

Chapter Seven

THE PINNACLE

The week passed sooner than expected, and David rushed into the office the morning of the fancy dinner purely on principle. He and Mercy had already orchestrated and implemented every possible detail, yet he'd come to the office early all the same. Even if he had to sit alone for the next ten hours awaiting the banquet, at least he'd be ready in case something went wrong.

He had just finished the first page of his favorite book, *House Law,* when the office door rattled. Looking as stunning as ever in a simple, knee-length blue dress with red heels and a matching red flower in her hair, Mercy walked in carrying a broad hang-up bag. She skittered across the office, heels tapping some offbeat tune, and laid the awkward bundle across her desk with a huff. She blew a strand of hair out of her face and looked up, eyes going wide.

"David," she said, straightening up into proper

posture, "I didn't see you there."

"Sorry," David said. "I … I would have helped you with that bag, but you surprised me."

She smiled and smoothed her dress. "I'm guessing you couldn't stay away either, huh? Better to sit and wait here than sit at home."

"Precisely. I'd pace a hole right through my floor."

She snickered at that.

David nodded toward her desk. "What's in the bag?"

"My gown."

David shook his head. "Gown?"

"My gown for this evening?" Mercy said, rolling her eyes.

"What's wrong with the one you're wearing?"

"I couldn't wear this to a formal dinner," Mercy said with a little laugh. "It's not proper. Come now, you're just messing with me. Where's your formal suit?"

"Well … I mean, I planned on just wearing this." David said, feeling some color rise to his cheeks.

"What?" Mercy placed her hands on her hips and laughed. "Didn't your mother ever tell you that you can't wear a business suit to a formal dinner?"

"No." David looked down at his father's tattered old suit. "At least not for a long time now."

"David, I'm so sorry. I'd quite forgotten your situation in life." Mercy's face was as pink as a pull of taffy.

"It's alright. I have it better than some. It might be my only suit, but it's one more than a lot of people have."

Mercy smiled, but it didn't quite reach her eyes. She looked away and absently brushed some dust off her hang-up bag. "Why don't we go get you one?" she said, looking up again, emerald eyes sparkling.

"A gown?" David asked, raising his eyebrows.

"No, silly—a suit ... a formal dining suit. We have plenty of time before our dinner with Johnson."

"Well, I don't know. I ... well ..."

"What's the matter, David?" she asked, a devilish twinkle in her eyes. "Afraid to go shopping with me?"

"No, never, but ... I can't afford to buy a suit."

"And you don't have to," Mercy said. "I'm buying."

"I couldn't possibly let you do that."

"David, I avoid speaking of my family heritage. But the truth is, I come from a good deal of money, and I have more than enough to buy my friends a gift or two."

David shook his head, but it was a feeble effort. He wanted a new suit with all his heart. "I can't, Mercy. I can't accept charity. I'll accept it for my mother, but not for myself. If I go down that road, living off the benevolence of others, I'll never learn to provide for myself."

"Who told you that?" Mercy asked, brow furrowed.

"It's something my father used to say."

"Oh. Well then, I won't buy it for you. Consider it a long-term loan."

"What?"

"Come on, get your things." Mercy walked toward the door, her blue dress swishing with every step.

"But I—"

"Are you going to make a lady get the door for herself?" she asked in an admonishing tone.

"No, ma'am," David said, jumping up and rushing to the door.

She took his arm, and together they walked toward the orbital transportation dock. But as they neared, Mercy pulled him down a different corridor.

"Where are we going?" David asked.

"To catch an air-taxi," Mercy said with an obvious look.

"Air-taxi? Why not the orbital sky-liner? They're free."

"That will take hours. Not to mention they smell." She wrinkled her nose and tossed her hair.

David found himself smiling at her, but he wasn't really sure why. Mercy had never been this casual before, but then again he had never been with her in anything other than a work environment. She was playful, like a puppy out on a walk, or maybe it was the other way around. Easy laugh, easier smile, more genuine—this was the true Mercy.

As they walked, David looked around at the foreign corridor. He noticed a lot less day workers and security guards and a lot more aides and representatives. As they rounded a corner, the hallway opened up into a wide glass room with a dozen lines to a dozen glass doors. Every few moments one of the gates would open with a hiss, and cool, high-altitude air would rush in as those departing swapped places with those arriving. In this manner air-taxis offloaded and loaded at a steady pace. The room echoed with the hissing of the doors and the rush of cool wind. Indeed, it was a good ten degrees colder than the rest of the orbital.

The entire room glowed with muted light as the orbital currently sat in the middle of a cloud bank. David avoided looking down, knowing that beneath his feet were only a few inches of glass and then swirling mist. But the glass floor hardly unnerved him as much as what was holding his arm.

Mercy still clung to his arm, his mechanical one, as if it was the right and proper thing to do. Her thin dress looked to be providing little in the way of warmth. For the moment he didn't mind her proximity, but in a few hours David knew his arm would sweat fluid and soak his jacket, as it did every day. He shuddered to think of the beautiful Mercy grabbing his arm, as a lady should, only to recoil at the touch of sodden cloth. It was a shame; he liked it when she held his arm.

They were second in line for a taxi now, and David could see the little airships swirling around the dock like a hive. Each was a rear-excess Porter, distinct for its oversized pontoons. They weren't the fastest or most agile craft, but they had an extremely comfortable ride. As he watched, an air-taxi backed into the little dock in front of the glass door, and an automatic clamp fastened to the back of the craft. But when the rear hatch opened, David sucked in a gulp of air. Eric Himpton stepped out in a burgundy suit and walked toward their glass door. What were the chances?

The door opened, and the passengers in front of David and Mercy stepped through to occupy Eric's taxi. Eric bumped shoulders with one of them but didn't bother apologizing. The orbital doors snapped shut behind Eric, and he frowned as he saw David and Mercy. Mercy's face remained the same as always—pleasant and impassive—but now she gripped David's arm with both hands.

"Hello, Mercy," Eric said, not even acknowledging David. "Stooping a bit low, don't you think? I would have thought Blythe could find someone else to take the trash out."

David had been called much worse than trash, so the comment didn't bother him—much—but Mercy didn't look interested in letting it go.

"Trash?" she said as she looked up at David, eyebrows furrowed. "Now that is embarrassing. How on earth did trash beat your score on the PLAEE?"

Eric glared for a few more seconds before stomping off.

David looked at Mercy, but she kept her gaze forward, hands gripping his arm, only the corners of her mouth betraying a hint of a smile.

The glass doors opened for them, and Mercy squeaked in terror. She ripped her hands from David's arm as her loose skirt caught the wind and flew up. David did his best to find very interesting things to look at everywhere *but* Mercy's general direction.

"I hate this dress," Mercy said, reasserting control over her wayward skirts, pinning them to her legs.

"Really?" David grasped for something to smooth over the situation. "Because, well, everyone else loves it."

Mercy shot him a look.

"I mean … Oh. That was poorly said, I think."

Mercy snickered a little, but as they entered the taxi, it was difficult to tell who was blushing more.

"Royal's, if you please," Mercy said to the air-taxi driver.

They took their seats in the spacious cabin with room for eight. David took note that they sat on comfy leather seats, and the floor was actually carpeted. The docking clamps released and the ponderous craft listed slowly through the sky into the cloud bank below. Unlike Blythe's Cloud Cutter, which sliced through the air like a knife, the Porter plowed the wind, trading speed for relaxation. The all-glass cockpit covered a front third of the airship.

The windows fogged as the craft dropped into Swollock Season's humidity. The driver dipped the ship into the low-altitude air traffic lanes in between Capital City's skyscrapers. David looked out his window at the thousands of personal craft: agile skiffs, delivery barges, an occasional orbital guard ship brisling with chain-guns, and lumbering tugs pulling pontoon crates. Their air-taxi pilot banked around the residential section of the city and into the commerce sector, docking at one of the top floors of a gorgeous glass-and-silver tower.

"Thank you, sir," Mercy said, handing the pilot a sterling.

"Thank you, miss," the pilot said, eyes gleaming as he touched his cap with the coin in hand.

David offered his right arm to Mercy before she had a chance to take his fake left one, his sleeve already beginning to soak with mechanical fluids. She accepted it with a smile and pointedly grabbed a handful of skirt with the other, this time prepared for the gust of wind that rushed through the open door. Here the wind felt hot and thick, unlike the high-altitude air around the orbital. Somehow the hot air felt as though it pushed with more force than the cold. Cold air would bite and sting, but hot air sapped and drained. The air-conditioned shopping center called them to it as they walked through the sticky smog.

They stepped through the tower door onto a halo-shaped balcony circling the entire tower, its center consisting of an enormous waterfall. David staggered as he gazed at the opulence around him, yet something about the waterfall was odd. As he drew nearer, he noticed that it flowed all thirty stories, from the ground floor to the penthouse … against gravity. David leaned over the railing, watching the water flow up with lazy momentum. Bioluminescent fish sparkled within, glowing florescent greens, yellows, purples, or pinks.

"Pretty, isn't it?" Mercy said from his arm.

"When you've lived at the bottom for so long, you forget how many levels of luxury there are. It's gorgeous." After a few more seconds David added, "There is no way I will ever be able to pay you back if you buy me a suit from here."

"Now don't go changing your mind on me." Mercy exaggerated a groan as she pulled him away from the waterfall and toward a fancy store with a carved marble and filigree sign that read *"Royal's."*

As they entered the shop, David gawked at the racks

and racks of suits in more colors than he knew existed, not to mention just as many more mirrors. A store clerk in a gray suit and sky-blue bowtie greeted them.

"We are looking for a formal dining suit for this evening," Mercy said as the clerk favored them with a well-practiced, well-pasted smile.

"I see." The clerk looked up and down David. "That is the military semiformal suit from the 3230s."

David nodded. "That's quite right, sir. It was my father's."

"Hmm, yes, and I think it's seen better days."

The clerk walked around David, assessing him with a critical eye. He stretched a tape between his hands that David hadn't known he was holding and measured his shoulders and arms.

The clerk said, "Let's try something over here."

He led them to a rack of colorful jackets and held up a bright red one. David tried his best to look pleased. If Mercy was paying the bill, he wasn't about to be picky.

"No, definitely not," Mercy said. "Something that says power and not butterfly."

The clerk nodded and moved to another rack, pulling out an all-black jacket with black-velvet piping.

"Too much power," Mercy said with a shake of her head.

She proceeded to say no to the next dozen jackets, all for reasons David didn't quite understand.

After fifteen minutes the clerk grew frustrated. "Well, how about you show me exactly what you're looking for, then maybe I can help find the right size?"

Mercy clasped her hands behind her back and glided through the racks, heels clicking on the marble floor. She perused a few coats from the rack before shoving them back in with words like "Yuck" and "Ew."

"This one," she said on her fourth rack.

She walked back to David, carrying a midnight-blue jacket with a black, velvet shawl-collar and matching piping. He wasn't sure why, but he liked this one. It was impressive yet elegant.

"Can we get one in this size?" Mercy asked.

The clerk nodded and walked to a rack.

"Let me help you with your jacket," Mercy said, stepping up behind David and loosening it from his shoulders.

David shrugged it off and paused as he felt a breeze pass through his pants. He'd quite forgotten about the sizable hole in the back of his trousers until he heard Mercy giggle. Whirling around, he put his back against a coatrack. Mercy had a hand shielding her eyes, shaking as she fought against the giggles.

"Well, at least we're even now," she said. "You've shown me your knickers and I've shown you mine."

Then she clapped a hand over her mouth as if to trap the words that already escaped. David couldn't help but laugh. In the end it was probably much more embarrassing for Mercy, and if she could laugh it off, so could he. But the blush came nonetheless for both of them.

The clerk returned, looking puzzled at both their red faces. He held out the coat to help David put it on, but

BORN HERO

David opted to take the coat and shoulder it on himself, all the while keeping his rear to the wall. The clerk just shrugged and folded his arms.

It fit perfectly, better than anything he had ever worn. He smiled as he stepped up to the mirror.

"Do you like it?" Mercy asked.

"Very much. But …"

"But what?" Mercy asked with a frown.

"My arm will soil it in no time." David looked down at his mechanical appendage as lubricant dripped from his finger.

Mercy tapped her lips with a finger. "We'll be needing the pants too," she said to the clerk. "Sooner rather than later, for all our sakes." She gave David a secret smile as the clerk went to retrieve the pants. "When he gets back, you find a fitting room and try on the pants. I'll be back in a minute." With that she turned and walked toward the door.

"Where are you going?" David asked. He was fairly sure the only reason the clerk hadn't thrown him out the minute he walked in was because Mercy held his arm.

"I'll be back," she said again from outside the entrance.

The clerk returned with some midnight-blue trousers and David fought to keep the panic from his face.

"Um, she's run off," he said. "Is there a fitting room I could use?"

"Most women do, sir. Right this way." The clerk betrayed nothing more than a flat gaze.

David had just slipped the matching trousers on when

he heard Mercy's voice through the closed door: "David, I'm going to pass something over the door, okay?"

"Okay," he said, wondering what she had.

A second later Mercy tossed in what looked like a long black sock, except it had a hole on both ends and it was made of rubber.

"Slide that over your arm," she said. "Then put this on."

Now a white formal shirt plopped onto his head. It took some doing, but the rubber sock stretched over his mechanical arm, reaching from his wrist to his shoulder. After that he buttoned on the shirt and jacket. When he stepped out of the fitting room, Mercy stood with two cravats—one black, one silver. She held them to his chest and then threw the black one to the clerk.

"Nope," she said. "Silver looks better."

"This is amazing," David said as he pulled back his left sleeve and marveled at the rubber sock. "What is it?"

"Um … well," Mercy said as she slipped the cravat around his neck. "It's a type of ladies' accoutrement."

David looked up with a start, not liking where that was going.

"Women of a more … robust nature will slide these over their arms whenever they want them to appear more slender. They come in most colors and look about like a sleeve to a dress."

"Oh," David said, letting out his breath. "I thought you meant a different type of accoutrement."

Mercy's mouth twitched at the corners as she finished tying his cravat.

"Wouldn't this make their hands go numb?" David asked, flexing his mechanical arm.

"Oh they do. But then again, if their hands are numb, they won't be able to put as much in their mouths, thereby solving the original problem."

"That makes rather morbid sense," David said as he puzzled it out.

Mercy laughed. "It does. Now ... here." She took a handkerchief from a hidden pocket and rolled it under the rubber sleeve like a cuff. "That should soak up anything that tries to sneak out. Take a look." She pushed him toward a mirror.

David hardly recognized himself. His shoulders still slanted and his leg still buckled, but he looked ... refined, less like an invalid and more like a war hero.

"Do you like it?" Mercy asked.

"It's ... amazing. I'm never going to be able to repay you ... for everything."

Mercy looked away and walked toward the clerk. "You don't have to. You know that, don't you?"

"I'm going to try," David said.

She shrugged and handed the clerk a coin purse, not bothering to look inside. "Thank you, sir."

"You're welcome, miss," the clerk said. "Do come and visit us again."

A few minutes later they stood at the dock, and as David pressed a signal button to call a cab, Mercy said, "I'm a bit jealous. In that suit you're going to outshine me. And to think I worked so hard picking out my gown."

"Outshine you? That's impossible. You could put my old suit on and still make the most beautiful women envious." He shook the bag holding his old suit for emphasis. "Wait … you were fishing for that compliment, weren't you?"

"A woman is always fishing for a compliment, David," Mercy said as she stepped into the taxi, leaving David at the entrance.

As he watched her walk ahead of him, he wondered exactly how beautiful her gown really was.

* * * * *

In preparation for the evening's dinner with Don Johnson, David and Mercy had made reservations at the Pinnacle, one of the most extravagant restaurants in all Alönia. It resided on the top floor of the tallest building in Capital City. In fact it was so far up that on most days it poked into Alönia's lower cloud cover. Tonight Jeshua smiled upon them, for the clouds were sparse and low, and the whole restaurant glowed with the pale-blue light of the moon. The tower looked rather like a peculiar tree, multiple oblong discs all attached to a central structure. Its imposing edifice conveyed an unmistakable message: those who dined there rose above all others; those who dined there were at the pinnacle of society.

David had arrived a few hours early to harass the wait staff with nitpicky details involving matters he really knew nothing about. Now he loitered around the restaurant lobby in his new suit just a couple minutes before eight.

"David?" someone behind him asked.

David turned and saw Blythe in a black pinstriped suit with a bright green cravat. An elegant woman in her early forties clung to his arm. She wore a dress of forest green, accenting her blonde hair and pale complexion. Once she had probably been exceptionally beautiful, though she had not aged well. Cycles clawed her face with furrows of time around her eyes, through her forehead and beneath her jaw. However, what she lacked in dazzling youth, she made up for in sparkling gems. An emerald almost the size of Blythe's cravat clung to her neck like the vise it was—or perhaps *vice* in her case. Bracelets and rings, all shining and glimmering in the moonlight, covered her arms and fingers.

"I barely recognized you," Blythe said. "That is quite some suit, very dignifying."

"Thank you, sir. I have it on loan."

"Well, you couldn't have picked a better night to wear it. Allow me to introduce my wife, Bernice." Blythe guided the bedazzled woman toward David.

"Pleased to meet you, Mrs. Blythe," David said, offering his hand.

Mrs. Blythe gave David her dainty, rock-encrusted fingers. "So this is the young man responsible for your sudden rise to power?"

"Bernice," Blythe said with a forced smile. "Probably isn't the best spot to discuss that. But, yes, David has been invaluable to me, and without him I would never be where I am today."

Bernice gave her husband a mocking smile and turned

toward David. "Would that he said such praise to all of us. You must have done something truly spectacular to warrant that slobber."

Blythe offered an awkward chuckle, and David found himself in a precarious position. He decided to use his favorite weapon in his arsenal for social conflicts: he played dumb.

"That's very kind of you, ma'am. Such words coming from you are high praise indeed."

David bent to kiss her hand, but froze halfway in the act. Every thought in his head was raptured away—every action, every movement. His very body no longer answered his command. For, just as he bent to kiss Mrs. Blythe's hand, a woman with auburn hair and a ruby-red gown entered the Pinnacle. Still clutching Mrs. Blythe's hand, David turned and followed her with his eyes as she walked into the lobby and a greeter took her cloak. Wearing a red ball gown with gold trim, Mercy thanked the wide-eyed greeter and turned toward David and the Blythes. Her skirts billowed around her legs, coming together in a fitted bodice that praised her figure. It looked like a rose, with petals surrounding her chest, opening to display her bare shoulders and a shining face. Her auburn hair was up, but for a single lock that curled down her back. No jewelry—only a large white flower pinned in her hair, its sweet scent growing stronger with every step she took: modest, elegant, and utterly gorgeous.

"You look … beautiful. I don't think I've ever seen someone so beautiful in all my life." David hadn't really intended to say the words out loud, just as he hadn't intended to say them while still halfway in the act of kissing Mrs. Blythe's hand.

"Thank you, David," Mercy said, her eyes looking a little watery.

"Are you going to hold my hand like that all day?" Mrs. Blythe asked.

David straightened abruptly, nearly pulling Mrs. Blythe off her feet. "I'm so sorry, Mrs. Blythe. I'd quite forgotten."

Playing dumb! David thought. *You're the biggest idiot that ever walked the Fertile Plains.*

"Quite alright, David," Mr. Blythe said in an easy tone. "One can hardly blame you for losing your wits in the face of such a gorgeous creature." He offered Mercy a little bow.

How was it so easy for him? Compliments flowed from him as if they were right and proper.

Mrs. Blythe let out an exasperated sigh. "Are we just going to stand here, or is somebody going to get me a drink?"

"I agree with Mrs. Blythe," Mercy said. "Mr. Johnson, if he is true to form, will be fifteen minutes late. The proper thing to do would be to head up to our private dining room and take some refreshment."

"Smart girl," Mr. Blythe said, guiding his wife toward the steam lift.

"Yes, why don't we all just do what the *gorgeous creature* says," Mrs. Blythe mumbled as they walked.

David offered Mercy his left arm, sealed tightly in its

rubber sleeve.

"That is an exceptional suit," Mercy said as she grasped the proffered arm and lifted the hem of her skirts. "Whoever picked it out was brilliant."

David smiled. "Aye, she is that and more."

The four of them took refreshment in their private dining room, at the pinnacle of the Pinnacle. The oval room featured a glass ceiling that extended all the way down to the wainscoting along the wall. It felt a bit like walking inside a diamond with the moon and starlight glimmering off all the crystal dishes. The Pinnacle staff lit the room with glow stones so that one truly believed they were dining with the stars.

As Mercy had predicted, Johnson arrived exactly fifteen minutes late. He was enormous, not only tall but wide as well. Jowls wriggled and shook with every word, his voice resonating inside his impressive girth.

"Representative Blythe, it is a pleasure to finally meet you in person," Johnson said as everyone took their seats.

He had brought one assistant, Devin, though anyone who looked at him would know that his skill set was less in the way of *pharmaceuticals* and more in the way of *bodyguard*.

David flicked his fingers at one of the waiters, and the restaurant staff began serving them immediately. Johnson had come for the food, and David wasn't going to make him wait.

"I can assure you that the feeling is mutual," Blythe said. "May I introduce my wife, Bernice?"

"Yes, yes, charmed," Johnson said, rubbing his hands

together in greedy anticipation, eyes never leaving the trays of food the waiters brought to the table.

Francisco had spent the previous week collecting information on Don Johnson's eating habits, which largely revolved around two words: "lots" and "expensive." Dozens of waiters brought platters upon platters of steamed spider crab, crushed tuber salads, and rare quilled mollusk. The restaurant boasted specialized chefs who could cut the mollusk meat from the poisonous quills. One wrong slice could lace the delicacy with an incurable toxin. Johnson wolfed down the cuisine with ravenous delight. Flecks of food and spittle flew around the room as he chewed, spoke, and laughed at the same time.

David did his best not to gag at the sight. Very little in the way of actual conversation accompanied the meal. Mrs. Blythe said nothing, ate nothing, and drank much. Mr. Blythe picked at his food while doing everything in his power to facilitate Johnson's enjoyment. David orchestrated the waiters, accepting pointers from Mercy throughout the night. Johnson's assistant—bodyguard—ate his food while assaulting Mercy with roving eyes. Another few minutes and David promised himself he was going to put his metal fist through the man's presumptuous face.

"David, be so good as to pass the sweet buns," Mr. Blythe said after Johnson inhaled all three of the ones on his own plate.

David reached across the table with his mechanical arm, but the buns were just out of reach. He stretched a little farther, and then something dreadful happened. His rubber sleeve slid up his metal arm and some of the pent-up gas escaped. It sounded like something terribly similar to flatulence. David snatched up the sweet buns and passed them to Blythe, who pursed his lips as he accepted them, one eyebrow raised.

David leaned back in his chair, hoping nobody had noticed, but as he rested his arm in his lap, it happened again. The same fart sound, but this time it exuded from his lap. He sat very still. The first *incident* might have been mistaken for the rolls sliding against the table, and the natural ambiance of the room covered up the second from everyone's ears, save Mercy.

"Is something the matter?" Mercy asked as she leaned close to him.

"That ladies undergarment is causing my arm to fart," David said, attempting to whisper, but still sounding panicked.

Mercy sat straight again, taking a quick bit of salad and doing her best to listen to Mr. Blythe's current story. As David thought of the best way to fix the situation, he noticed Mercy shaking as though she were in a chill. David looked at her. Her face looked intrigued as she listened to the story, but her body shook as she stifled the obvious laughter inside. She wouldn't look back at David, probably fearing she'd lose her composure.

David frowned. This was a real emergency, and Mercy was laughing at him. All of a sudden Blythe reached the end of his story and delivered the punch line. As Johnson barked out a laugh, sending flecks of food around the room, David took advantage of the moment and squeezed his rubber sleeve. The rest of the pent-up gas wheezed out with a burbling hiss. Mercy exploded with laughter to go along with Johnson, finally having an opportunity to release her emotion and unable to hold it in any longer after David's closing performance. She did, however, laugh far harder than Johnson at a story that really wasn't that funny. The rest of the table laughed awkwardly, joining in only to avoid looking as though they were too slow to understand the joke. Mercy visibly restrained herself, reasserting her rigid posture as the humor simmered down. David let out a sigh. Crisis averted.

"Aww," Johnson said after stuffing one last bit of sky fish into his greasy jowls. Then he belched so loud that Mercy actually jumped. "Splendid! Absolutely splendid evening, William! I think I'll get on quite well with a man of such exquisite tastes."

"I'm glad you enjoyed yourself," Blythe said. "Perhaps we'll have more opportunities once we complete your new facility at the Third."

"But, Representative, next it will be my turn to entertain you. Yes. Yes, you must," Johnson said as Blythe put up dismissive hands. "We will have lunch on my yacht over the Desert Maw. How does a fortnight from today sound? No, wait. I'll be in Armstad then. Three weeks—what do you say to that?"

"We wouldn't want to impose on you, Mr. Johnson," Blythe started to say, but the fat man bowled right over him.

"Tell me, lad," Johnson said to David. "Have you ever sailed the Desert Maw?"

"No, sir, never," David said, surprised at being singled out.

"It's settled, then. I'll see you at 9:00 a.m. at Airship Landings three weeks hence. Put it on my calendar, Devin."

Devin grunted but did nothing as he continued to eye Mercy.

The little party rose together and bid their farewells after the appropriate amount of social slavering.

Once Johnson left, Blythe wrung his hands with delight. "I'd say that was a rousing success. Well done, David and Mercy. You've both earned the morning off."

"Our pleasure," Mercy said.

"Thank you, sir," David added with a nod.

Blythe rose and helped his tipsy wife to the lobby, then David offered Mercy his arm.

"Is it safe?" Mercy asked.

David frowned and squeezed the rubber sleeve. It sputtered one last, wet fart before fizzling out.

"Quite safe," David said before offering his arm again.

Mercy laughed and took his arm.

Once they all reached the lobby, Blythe bought David and Mercy each a taxi back to their respective apartments. David dreamed all the way home of a red gown, a sweet smile, and auburn hair. Life seemed like it could not be any better.

Chapter Eight

SPIES AND CONFIDANTS

David used the opportunity afforded by his morning off to visit the Capital City Water Station, famous for its wide and exotic variety of inventory. Since his supply of lubricant cartridges for his bionic arm was running low due to the incessant leakage, he decided to see what the station had to offer. He was not disappointed. When he stepped into the shop, he gasped at the rows upon rows of clear, bubbling tanks. David spared a frantic glance around at all the options. Unfortunately all the station assistants were otherwise occupied with other customers. He meandered through the tanks and gawked at the water prices; some of them sold for fifty sterling per milliliter. He paused at one tank and read the description.

Magnetic Water: Infused with micro-particulates for magnetic manipulation. Uses include solid-state pumps and steam projectors.

David marveled at the glass tank, leaning forward and looking through its blue-tinged depths, but when he cupped his hands over his eyes, his metal hand stuck to the side of the glass and vibrated something fierce. He pulled his hand with all his might as it rattled against the tank and the water within began to churn. Finally the hand pulled free with one last buzz and a pop. The air smelled of ozone, and David spun around to see if anyone had noticed the incident. Luckily all the salesclerks were still preoccupied with describing products with well-rehearsed, exaggerated descriptions. David breathed a sigh as he continued down the aisle, rubbing his metal arm where it attached to his shoulder, skin still prickling.

But another tank of water interested him as he walked down the next row, and he couldn't help but take a peek into the gray depths as they arced and sparked with current. This time he held his bionic arm well away. The plaque read *Thermal Water* and described its uses within hydroponic generators. He sucked in a breath with fascination, a feeling that only compounded as he continued to meander through the station and read descriptions. *Boiler Water*, which boiled several times faster than regular water. *Antifreeze Water*, which did not freeze at any known temperature. *Easy Ice*, which froze solid at most temperatures. These were just a few of the more interesting ones.

As he walked toward a salesclerk, he got a peculiar look from the customer the clerk had just finished helping. He shrugged off the cheekiness and gave the salesclerk his best smile. The freckle-faced lad smiled back with a toothy grin—a grin that was perhaps a bit more excited than the situation called for.

"Good morning, sir. Can I help you?"

"Yes, good morning, um ..." David squinted down at the lad's name tag before continuing, "Dillon, I was hoping to resupply with lubricant cartridges for my bionic arm."

"Excellent, sir. I know just what you're looking for," Dillon said with another grin.

He turned and led David down a few aisles.

"Begging your pardon, sir, but did you happen to look into the magnetic water tank?"

David sucked in a breath and cleared his throat. "Yes, um, as a matter of fact I did. Fascinating stuff."

"Yes, sir. The reason I ask is, well, your hair is still filled with static." Dillon turned with the same smile and pointed up at David's hair.

David put his real hand to his head and felt the hair stick to his fingers as it stood on end. "Oh. ... That would explain the look that customer gave me."

"Quite so, sir. You may want to wet it down before you meet up with any young ladies."

"Thank you, Dillon. Much appreciated," David said as he did his best to brush his hair flat, but it was a lost cause.

"Absolutely, sir. Now, as for your lubricant cartridges, might I suggest some of our custom-mixed water?" The lad stopped at a shelf with a box of prefilled ten-milliliter cartridges. "These here are a mixture of noncorrosive water and standard lubricant water. It will lubricate just as well but it has the added bonus of never causing any rust or other corrosion to any of the internal parts. Users find their bionics last several times longer."

David held one of the clear glass cartridges up to his eye and watched the light sift through the liquid. "Is it expensive?"

"Well, given we mix it ourselves and you can't get it anywhere else in the Houselands, it is a tad more expensive than standard lubricant water. Say, about fifteen sterling a cartridge."

"Fifteen sterling a cartridge?" David's mouth fell open as he looked at Dillon.

"Plus tax."

"I see. Well, it sounds like a wonderful product, to be sure, but maybe a little out of my price range. Do you have any regular lubricant cartridges?"

Dillon's toothy smile melted away as he took the cartridge and dropped it back into the box. "Right this way."

As it turned out, the standard lubricant cartridges the Water Station carried were the exact same ones David bought in the Third, though at a considerable markup. David bought only one, to the chagrin of Dillon, and decided to wait until he had time to purchase some back home in the Third. It was a wonder anyone could afford to reside in Capital City, considering the increased cost of living.

Half an hour later David walked into the Third's office area on the orbital—later than he usually arrived, but still plenty early for what was supposed to be a morning off. After a brief trip to the washroom to comb his static hair back into place, he found he'd arrived before Mercy, for once. Not Francisco, though. He already sat at his desk reading the newspaper. Bethany was late, as usual.

"Morning," David said in a cheerful voice, but Francisco only grunted and turned the page. "Is anyone else here yet?"

"Not since I've arrived," Francisco said, never looking up from the paper.

"Well ... fancy a cup of tea?"

Another grunt, which David took to mean *yes*. David walked across the main office to the refreshment station. The only problem was, no tea. Bethany literally only had one job. No matter, Blythe had some in his office. David would pop in and grab some before anyone was the wiser.

David walked to the double doors, paused to knock, and then felt like an idiot. No one was in the office. He slipped through one of the doors and stopped so quickly that he nearly fell on the glass floor. Blythe and Samantha broke apart from something that looked like a kiss. Blythe looked at David with his usual smile, but his eyes burned like smoldering coals.

"I ... I ... um ... just came in to borrow some tea." The words tumbled out of David like so many stones.

"You really should learn to knock," Blythe said as he let go of Samantha's hands. "That will be all, Samantha."

She turned and walked toward David with an indignant look, hips swaying with every step. David turned to exit as well, but Blythe stopped him.

"A moment, David."

David groaned inwardly. He was in for it now.

Blythe waited until Samantha closed the door. Then he turned and walked over to his private refreshment station and began making tea.

"My wife and I are married, but for political reasons only. Both of us see the benefits of the union, but we haven't lived as husband and wife for quite some time. As far as either of us is concerned, we are free to pursue any relationship we choose, as long as we maintain the public appearance of matrimony. Do you understand what I'm saying?" Blythe looked over his shoulder at David.

"I think so, sir."

"I am like any other man, David. I desire a relationship with a woman as much as any of us. I am lonely, and Samantha is beautiful. Sure, she's only seeking a relationship with me because of my status as a representative, but such is the way of all relationships, one way or the other. They thrive as long as the benefits remain mutual and consensual. Truthfully I actually think I could love her. She makes me feel young again—young and full of hope. Could you deny that to a man?" Blythe turned away from the station with two steaming cups of tea and looked at David.

David accepted the cup of tea and gazed into it, hoping to find an answer. "No, sir, I couldn't. I was just a bit surprised. I had no idea you and your wife weren't, well, cohabitating."

Blythe laughed as he sat behind his desk. "Cohabitating? That woman hasn't shown me more than her face in the past ten cycles." He took a slow sip of tea and let out a satisfied sigh. "The public can't know of this, David. They wouldn't understand. They'd think me like all the other representatives who keep secret mistresses behind their wives' backs. My wife knows full well that I'm seeking love in the arms of other women, just as I know she is doing the same with other men. Can you keep it a secret, David?"

"I will, sir. I find it ... strange, but you can count on my silence."

Blythe gave David a short nod and took another sip of tea. "Very good. By the by, how is your mother?"

"She's fine. The funds from the nonprofit have really helped, enough to keep Ella on as a nurse. I really can't thank you enough."

"Least I could do. Now get out of here. You already ruined my morning; I don't want you ruining this cup of tea as well." He gave David an exasperated look, but his eyes were smiling.

David walked out of the office and felt Samantha's smug stare boring into his back all the way to his desk. Francisco still read his newspaper. How could the prick not have known Blythe was ... *entertaining* a guest? If he had, why hadn't he warned David?

And why did it bother him anyway that Blythe felt affectionate toward a beautiful young lady? True, she was half his age, and he technically still had a wife, but that was just it: a *technicality*. All interested parties to the marriage consented to his extramarital activities. It really wasn't a marriage at all—more like a business arrangement. So why did it bother David?

Bethany walked in, a full hour late, as usual. She sat at her desk, bright-eyed. Like a cat in a window she watched Blythe's shadow flicker across the seam beneath the double doors. David looked around on his desk, searching for anything to do that would take his mind off his embarrassment and confusion. He settled on the past week's district financial report and busied himself in the numbers.

At half past nine Mercy walked in with a disposable teapot and a bag of steaming pastries.

"Tea, anyone?" she said.

"Yes please," David said as he jumped up and walked over to Mercy's desk.

She smiled as she handed him a pastry—a sweet tuber bun filled with cream and caramelized berries. David took a bite and breathed out in sweet satisfaction. It was so much better than that morning's Charra gruel.

"Slow down, David. You're going to choke yourself," Mercy said, placing a hand on his arm.

"I can't help it," David said around a mouthful of bun. "My mom used to make these as a special treat. I haven't had one in four cycles."

Mercy chuckled as David stuffed the rest of the bun in his mouth and reached for another. Francisco and Bethany joined them, but Samantha turned her nose up at Mercy's invitation. That was fine with David. The four of them passed around tea and buns. Bethany nibbled at her pastry like a rodent. Francisco picked up a cup of tea in one hand and two pastries in his other before he returned to his newspaper.

"Any word on what we are doing today?" Mercy asked. "How are we saving the Houselands?"

David shook his head as he took another bite of a pastry. The sweet taste in his mouth almost covered up the bitter embarrassment.

"Mercy? I'd like to meet with you at your earliest convenience," Blythe said as he poked his head out of his office for an instant.

David gagged a little on the half bun he had in his mouth.

Mercy laughed, a sweet tinkle of rain on a clear glass window. "I told you not to eat them so fast." She turned toward her desk to retrieve a pen and notebook, red-and-white-striped dress swishing behind her.

David looked back at the double doors, and then at Samantha, who wore a pout on her face, and finally at Bethany, who at that moment seemed to be daydreaming in Blythe's general direction.

A thought flitted across David's mind. He gulped. *Not Mercy.* Would he enter one morning and find her in Blythe's office? He wouldn't. She definitely wouldn't. But if Blythe made advances toward her and she refused, what would happen then? Blythe was a good man. *He'd never send Mercy away. … Would he?*

David watched as Mercy walked across the office toward Blythe's doors, a strange mixture of jealousy, horror, and desire welling up inside him. He looked around the room, frantic for a solution. His eyes fell on Francisco.

"Mercy," David said just before she reached the

double doors.

She turned and acknowledged him with a sweet smile.

"Um," David said, "maybe you should take Francisco with you to scribe, just in case."

Mercy's sweet smile morphed into one of curiosity as her head cocked and an eyebrow rose. She regarded David for a few seconds before giving him a slow nod.

Francisco didn't need to be told. He jumped up with a pad and pen, grabbed another tuber bun, and slipped into Blythe's office behind Mercy.

David pondered as he reached for another bun, but Francisco had pinched the last one. He chastised himself as he retook his seat and got back to his financial report. This line of thinking was getting him nowhere. Blythe was the only representative who actually cared about the people.

The rest of the day meandered by. Blythe sent Mercy on a negotiation mission to the mainland houses to propose a trade deal for House Braxton. The mainland houses were the breadbasket for all of Alönia—all of the Fertile Plains for that matter. More food came from those four houses than all of Viörn itself.

The office hummed along for the next few days, and David was just starting to relax after his awkward interruption of Blythe and Samantha when the storm clouds broke and rained all over his happy little career.

David arrived early as usual and busied himself with different house reports and constituent letters. Francisco arrived next, clutching a newspaper in his hand. David smiled and said hello. Francisco grunted—what a surprise. Next was Bethany, late as usual. Lastly in walked Blythe and Samantha, arm in arm.

David did his best to smile at them, but it was an awkward attempt and not well met. Samantha sneered, and Blythe nodded in a cordial but stern manner.

After depositing Samantha at her desk, Blythe said, "David, in my office."

It wasn't the words, but something in the way he said them that made David feel he was about to be in big trouble. David scrambled to his feet and followed Blythe into his office.

"Sit," Blythe said as he paced back and forth across the glass floor like a caged animal. He held his hands behind his back, one of them clutching a section of newspaper. After a few more laps he proffered the paper.

David took it and smoothed it out, then he glanced through the articles. It was the political section of the *Voxil Tribunal*, a newspaper suspected to be in Speaker Walker's pocket and, unfortunately, the most widely read in the Houselands. However, despite its partisan reputation, the main article made David's stomach contract and churn:

WOMANIZER AND ADULTERER

A secret informant closely connected to the Blythe political office reports that William Jefferson Blythe IV is engaged in an extramarital affair with a woman half his age. ...

David read on and finally looked up at Blythe, whose mouth was working but with no sound coming out.

Blythe regarded him with an unyielding gaze. He scooted a chair across the glass floor with a screech and sat at an uncomfortable distance from David.

"I'm only going to ask you this once, David. Did you issue this report?" His face was stern, and his eyes bored into David's very soul.

David shook his head. "No, sir! I didn't do anything of the sort." David's voice cracked a little at the end as he poured every bit of honesty he possessed into the words.

"Don't you think it is at least a little curious that only three days after you discover my situation in marriage, the *Voxil Tribunal* accuses me of adultery?"

"I find it very curious indeed, sir, but I did not submit that article."

Blythe pursed his lips for a moment before standing and resuming his pacing. David didn't know what else to say. The facts were stacked against him, and the only defense he had was his word. He'd never seen Blythe like this before, wild and functioning on full burn.

Finally he stopped and looked at David. "I'd like to believe you David, but you're going to have to prove it." Blythe visibly forced his frustration into some dark prison deep within him. "You have three days to find out who did this. After that I have no choice."

"But, sir—"

"Three days, David. Go. Time is short, and I need to figure out how to get out of this mess."

David jumped to his feet and walked, head down, toward the door; but before he opened it, he had a thought. He turned back to Blythe. "Sir, not that you want my advice, but if I were going to try to get out of this mess, I wouldn't deny it. The public is all too eager for sex scandals these days. They assume all people who deny it are guilty. If you accept it and explain that you and your wife have been estranged for the past ten cycles, most people will forgive you, and everyone else will forget about it since it's not the juicy tabloid fodder they were hoping for. Some might even feel sorry for you."

Blythe looked at David for a moment before saying, "Thank you, David. That will be all."

David sank into the chair at his desk with a solid thump. By now the rest of the office had read the article, and a somber mood hung over them. Three days … David had three days to fix this or else he'd lose his job. He'd probably lose his apartment and Ella too, and then what? Where would he go? What would happen to his mother? David stopped himself from sinking into despair. He had three days. *Best make the most of them.* Whatever happened would happen. If he wanted to control that, then he'd better stop worrying and start thinking.

He looked around the room. Someone in their office was a spy—Francisco, Bethany, Samantha. David replayed every moment of the past three days in his mind. The only day that really mattered was the day he had stumbled into Blythe's office and made a fool of himself. Something had happened that day, and if it was that day he was examining, he had to include Mercy in his list of spies. He shuddered, not wanting to think ill of her. She was wonderful, and if he was being honest with himself, he liked her very much. However, that was all the more reason to include her. *Look where no one else is.* She had been gone that morning and so she had a perfect alibi, but it was still possible.

David took out a sheet of paper and wrote the names down. He marked Mercy as number four, not because he liked her, but because she'd been absent on the morning in question.

Bethany was next of the least likely culprits. Her head was full of a bunch of cabbages. True, that could be a perfect cover, and she did have a motivation. Even now she gazed with longing eyes toward Blythe's door. If she had discovered Blythe and Samantha's little secret, how would she react? She had the motivation, but did she have the intellect?

Next was Francisco. He seemed perfectly content in his situation. Competent and diligent at every assigned task, yet zero ambition to pursue life any further. He'd been there the morning David interrupted Blythe. Had he known the whole time Samantha and Blythe were in there? Had he known what they were doing, or had he just suspected? The opportunity and knowledge were there, but not the motivation. Francisco didn't seem to care. He had his job, and he did it well. He had also come on a personal recommendation from one of Blythe's close friends. Of course, money could be a powerful motivator. And besides, that eye was really creepy. How could someone ever trust a person who could look two places at once? David wrote a number two next to Francisco.

Lastly was Samantha. David really didn't like her. She

was the only person in the office who had come without a recommendation from either a known associate or personal friend of Blythe. It was also clear from day one that she had seductive intentions toward Blythe. She had personal knowledge, plenty of opportunity, and motivation. Seduction was a favorite political tool. Send in an attractive, well-endowed assistant, eager to please either in public or behind closed doors, catch the politician in an affair, and then blow the whistle. It happened every single day. Blythe was more vulnerable than most, easy prey for such a move. If this was true, that meant this was only the beginning. They would wait for Blythe to deny the affair, and then they would present the evidence. Moreover the position Samantha now filled had been conveniently vacated at the time of her application. Paula's torturous death and the close proximity of her secretarial position with Blythe created simple, scandalous stepping-stones for any seductress. David put a number one next to Samantha's name.

He looked at his notes. What now? Questioning them wouldn't do any good. They'd already fooled him once; they could just do it again. He had to lay a trap and hope it caught a traitor within three days. David winced.

He tapped his pen against the side of his head. It stood to reason that if Blythe survived this first attack, there would be another. However, it would take quite a bit for a spy to strike twice within one week. They needed an extra little push.

David looked down at the mess of financial documents he'd been perusing the past few days and had a thought. He pulled a document from the file cabinet and filled in some of the requisite blanks. Once done, he slipped a vial of fine powder out of his satchel and sprinkled it across the document, brushing the excess into the wastebasket. Lastly he penned an affidavit and autographed it. David reviewed his work and took a deep breath. This would either work or he would be homeless. He got up, pocketed the affidavit, and took the other document into Blythe's office.

Thirty minutes later he walked out of the office in shame. He'd been fired.

* * * * *

Three days ... three days of anxiety and terror. That's what he had to wait through. He should have enjoyed the time with his mother, and the extra rest, but he spent the days and nights pacing his apartment floor. He could see the new transportation facility from his window, scaffolding and steel girders poking at intricate angles like a giant briar patch. Another month and Public Pharmaceuticals would be finished, fully operational with a full three weeks to spare before the census. It was all going so smoothly, until now. They had a rat in the office; a rat that somehow had placed the blame on David. A rat who, in David's opinion, worked for a bigger rat. David only accomplished one productive activity throughout the entire time he paced his apartment: he'd added a person of interest to his wall. He didn't have much, only a blank sheet with a question mark and, after some consideration, a title: the man in the shadows. Someone was pulling the strings.

Blythe had released an article the same day he fired David. It described his situation in life and marriage in such eloquent terms that David even found himself feeling sorry for the man—alone, in love, and looking for someone to share the rest of his life with. Mrs. Blythe wrote a supporting article admitting that she and her husband had separated over ten cycles ago for irreconcilable differences, but had kept up the pretense of marriage for political reasons. The whole episode blew over the public's head like an early-morning breeze. However, it wasn't over yet.

On the morning of the third day, the last day of Blythe's ultimatum, the public gasped as the front page of every Alönian newspaper—not just the *Voxil*—presented the same article:

PUBLIC FUNDS USED FOR PROVOCATIVE ACTIVITY

New evidence presented against the Blythe administration that proves the representative used public funds to pay for dance clubs and courtesans.

David didn't waste any time. The moment he saw the article, he rushed to the office, even going so far as to hire a taxi. When he arrived, the other staff looked at him openmouthed, even Mercy. That he would presume to come back here at such a time surely seemed absurd to them. David found Blythe alone in his office, just as planned, though David still knocked—lesson learned.

"Ah, how was your vacation?" Blythe asked as David entered.

"Um … exciting and boring at the same time."

"I think that's called *restless*."

"Precisely, sir."

"Well, time to see if your little gambit worked. Are you ready?"

David nodded, and the two of them stood and walked into the main office, where everyone else still gossiped about David's re-emergence. Mercy smiled kindly at David, but something in her eyes spoke of lost respect for him.

Blythe pulled out a little luminous-torch as he and David walked into the file room. David rolled the ladder down the closet to the financial section, and Blythe climbed a few rungs and switched on the torch. One of the files glowed florescent purple under the light of the little torch. Blythe nodded at David. Then he waved the torch around, shining its faint light around the file room. The same florescent splotches appeared on the ladder, across a few other files, and on the closet door and doorknob. Together Blythe and David walked out of the office looking a curious sight, to be sure, as they waved the little light around, following an otherwise invisible trail across the main office—until, that is, the trail stopped at a desk. Blythe shone the light around the desk and the whole surface glowed purple—the whole surface of Samantha's desk.

"Ew," Samantha said. "William, what is this? It's on

my dress!" She brushed at the substance, but it only smeared under the glow of the torch.

Blythe didn't answer. He shone the light around the room, but none of the other staff had anything like Samantha's level of luminescence.

Blythe looked at Samantha, his eyes a mixture of sadness and fury. "Samantha, hold out your hands."

Samantha puzzled at the request but did as asked. Blythe shined the light over her hands, and then blanched at the violet sheen.

He shook his head. "Why? Why would you do this?"

"Why what?" Samantha said, posturing herself in her chair and fluttering her eyes. But her feminine wiles would not work any longer. The spell was broken.

"Why would you betray me? What did you think you would gain that I could not provide for you?"

Samantha shrugged. "I haven't the faintest idea what you are talking about. The only person here that betrayed you is standing right there." She pointed at David. "Remember?"

"What do you think you have on your hands?" Blythe asked. "What do you think is all over your dress?"

Samantha rubbed her fingers together. "I really don't know, but perhaps you could tell me how to get it off? I probably have it all over the place." She sighed dramatically.

Blythe didn't look the least bit interested in Samantha's innuendoes. He beckoned to David to explain.

"Before I was fired a few days ago," David said, "Mr. Blythe and I had a discussion. We knew there was a spy in the office, and all suspicions pointed toward me. So we decided to fire me and make the real spy think they were no longer under scrutiny. Then Mr. Blythe issued his marital statement and cleared his name after the adultery accusation. We suspected at the time that the spy would strike again as soon as they realized that their first attempt to soil Mr. Blythe was unsuccessful. This …" David pointed at the substance on Samantha's desk. "… is a florescent powder that only becomes visible under luminescent torchlight. I sprinkled it on a document I crafted just before Mr. Blythe fired me—a document that, to a sophisticated observer, recorded the use of public funds for explicit activity. Blythe planted that document in the file room the night after I left. At some point between that night and this morning, someone removed the document and leaked it to the newspapers, creating a florescent trail in the process." David pointed from the file room to Samantha's desk.

Samantha slit her eyes at him, then huffed. "Oh, you think you're so smart Mr. 'I got the highest score on the PLAEE,'" she said, rolling her eyes and fingering quotation marks in the air for emphasis. Her eyes flashed toward Blythe. "Did you really think of this, dearest? Seems to me that David is framing me to get his job back. He dislikes our relationship and will do anything to displace me. How easy would it have been for him to sprinkle that same powder on my desk three days ago? Hmm, did you think of that?"

Blythe looked at her for a moment before saying, "I searched the room with the torch the same night I planted the document. There wasn't a trace of the substance at your desk, and David hasn't left his apartment since the day I fired him. I know, because I had him watched."

When David raised an eyebrow at this, Blythe only shrugged in apology, and David could only shrug back.

For the first time in the confrontation Samantha started to panic. She looked around the room, eyes darting from person to person, ending on Blythe. "You think you can just use me and cast me aside as easily as an old towel. What? Is this not enough for you? Now you want *that*?" She gestured to herself and then to Mercy, who shuddered at the accusation.

"Samantha," Blythe said, "if you would be so kind as to collect your belongings, your services will no longer be needed at this office."

"Oh really? And which services would those be?" She picked up a teacup from her desk and hurled it at Blythe.

He ducked just in time, and the mug shattered against the wall. Samantha grabbed her purse off her seat with such force that the chair fell over, though she had stomped halfway to the door before it clattered across the ground. No sway of her hips this time, no fluttering lashes or pouting lips—only fury.

How often overt seduction and hatred walk hand and hand—as often as guilt partners with sin, David mused.

Samantha Samille slammed the office door so hard that a pencil rolled off Bethany's desk and skipped across the floor. Silence followed.

"Well, David," Blythe said after a sigh, "welcome back

to the Third."

He began clapping and the others joined in, the clap becoming an applause.

Blythe gripped David's shoulder and pulled him close. "I'm truly sorry for all I put you though these past few days. I didn't want to believe you were a spy, especially after how much you have helped my campaign. Please accept my sincerest apologies and … I hope we can put all this behind us."

David nodded. "There is nothing to forgive. I understand why you did what you did. We are too close to the census to risk anything."

Blythe smiled and looked down. "You're a good man, David."

The clapping died down as Blythe walked back into his office.

But then Blythe's head poked back out. "Oh, David, be a dear and file that affidavit and the falsified bank transaction with the newspapers. I'd like to have a clean name again."

David nodded, noting that Blythe looked both sad and relieved. David returned to the desk he'd thought he might never see again only a few days earlier—his desk, his very own desk.

Bethany sat up abruptly, eyes wide as she turned toward David. "Wait … Blythe and Samantha were having a relationship?"

Chapter Nine

SINCERITY

Mercy puzzled as she floated away from the Capital Orbital in an air-taxi. David was so much more than she'd originally assumed. Any other aide would have crumbled under the kind of pressure he withstood every day. He not only stood strong, but also excelled. She pulled a small book from a pocket hidden in her billowing skirts, opening it to a page titled *David,* though the rest of it was blank. She pressed a pen to the page, but couldn't think of what to write. *David is … what?* Mercy thought. She looked out the window as the taxi soared between buildings toward her apartment, all the while searching for words that might be hidden between the raindrops.

The towers were a little shorter here, sacrificing height for elegance. The residential sector had less edifice and more shrubbery dangling from the thousands of private balconies bulging out from the different complexes. Giant orchids drooped hundreds of feet, flaunting their bioluminescent flowers, great epiphytes drawing nutrients from the moist air. Large, rubbery leaves pooled with water until they overflowed and dumped their contents onto the leaves below.

As the taxi rocked a little, Mercy roused from her musings. She realized she was already docked and the pilot was muttering to himself about the long night ahead and needing to get along and how very lovely it would be to have an extra tip. Mercy pulled a sterling from her coin purse and handed it to the pilot. The man's eyes widened, and he pocketed the coin with eager fingers. He tipped his cap and let the ramp down in the back of the taxi. Mercy exited and held her hands over her head as rain pelted her hair and threatened to run down her back. She ran across her spacious balcony, between tree ferns and philodendrons, to her door.

Yet she couldn't get David out of her head. David was different—different than anyone else in politics. She fiddled with the door for a moment, wet fingers slipping on the combination lock. Finally it clicked and she walked inside, shivering as she moved across the marble floor and plush carpets. It smelled fresh and clean, like a new skiff off the sale dock. Mercy wanted nothing more than to slip into a hot bath and soak away the evening, but her day wasn't over yet. Instead she changed out of her pretty but restricting dress, hanging it in an expansive closet along with hundreds of others. She swapped it for a pair of fitted black trousers; a black, knee-length raincoat; and matching boots and gloves. After walking to the mirror, she piled her hair beneath a wide-brimmed hat and frowned at her final appearance. She much preferred the pretty dresses to this boyish appearance, but duty called.

She walked through her cozy apartment, weaving between comfy couches and plush chairs until she entered a glass greenhouse that extended off the backside of the tower. The moment she stepped into the glass-enclosed room, a dozen sweet smells rushed to meet her, each competing for her attention. Broad leaves and lush flowers filled the room to capacity, a veritable jungle. A few of the flowers glowed florescent colors, casting a dim light around the greenhouse. Mercy removed a glove and ran her fingers through the leaves of her plants. A girl had to have at least one vice. She stopped after a few steps and bent to smell a cymbidium, breathing in the spicy scent and feeling it soothe her fatigue. She cupped the delicate flower in her hand, a wondrous creation. After a few moments of appreciation—moments she couldn't spare—she pulled herself away from the flower.

A skiff sat amidst the lush plants, concealed in their greenery. David would have known exactly what type of skiff it was, down to the last detail. Mercy snickered at that thought. She, on the other hand, knew it would get her from where she was to where she needed to be. She pulled back the cloth top, climbed in, and powered up the burner. The ship hummed as the burner flash heated the gas-filled pontoons, growing lighter by the second. After a moment she put the top back up, then pulled a lever and the glass roof of the greenhouse opened to the night. Evening fog poured in through the opening like the milky froth on an exotic drink. Warm rain pattered on top of the skiff's cloth roof as it rose out of the greenhouse, and Mercy guided it into the night toward the industrial district.

Yes, David knew a lot of things, Mercy thought as she guided the skiff, but it wasn't his intelligence that had her stumped. There were plenty of intelligent politicians. As she weaved through capital traffic, the structures changed from posh apartments to industrial complexes with cooling towers and loading docks up and down their multiple stories. Massive gears rotated on the sides of the buildings as they labored away the evening hours. The airships changed too. Hers was now one of the only skiffs bobbing between freight haulers and tugs, each pulling immense loads of goods and materials. Mercy guided her craft down a sky alley between two enormous factories. It barely fit, bumping against one of the towers as she turned it into a large bay door and docked along some scaffolding. She pulled open the cloth roof and walked across the scaffolding, each step echoing in the empty bay.

As she walked through the warehouse, she continued to puzzle over David. *Innocence* … That might be the word she was looking for. David was innocent, but that was still only part of it. Innocence often paired with ignorance, and David was not ignorant. Perhaps he was innocent of the lie that was politics, but not innocent in a way that made him vulnerable.

She turned one last time in the dingy hallways and knocked on a metal door, issuing four solid thrums. The door opened, and Mercy walked into a small room with a table in the middle and an assortment of stools around it. On the far side sat an imposing figure, cloaked in the shadows. The only light in the dirty space illuminated the table, leaving the outskirts dark. Dust sparkled in the air as it floated in and out of the light. Two other figures stood to the right of the table, a male of medium height and a female of more petite stature, both wearing wide-brimmed caps that obscured their features. As Mercy walked to the table, the door shut behind her with a clunk. She knew a guard stood hidden behind the door, opening and closing it, but the door seemingly moving on its own accord still gave her the jitters.

Mercy removed her hat and gloves and reached to place them on the table, but opted to hold them when she saw the accumulation of dust on the tabletop. "I told you not to move until I got back," she said to the man standing to the right of the table. "As it is, we nearly lost everything in some pointless gambit." She perched herself on a stool and crossed her legs.

"I nearly succeeded in bringing down Blythe and extricating the boy," Francisco said. "I wouldn't call that pointless."

"If I had been there, it *would* have succeeded," Mercy said. "But instead we revealed our hand, spent one of our most valuable cards, and cemented Blythe as a man longing for love in the hearts and minds of the public. He'll have every lady, eligible or not, moving to the Third District from three houses over. And if it wasn't for that eye of yours, you would have been caught in the act."

"You approved my actions before you left," Francisco

said. "You said nothing of waiting until you got back, and if I had, we would have missed our opportunity to hang it all on the boy."

"I approved of the original news article, but I expressly told you to wait for me before taking any further steps." Mercy crossed her arms and looked at the man in the shadows. "You transferred me away from Representative Herald because Blythe presented a greater threat to your plans. You tasked me with sabotaging the Blythe campaign because *I* was the best. Let me do what you hired me to do."

Francisco snorted at that.

Mercy looked at him with narrow eyes. "You are an assassin, Francisco, not a politician. You are my bodyguard and an insurance policy if I fail. I won't interfere with your job if you stay out of mine." She looked back at the man in the shadows. "I can do this."

The man didn't speak, though his eyes glowed like two embers in the night. The silence drew on for a few moments before his deep voice rumbled out of the darkness: "Samantha Samille was a liability … an uncalculated variable. She might have been usable, but that one was always a wild card. Having her out of the picture will clear the way for you, Bethany." He nodded at the female standing next to Francisco. "I trust you are ready, my dear."

Bethany nodded. "Samantha certainly made it harder. He is expecting overt sexual interaction now, and I'm not willing to go that far. I'm not sure my vulnerable routine will be enough to interest him anymore. He wants something exciting, not easy."

The man's dark figure shifted, as if he were nodding. "However, from now on, Francisco, consult Mercy before making political decisions. We don't want any more close calls. What of the rumor of hidden population within the Third?"

"I searched some of the records at night," Francisco said, "and I can't find anything to prove those assertions. But ..." He paused and glanced toward Mercy.

"Blythe and David speak and act as if the speakership is already secured," Mercy said, finishing Francisco's thought.

"A ruse?" the man asked.

"Not likely," Mercy replied. "That kind of ruse could only harm a district, given all the poaching after a census."

The man in the shadows breathed a sigh. "Blythe is smarter than we think. He's planned this for cycles without anyone knowing."

"With all due respect, sir, I don't think it's Blythe doing the planning," Mercy said.

The man in the shadows looked at her for a moment. "Explain."

"Blythe is eloquent, charismatic, handsome, and smart, but he was never a threat in the past, because he possessed the same fatal flaws as any other politician. He's a philandering cheat. From what I've been able to glean, the transportation facility was David's idea. Successfully transporting Public Pharmaceuticals was David's idea, as was Beldon Construction, Linden Airsail condemnation, the false courtesan transaction documents, even Blythe's confession of his marital status. Blythe was never a threat. In fact he would have fallen on his own face by now if it wasn't for David."

Francisco waved a hand in the air and interrupted, "The boy is a nobody. No formal education, no previous training, no parents to speak of. In fact his house record doesn't even begin until his aideship. I find it hard to believe an aide could accomplish all that in a matter of weeks."

Mercy shook her head. "David is different. He's … He's …" She racked her brain for the right word that she hadn't been able to think of throughout the entire night. "Sincere. David is sincere. He does these things because he honestly believes that they are right. That makes him different than any other Equalist out there. When you add his sincerity to his intellect and work ethic, it also makes him extremely formidable."

The man in the shadows looked at Mercy for a long time, then shifted his gaze. "Bethany, you're his assistant. What have you been able to glean about him?"

"Nothing. He never allows me to do anything more than make tea. I've made it wrong for the past three weeks out of spite."

"What if you switched your affections toward him?" the man asked. "Could you get him to talk?"

"Ha!" Bethany said. "There is only one woman in his eyes. I think he's wholly smitten with this one." She pointed toward Mercy, who flushed and looked away.

"Is this true?" the man asked.

When Mercy looked up, the man was staring at her with his piercing eyes. "Yes," she said, before looking at her knees.

"Then seduce him," the man said. "Get him to trust you and then—"

"Now you wait one minute!" Mercy said, feeling her flush spreading down her neck as she pointed a finger at the man. "I might be a political spy, but I have my limits."

"Relax. The boy is an invalid," the man said. "He won't touch you, and if he does, he's hardly a threat."

Mercy huffed and put her hands on her hips. "What do you expect me to do? Go to his house and perform a dance club routine?"

The man shrugged. "I expect you to talk to him, and nothing more. Encourage him, smile at him, confide in him. A woman has many wiles that don't involve the physical. If he already likes you, he'll be putty in your hands."

Mercy cringed and looked down again. "He didn't ask for this, you know—none of it. He's just unfortunate enough to be on the other side of the aisle."

"Need I remind you of the consequences for us and our loved ones if we fail?" the man asked, his voice a little more firm.

Mercy took a deep breath. "You need not. I know better than most."

The man went on, "We don't have the luxury of feelings. Time is running out. Our window of opportunity is shrinking with each day. All of us will be stepping outside the original job parameters before the end.

However, I am still not convinced that Blythe is no longer our main target. We will proceed as scheduled for the pleasure cruise with Don Johnson. If all goes according to plan, we might be able to put this entire matter behind us a few weeks hence."

The meeting ended, and Mercy's chest ached as she left the dingy room and climbed back into her skiff. It might have been her imagination, but it seemed drearier now than when she'd arrived. When she took this job, she'd imagined herself swindling some wretched politician, not a hardworking young man. David was sincere, and sweet, and innocent, and … kind. What was she? Deceptive, conniving, subversive, and now she had to add seductive. Who was she becoming? Where would this path lead? How far would she go to save the ones she loved?

Chapter Ten

THE MAW

In the far northern corner of Alönia, where the dunelands of House Floyd met the foothills of the Rorand Mountains, lay the Maw, the mouth of Northern Desert. Fathoms and fathoms of sand and dust covered the vast, unnegotiable plain. It was said that by the time the clouds passed over the Alönian lands, they had no rain left for the desert. Truthfully the ocean winds and the high mountains held the clouds back. Not a drop of their life-bringing vapor ever touched the barren lands of the north. No airship had ever crossed the sands, though many had tried. Rumor had it that the desert went on forever or until the land dropped away into empty space. However, it wasn't the heat, or the aridness, or the vast size of the desert that created fear in the hearts of all who knew it. The desert drove men mad. Any airship crew that sailed the sandy seas too long never returned the same. Their minds broke in that lifeless place. Some believed ghosts roamed the sands and possessed any who ventured there. Though, more reasonable minds knew it was a combination of heat, thirst, and overexposure to sunlight.

For these reasons and more, the Northern Desert presented a perfect hideout for Outlanders, criminals, and outcasts from the civilized sections of the Fertile Plains. Criminal overlords divided up the different sections of the sands into their own little kingdoms, harassing the borderlands and snatching up shipping vessels. At least that was what it had been like half a decade ago. There hadn't been an Outlander attack for cycles now. Military intelligence believed the overlords had killed each other off in a great war over territory. While the Outlanders were seemingly gone, the thrill of visiting the Maw and gazing into the hostile territory still drew a good many tourists.

That same thrill had induced Johnson to invite Blythe and his aides to join him for lunch on his yacht, *The Reverie*. The little party met on the docks of the Capital Airship Landings at 9:00 a.m. The sun made a rare appearance, shining like a beacon through the parting clouds, an occurrence that Johnson believed a good omen—however, not nearly as good of an omen as Johnson's airship. David gasped as the rotund man led him, Mercy, and Mr. Blythe toward the most beautiful airship at the Landings. Mrs. Blythe had opted not to come, recent events being what they were.

"That's a Sunbeam," David said to Mercy as they approached.

She looked radiant in her red sailing dress, with her hair in a ponytail beneath a captain's hat. David noticed some tights poking out from under her ruffling dress. Clearly she took precautions this time in anticipation of the wind.

"Is that supposed to mean something?" Mercy asked, head cocked with a half smile.

"Ra*ther!* That's one of the most expensive airships you can buy," David said, but he had a hard time rolling his eyes at such a beautiful face. It came off more like a spasm.

Mercy giggled behind a hand. "You need to work on your sarcastic face. I'm having a hard time believing it."

"Hey, my sarcastic face works on everybody else. Maybe you're the one with a problem." David tried to roll his eyes again; it didn't work.

As they got closer to the Sunbeam, David's mouth almost watered over the magnificent vessel. Sunbeam was the first Alönian company to implement an internal balloon. The center of the ship consisted of one sectioned cylinder filled with buoyancy gas, though it remained invisible from the outside of the ship. Supposedly the sectioned balloon allowed the captain to shift buoyancy to counteract an imbalanced load. If all the pleasure cruisers wanted to dance beneath the stars in the glass observatory at the front of the ship, that could happen on a completely level deck. From the outside the 150-foot airship looked like a sailboat out of water, constructed of brass, glass, and wood planking—actually, David knew it was polymer made to look like wood. One massive deck extended the entire length of the ship's top deck, a strange mix between old-fashioned and modern with its planking and brass railing. The control tower poked a fathom above the rest of the deck, where the captain leaned against the wheel in anticipation of liftoff. The ship's three decks encased the internal balloon. The middle one wrapped around the outside, glass windows sealing it from the elements. The bottom deck had small porthole windows, hiding all the intricate machinery that propelled the magnificent ship: two burners, three generators, and a variety of gears, turbines, and cooling vents. The iconic prow of the vessel provided Sunbeams with their name. The entire front of the ship was one massive glass cone, all three decks conjoining into one observatory. The glass glinted in the sun, making the ship look like a ray of sunshine as it sailed through the air. Said observatory included one of David's favorite features: a glass floor, which he hoped wouldn't bother him like Mr. Blythe's window-floor did. David hoped they would have lunch on the open-air top deck and not in the observatory. It would be a shame to make a mess in such a magnificent ship.

David couldn't wait to see the turbofans in action. The huge disks were currently folded against the ship's sides, allowing it to dock, but once airborne they would lift out like great cylindrical wings. Their gyroscopic mobility made the Sunbeam the most maneuverable ship in the air despite its size. Once close enough, David ran to the railing of the dock and looked over the edge. The folded disks covered a full third of the ship's length, spanning across all three decks. David looked below the fans and saw the keel resting against the landing like a giant fin. It made the ship almost as tall as it was long. The keel's front side had a wicked serrated edge, and its back one enormous rudder, reaching the entire height of the ship and adding yet another degree of maneuverability.

She was a gorgeous vessel, the most beautiful David had ever seen.

Mercy joined him at the railing. "If eyes could steal, you'd be a thief," she said.

"Do you think I could fit it in my pocket?"

"No." Mercy smiled as she looped her arm through his and steered him toward the gangplank.

As David tore his eyes away from the gilded vessel, he happened upon something absolutely hideous: Devin stood on the deck welcoming Blythe and Johnson aboard. David could already see the pervert's eyes roving over Mercy. As he and Mercy walked up the gangplank, David was sure to always keep himself between Devin and Mercy. He gave Devin a polite nod, extending his metal arm to shake hands and then squeezing hard enough to make the bodyguard's eyes wince.

As David stepped onto the top deck, he realized why Sunbeams were so coveted as pleasure yachts. Built-in loungers lay intermittent with wet bars and a full-sized shuffleboard court. Waiters and waitresses meandered across the deck in matching white sailor uniforms serving refreshments. A circular staircase reached through the floor at both bow and stern.

David heard a bell ring and realized they were already

shoving off from the Landings. He wanted with all his heart to run to the railing and watch the famed turbofans engage, but he was caught between watching a wonder of machinery and leaving Mercy alone with Devin on the prowl.

Mercy saved him the discomfort: "Come on. You're going to miss the fans unfurl."

He smiled as she tugged him over to the railing, and together they watched as the massive disks lifted away from the ship's sides and whirred to life. A breeze blew across the deck, and the ship gained speed. The captain was brilliant, maintaining constant lift and acceleration so that the passengers could move about with ease, hardly even knowing the ship was in motion. True, it only utilized a tiny part of the ship's capability, but it was enthralling all the same.

Mercy laughed and David looked up to see her smiling at his fascination.

"What?" he asked.

"You look like a child on his first day of school," she said as she guided him back toward the others, who were chatting around the wet bar.

Truth be told, that was exactly how he felt.

"So, Mr. Ike, your Mr. Blythe here tells me you live next to my new pharmaceutical plant," Johnson said as David and Mercy joined them. "How does she look?"

"Better and better every day," David said. "The original facility was always something impressive; it just needed a good cleaning. But the new additions and modernizations will make your new headquarters the epicenter of the Third."

"That's exactly what I wanted to hear," Johnson said, his jowls jiggling as he nodded.

A waitress walked by with a platter of raw sky fish fillet over grasswheat wafers and offered them to the little gathering. Johnson sucked in his breath and took the whole platter from her arms right as Blythe reached for one of the hors d'oeuvres. Johnson slipped one after another into his mouth, barely taking the time to chew while smacking his lips and moaning with pleasure. David thought he might be sick.

"Let me show you around the ship," Johnson said after emptying half the platter.

He turned and waddled his enormous body toward the circular stairs at the front of the airship. The group followed Johnson down the stairs, which ended at the glass observatory.

David felt a trickle of sweat run down his back as he stepped onto the glass floor. The airship was flying over water now, and would be for the next two hours. After that they'd sail for an hour and a half across farmlands until they reached the Maw, excellent time for an airship. He gulped when he saw a luncheon set up in the middle of the glass observatory. Johnson was prattling on about what they had planned for lunch when Mercy elbowed David and motioned toward a hallway. She tugged his arm and together they slipped out of the unsettling room onto the second level of the airship, which was like a circular track wrapping around the whole ship: one side glass windows, the other smooth paneling. It was a splendid view: clear blue sky and green-blue ocean divided by the hazy mountain cliffs.

"Beautiful, isn't it?" Mercy said.

David looked at her and nodded, but he wasn't quite sure if he meant the view of the beautiful girl or the beautiful mountains. "I've never seen anything like it. Most of my sailing took place over land."

"Oh, have you sailed much?"

"Some, though not for a long time. My father wanted me to join the armada, so he had me practice with our family's yacht."

"I should like to meet him sometime."

"Well, I'm sure he would have loved to meet you too, but he died on our last airship voyage."

"Oh. I'm so sorry." Mercy looked down, seemingly embarrassed.

"It's okay. I love flying. Doctors said I'd come to hate it because that's how my dad died, but every time I'm in the clouds, it feels like I'm closer to him somehow. Flying is what he loved to do, and it's what he wanted me to love too."

"He'd be proud of you, even if you aren't in the armada."

David smiled. "I hope so. I've done the best I could. I know he'd be happy about that."

They walked for a while circling the ship and chatting on about this and that, pausing here and there to admire the view—sweet nothings really. In fact they walked and talked for so long that David barely even noticed the scenery change from ocean to farmland. The hills of

House Floyd rolled by, their irrigated land looking like giant splotches of blue and green paint. David was shocked when a sweet waitress excused her interruption and announced that, presently, lunch would be served in the observatory.

David and Mercy took their seats, the other passengers hardly even knowing they had left, all save Devin, who eyed them suspiciously. The party of five sat around the small white table as a team of servers twice that size brought platters of food, replaced platters of food, and refilled drinks. David could hardly take a bite of something before another delicacy miraculously appeared on his plate—rare fruits from Viörn, exotic meats from Berg, and giant squid caught by fisherman who braved the Southern Ocean storms. Having Mercy beside him made David forget about the three inches of clear glass separating him from death. Plus he was a bit preoccupied keeping an eye on Devin, who was keeping his eyes on Mercy.

The food was stupendous, but to David, perhaps a bit much. Life had taught him that food was nothing more than sustenance—anything more than that and it became a vice. He looked at Johnson and shuddered.

Conversation centered upon the increased sales of Public Pharmaceuticals' latest adolescent behavior-correction drug. It was evidently a sensation amongst dual-working households in the big cities. David didn't care much for the topic, but he had little excuse to leave until a bell chimed and the captain announced over the loudspeaker that they were approaching the Maw.

While the rest of the table stood and walked toward the front of the glass observatory, David grabbed Mercy's arm and said, "I want to see it from the top deck."

She nodded, and the two climbed the circular stairs.

"Why do you want to see it from here?" Mercy asked as they reached the top of the stairs. "It's just as good of a view in the observatory."

"I'm not a fan of standing on glass, if you hadn't noticed," David said even as he winced. "Plus it just doesn't feel real unless the wind is blowing through my hair."

Mercy laughed as they rushed to the front of the ship and looked over the glass observatory from the top deck.

The Rorand Mountains rose up on the right, extending all the way back to the sea, their peaks lost in the sky. On their left, hills and farmland dissipated into desert and dust. In between the two lay a grassy plain that faded from green to brown to barren. Dozens of dust devils churned in the air, welcoming all who dared to enter the wastelands. Even as David watched, dry lightning arced out of sandy skies and scorched an unfortunate tuft of grass. This unique piece of landscape marked an area where three distinct climates abutted each other, battling over a worthless patch of dirt. It was intimidating to behold and would have been ten times worse a decade earlier when Outlanders frequented the Maw, snatching up any ship that ventured too close. However, the Outlanders' legacy grew more visible the closer they got to the desert. Airship wreckage littered the plain from a hundred different battles over the past few centuries. Rib cages of mining vessels—large enough for the Sunbeam to maneuver within—lay strewn around from back when Alönia sought minerals in the Rorand Mountains. Those same mining vessels were the reason Outlanders had started roaming these regions.

Originally six different mining companies had divided up the Rorand Mountains into six different regions. Great cities grew out of the profitable venture along the mountain range, one for each company. But when the minerals depleted and finances grew thin, boundary disputes escalated into a full-fledged war. The mining companies degraded into six Outlander syndicates even as their members' minds shriveled in the heat. Outlander Prowler ships would swoop in on a rival's cargo vessels, filch the minerals, and escape back into their desert fortresses. As mining ceased, the Outlanders started raiding the Alönian borderlands.

The Sunbeam dropped in elevation as it neared the Maw, and David noticed the rock and sand blurred beneath his gaze. Just how fast were they going?

"I want to speak with the captain," David said as he spun toward the stern.

Mercy smiled at his enthusiasm and followed at a more ladylike pace. David crossed the ship with ease over the steady lift of the balloon; it felt almost like solid ground. As he reached the pilot's tower and climbed the dozen stairs, the captain nodded down at him. He stood a half a head over David with salt-and-pepper hair sprouting from beneath his cap and a name tag that read *Captain Arold*. His hands flicked switches and turned knobs with inhuman speed.

"Mind if I have a look around?" David asked as he finished climbing the tower stairs. "I've never seen the cockpit of a Sunbeam before."

"Not at all," Arold said, seeming all too eager to show off his ship. He appeared to be as stereotypical as pilots came: cocky and eager for everyone to know it. "Have you ever flown an airship before? It's a bit like driving a steam car except it goes two additional directions, and if you crash, everybody dies." He flashed a smile and chuckled at a joke he'd obviously told a thousand times.

"I have actually," David said just as Mercy caught up with him and looked around his shoulder at the controls.

"Really?" Arold said, staring at David like he'd robbed the cookie jar. "What kind?"

"A Seeker 17, a Condor Light, and a couple different skiffs. Never anything this nice," David said as he admired the altitude control.

"My, that's quite a portfolio. This ship isn't much different than a Condor. Newer and fancier, but it really only has one additional mode of steering. See there." He pointed to a couple levers next to the altitude controls. "Those allow you to roll the ship a degree by heating one of a pair of balloons in the bottom of the keel."

David looked at the controls and nodded. "It is similar. What about the sectioned central balloon controls?" He pointed at a row of six switches. "Could those also be used for pitch control?"

Arold thought about it for a moment. "Yes, I suppose they could, but I think that might make your pleasure cruise passengers a bit unhappy."

David smiled. He had never flown for pleasure cruisers before, but that made sense. He looked out the cockpit window and saw they were near the middle of the Maw, only a few hundred feet off the ground. "How fast are we flying? The ground is passing faster than it feels like we're moving."

Arold squinted at a dial. "We're at … 176 grandfathoms an hour."

David's mouth fell open. "Really—176? But the wind … Why aren't we being blown off the back of the ship?"

"Ah, that would be the Sunbeam's aerodynamics. They really are amazing ships. You see those glass plates at the bow?" He pointed to some glass fins glittering in the sunlight that David hadn't noticed before. "Those direct the air over the top of the ship. We could move like a hurricane, and you'd still only feel a light breeze."

David gawked, looking first at Captain Arold and then at Mercy.

"If you don't believe me, try reaching a hand over the side as far as you can, though I'd take a good firm grip on the railing before ya do."

David climbed down the tower stairs and walked to the railing, Mercy at his heels. He gripped the railing with his mechanical arm and reached out as far as he could with his other hand. His fingers passed an imperceptible barrier and dipped into such a strong wind that it flung his hand away. David turned a giddy smile to Mercy.

"Hold on to me," she said. "I want to try."

She stepped close to David and presented her hand.

David took it as she leaned over the railing and let her fingers bounce off the wind wall.

Mercy laughed and said something, but David wasn't listening. A flash on the horizon behind the ship caught his eye, something that looked like a glint of metal off the mountains to their right.

David pulled Mercy back onto the airship and walked slowly to the stern, his eyes never leaving the point where he saw the glint.

"David? … What is it?" Mercy asked, but the words didn't penetrate David's wonderings.

The mountain where he'd seen the glint led back to a crevasse reaching some unknown depth into the Rorands. Then he saw it again, the same glint.

"Look," David said, "right there … in the split of the mountain. Do you see anything?"

Mercy looked for a moment. "No. Did you?"

"I thought I did. But I don't see it anymore."

David climbed back up to the control tower and borrowed Captain Arold's spyglass. Then he walked to the edge of the stern and looked through the glass. It wasn't a crevasse at all; it only looked like one at a distance. The mountain split and a cave burrowed deep into its depths, but there was nothing glinting there, just rock and dust. David scanned along the mountainside for a moment with the glass. Then he saw it yet again, the same glint. As he focused the glass on the spot, he saw the top of an airship rise above the foothills of the Rorand Mountains, and then dip back down into concealment. He only saw it for a moment, but he would know that kind of ship anywhere. A low-profile build and a long, slender balloon enabled it to fly close to the ground, gliding in and out of mountains and hills without ever being seen. He only saw a glint because most of the ship, save the prow, was dust brown in color. All in all, the ship resembled a voxil, stalking through the grassland, seeking prey—exactly like an Outlander Prowler.

Chapter Eleven

PROWLERS

David gasped, leaning forward on the rail and peering through the spyglass at the last spot he'd seen the ship before it had dipped down beneath the hills. It couldn't be a Prowler. Nobody had seen one of those in half a decade. He gazed at the next foothill for a space of heartbeats, each one thudding in his ears, praying he was wrong. When nothing emerged, he exhaled the breath he hadn't known he was holding. But then the ship crested another hill, dusty brown and blending with the surrounding landscape. David stiffened.

What should he do? Run to the captain and yell like a little girl that Outlanders were chasing them? That was exactly what he should do. Well, maybe he could scratch the *little girl* part. But what if he was wrong? No one had heard of or seen a Prowler in cycles. Why should he see one on his first trip to the Maw? On the other hand, what if it was a Prowler? What of Blythe? What of the speakership? What of Mercy? That struck a chord with David. He snapped the spyglass shut and ran for the control tower, nearly knocking Mercy down.

"Captain Arold, I ... I think I saw an Outlander Prowler, sir," David said, even now losing his nerve.

Arold looked at him for a moment, eyebrows tickling his hairline. Then his lips puckered and his eyes crinkled as he threw his head back and laughed.

David felt the idiot, but he endured. "To the southeast, sir. If you will just have a look."

Arold kept laughing until David nudged him with the man's own spyglass, and he noted David's troubled face.

"Nonsense, my boy," Arold said. "There hasn't been a Prowler sighting for almost six cycles. Poor devils finally died out in that wretched desert."

"Sir, I'm sure—I mean, I'm pretty sure I can identify one. We studied them at the academy. It might be prudent to have a look yourself." David felt fully flushed by this point.

Arold took his spyglass back and, with no small amount of amusement, held it up to his eye with a sigh. "I don't see anything."

"Right there," David said as he saw the same prow crest a hill and dip into a ravine. It was getting closer.

"Where?" Arold asked between smiling lips while squinting through the glass due south. Did the man not know what southeast meant?

David reached up and nudged the glass toward the correct place right as the Prowler crested yet another sand dune even closer. David didn't even need a glass anymore to make it out.

"Okay," Arold said, "so there's a ship out there. No telling if it's a Prowler or not. Probably just a House Floyd citizen having a bit of fun in a Sand Sailor."

"But there isn't a sand tail or any dust," David said, losing his confidence.

Yet, if it was a Prowler, precious seconds were slipping away, each one diminishing their chance for escape. The Sunbeam was magnificent and toothless. If it came to a fight, they could not bite back.

"Come now, lad. I've sailed these sands many times, and I've seen a few Prowlers in my day." Arold patted David on the back as he spoke. He snapped his spyglass shut, slid it into a pocket, and turned back to his controls. "That was a particularly good spot, though. You must have good eyes."

David melted a little bit as he turned back to Mercy, who had followed him up the stairs. "I don't think Prowlers exist anymore, David," she said.

Her tone was sweet, but it still made David flush with embarrassment. He didn't answer. Instead he took one more look at the foothills. The same ship crested a sand dune not a grandfathom back. It was getting closer, but he put it out of his mind and watched the captain level off their descent to the floor of the Maw.

"Yes, my boy, I don't think we will see Prowlers in these parts anymore. Simply isn't profitable with our Border Armada keeping watch." Arold turned around and smiled at David, but as he did so, his eyes went wide.

David looked over his shoulder and saw the ship soar

over one last rocky ledge and race into the Maw directly behind the Sunbeam.

Captain Arold cursed and slammed the throttle down, throwing David to the back of the control tower. Mercy nearly fell down the stairs as the Sunbeam surged forward. David gripped the railing and pulled Mercy to her feet. When next he looked out the back of the control tower, the Prowler was right on their tail.

"What is it?" Mercy asked as she also grabbed the railing.

"*That* is a Prowler," David said. He wasn't rubbing it in—how could he when all their lives were in danger?

The long, narrow Prowler had behaved in typical Outlander fashion: hide in the low hills until it could sneak up and pounce on the wayward ship. Prowlers had no real manufacturer; rather they were crafted from scavenged parts taken from freight haulers, miners, and the occasional pleasure cruiser. This particular Prowler sailed slightly off kilter, its balloon and decking unbalanced. Whether this was on purpose or just a construction flaw, David didn't know.

However, he did have a rather good idea what its capabilities were. His father had fought a few Prowlers, and he'd said the slowest could top two hundred grandfathoms an hour, which was about as fast as a Sunbeam could fly. What a Prowler couldn't do was turn. All its engines were affixed to the rear of the long ships, giving it excellent top speeds, but only in a straight line. In addition a Prowler's low-profile balloon limited its maximum altitude. All these limitations were fine when matched against heavy mining haulers, but against a Sunbeam?

So the question was: Why was Arold trying to evade the Prowler in a manner that pitted his weaknesses against their strengths? David looked at the captain. The man was angling the Sunbeam toward a dust storm, its center flickering with dry lightning. David looked back again. The Prowler was so close that he could see its guns tracking the Sunbeam's every move, but they weren't firing. Why?

Never forget to look where no one else is. This was a trap. They were being herded, but where? David peered into the dust storm as it swirled a few grandfathoms ahead. If Arold hoped to hide a golden pleasure cruiser in that, he would be sorely disappointed. Dust storms were perfect for hiding Prowlers, but not Sunbeams.

David sucked in a breath. "Captain."

"Not now, lad."

"But, sir, there is another Prowler in that dust storm."

Arold said nothing as he pulled back the throttle a little and pointed the Sunbeam straight toward the dust storm. David's mouth fell open. Why would he slow the ship? And why hadn't he heated the balloon and risen above the Prowler's range? Every lesson David's father had ever taught him screamed in protest. What was this idiot doing? Perhaps the captain had a trick up his sleeve. After all, he had fought Prowlers before, hadn't he? But on the other hand, if the situation didn't change soon, they would all be slaves within the next five minutes. Unless that's what the captain wanted? How easy would it be to thwart Blythe's rise to power with a simple kidnapping? How much easier to bribe a simple pleasure cruiser captain? David knew he was thinking nonsense, but this was no longer a game. Their situation was dire.

As the dust storm loomed ever closer, David peered into its depths, looking for a second Prowler. Perhaps there wasn't one. But just then he noticed Captain Arold doing something very peculiar. The captain took a small rope and tied the wheel in place. Then he opened a small cupboard and pulled out a life-balloon.

"Last time I flew through a dust storm, I nearly died of a lung infection," Arold said as he strapped the vest on. "I'd recommend breathing through a cloth if you can."

With that he ran from the control tower, hopping down two steps at a time. He reached the deck railing and hurled himself overboard. As the wind caught him, he shot back in the Sunbeam's jet stream, inflated his life-balloon, and bobbed along in their wake, disappearing into the distance.

"What is he doing?" Mercy asked with wide eyes.

"Abandoning ship, I should think." It all made sense now. This was his plan all along.

"But ... But who is going to fly the ship?"

David looked at the wheel for an instant, hesitating. The last time he piloted an airship was the day his father died. He gulped. That was the past; this was now—and people needed him. He shoved his pain into the deepest part of his soul and answered Mercy by stepping up to the controls. He ripped off the rope and spun the wheel thirty degrees. The ship hummed as it veered to the left and carved the air. He pushed the throttle down to full speed and, despite the circumstances, felt a thrill as the vessel accelerated to two hundred grandfathoms an hour. Mercy grabbed the railing when the deck leaned. David heard some angry calls echo from the stairways when pots and pans, and perhaps a few people, rattled around. He bit his lip as the ship answered to every flick of his fingers and turn of his wrists. Not to worry—if he made a mistake, they would only die. Piloting an airship he'd never even seen before—surely the stupidest thing he had ever done.

"It's just like a Condor. It's just like a Condor. It's just like a Condor," David muttered to himself amidst some flashing lights on the control panel.

He looked back at the crooked Prowler. It couldn't match the Sunbeam's turn and instead rocketed toward the dust storm. He still couldn't see any other Prowler within the dust storm … yet. He was sure it was there, waiting for the perfect moment to strike. He maneuvered the Sunbeam, skirting the outside of the dust storm even as he superheated the balloon. They needed to leave the prowling ground. Wind buffeted the side of the airship, and sand rattled and hissed as it swept across the deck. But then a second Prowler emerged from the dust storm, fine particulates billowing around it like a cloud of vapor, blocking the Sunbeam's ascent. This one had none of the imbalance like the other; rather its prow divided into two points, a gun emplacement on each. David slammed a lever down and vented the balloon moments before the

Sunbeam slammed into the bottom of the second
Prowler. Mercy shrieked as the control tower missed the
bottom of the Prowler by mere fathoms. As David tried
to maneuver around the new Prowler, the first one pulled
up along the right side of the Sunbeam. They were trying
to force them into the dust storm. David didn't know
much about dust storms, but Captain Arold's warning
about breathing through a cloth gnawed at him, and the
particulates couldn't be good for the Sunbeam's fine-
tuned turbofans. Besides, if Outlanders wanted him to go
into the storm, it was definitely a bad idea.

He looked at the first Prowler beside him as it nudged
closer and closer. They were so close that he could see
the crew. Every man wore a mask and a pair of tinted
goggles. So that's how they managed the dust. He spun a
knob and his gyroscopic turbofans rotated into full
reverse. The Sunbeam bucked with the change in
momentum, but the Prowlers were waiting for just such a
move. Each ship reversed engines and slowed to match
the Sunbeam, but the first Prowler wasn't quite fast
enough. David spun the wheel and the Sunbeam cut
behind it. He saw the captain waving his arms and
screaming at his men. David marked that ship as the
weaker of the two. A captain with a hot temper always
presented less of a threat.

However, the second Prowler was not so easily
evaded. That captain amazed David as he loosed an old
fashion sail, which spun his ship 180 degrees. This man
knew his ship. Instead of using conventional measures to
turn, which on his ship were lacking, he used wind and

sail. That was the thing about Outlanders and their eccentric ships: no one could ever depend on specific restrictions, as every ship and captain proved unique. The captain wasted no time after his maneuver, racing forward and again blocking the Sunbeam from ascending, forcing the golden ship toward the ground. David worked the wheel back and forth, but it had been a long time since he'd flown an airship, and this particular Outlander captain proved superb. He matched David's every move, releasing sails and drawing them in, his expert crew outflying a wonder of machinery using a method two hundred cycles old.

The funny thing was, even still, neither Prowler had fired a shot. While they were obviously tasked with eliminating Blythe, maybe they wanted to capture him and hold him for ransom. Or they meant to take the Sunbeam as a prize and would only fire on the ship when they thought they might lose her. David wished he knew their munitions load-out, but he couldn't spare a moment to look. Maybe Mercy could. She still stood at the top of the control tower stairs, clutching the railing and wincing at every turn.

"Mercy, I need you to find another spyglass and tell me what type of guns are on the Prowlers."

"What? But I don't know airship guns."

"If you describe them, I should know what they are," David said as she rifled through some cabinets.

He tried to keep the Sunbeam as level as possible for the next few moments while Mercy moved about. Then he had a thought: he'd never sounded the maneuvers alarm. He slapped a hand down on a red button and a klaxon rang across the ship. *Better late than never.*

Mercy cried out in triumph as she held a spyglass to her eye. "Okay ... I can't see all the guns on the ship above us, but the ones on the lower decks are either long and narrow with multiple barrels, or short and stubby with canisters of fluid attached."

David nodded. "Chain-guns and chemical throwers. Good for killing crew but not so good at taking down airships." He puzzled at that. It didn't surprise him that the sides of the ship were stacked with short-range weapons, but if they meant to take the ship, why hadn't they swept the deck with chain-gun fire? Taking Blythe alive, then. "Any others?"

"There's a pair of guns sticking out of the front, but I can't see anything other than the barrels. They're ... large."

Some sort of heavy cannon. Something like that could bring down an airship, and it could do it from a long way off. But guns like those had limited maneuverability, and if the Sunbeam could gain some elevation, they might be able to avoid them. David looked back. The first Prowler had finished its clumsy turn and was even now careening toward them. He only had a few more seconds until it caught up. Then it happened: the first shot of the engagement—but not from the second Prowler. The hot-tempered captain of the first one had burned through his limited supply of patience in the first maneuver. The shot went wide, exploding a hundred fathoms in front of the Sunbeam.

"Incendiary rounds … great," David muttered.

He looked for something to level the playing field. He hadn't much time before things would get messy. He couldn't flee, and he couldn't climb if there was a ship above him. But he had another option, one that made him grin.

David dropped the ship's elevation, a move that appeared foolish when pitting a Sunbeam against a Prowler. He flew so low that the bottom of his keel kicked up dust from the ground, and he angled directly toward the wreckage of an old behemoth-class mining vessel.

"Try using sails in here," David mumbled as he speared his narrow ship between two steel ribs of the wreckage while rotating the turbofans into full reverse.

Mercy shrieked as the Sunbeam passed through the space with only a fathom to spare on either side.

David spun the wheel hard, placing the ship in full reverse and narrowly missing several rusty girders and a partially intact cargo bay door. He looked behind them, breathing a sigh of relief when the second Prowler did not pursue, choosing rather to fly above the wreckage. As the Sunbeam rounded a bay door, David saw the entire length of the old mining ship, the Sunbeam floating along its keel. The whole wreckage looked like it might collapse in a light breeze, rust and time subduing metal.

The Sunbeam entered at the middle of the oblong ship. The old girl's disintegrating top deck acted as a kind of ceiling, shading the rest of the ship from the desert sun. Here and there hundred-fathom shafts of light speared through the top deck and illuminated fine dust particulates. The bow of the old miner had disintegrated away, perhaps decades earlier, leaving the front as a gaping hole that cast a shadow onto the sand beyond. That's where the second Prowler had most likely gone. At the stern of the old ship, a jagged crack slashed at an angle across the hull, a rift probably caused when the vessel impacted against the desert sands.

After taking stock of his surroundings, David did what all excellent captains do: he gambled, hedging his bet off a momentary glimpse at a hot-tempered man.

He put the ship in full reverse and rotated his turbofans. The Sunbeam spun 180 degrees along its axis. The belly of the mining vessel clouded as cycles of undisturbed dust filled the air. He halted the Sunbeam in the shadow of the rusted cargo bay door. From his vantage point David saw the space between the ribs where he'd entered the wreckage. There, David waited, counting off seconds in his head.

"David, what are we doing?" Mercy asked.

"Something stupid."

"What?"

But David didn't explain any further, for the moment he'd expected had arrived. The first Prowler plunged through the same gap in the miner's ribs, the heated captain throwing caution to the wind. His wider ship fit through the gap, but not as clean as the Sunbeam. The Prowler's right side scraped along a steel rib, bending the barrels of the port-side guns. A loud screech reverberated within the wreckage, each echo gaining volume.

David didn't waste any time as he pushed the turbofans to max power, accelerating the Sunbeam along a collision course. The captain of the first Prowler didn't have time to maneuver away from him; in fact he probably didn't even see him. The hot-tempered man had entered the wreckage at twice the speed as David and had to place his ship in emergency reverse before he smashed into the miner's opposite side. The Prowler stopped directly in front of his course.

David adjusted his aim, increasing altitude and squeezing the bars of the wheel so hard that even his mechanical knuckles turned white.

He flicked on the ship-wide intercom. "This is David Ike. Brace for impact."

"Oh no!" Mercy said, closing her eyes as she laced her arms around the control tower railing.

David held his breath, adjusting his altitude one last time and praying he was accurate in his approximation of the keel's length. The Prowler disappeared from David's view as the Sunbeam passed over it. For a moment David wondered if he'd missed. But then the Sunbeam bucked, throwing him against the wheel. It felt as if the air around the Sunbeam had changed to tar and the vessel struggled to break free of the viscous substance. When he heard the tear of cloth and the hiss of aerosol, he knew his aim had been true.

He'd sliced the top of the Prowler's balloon with the Sunbeam's serrated keel, its tip piercing through the heavyweight fabric, catching in the fibers, and ripping it apart. David laughed and shot Mercy a half grin, but his expression vanished when the Sunbeam pitched forward. His feet slid on the deck as he fell hard against the wheel. He looked up and saw the sand rapidly approaching. He hadn't accounted for their keel catching in the fabric of the Prowler's balloon. The Sunbeam's turbofans, which had previously been directing them forward, now propelled them nose-first toward the dirt and what would be a very messy impact. He reached for the gyroscopic controls and spun them to the reverse position, halting the Sunbeam's glass observatory mere fathoms above a dusty demise.

As the ship righted itself, he heated the balloon and propelled the Sunbeam up and away from the first Prowler. The ship moved sluggishly, so he added more power, and then more power. He was about to throttle up a third time when he realized the problem: the Sunbeam's keel was stuck fast. They were dragging the Prowler through the air by the sinews of its own balloon. The danger was that if the Prowler ripped free, David risked smashing into what was left of the miner's top deck before he could throttle down.

In retrospect, if David could have seen the sight of a Sunbeam with its keel stuck fast in a Prowler filled with angry Outlanders while hovering in the middle of a rusting old miner wreck, he might have paused to admire the airmanship. As it was, his hands moved in a blur as he did everything he knew to keep them airborne. As he reminded himself to never again underestimate the tensile strength of a Prowler balloon, he decided one more gamble was in order. Jeshua had smiled on them so far;

perhaps He would see them through.

David cut power to the turbofans, vented the balloon, and waited as gravity reached up and tugged on the airship. A moment later—once he'd felt a familiar tingle in his stomach—he reheated the balloon and directed the turbofans straight down at full power. The Sunbeam jerked, and he heard a tear as the Prowler balloon ripped free. He leveled off the Sunbeam's balloon and directed their craft forward, narrowly avoiding the miner's top deck. As the Sunbeam lurched toward the miner's stern, he chanced a glance backward. He watched the first Prowler fall at an angle, one half of the balloon still providing lift, and then collide with a steel beam. He smiled as he heard the impact echo through the ship—until he realized that it wasn't an echo, but rather secondary impacts as the weakened state of the mining vessel protested the abuse. Sheets of metal as long as the Sunbeam fell from the deck above them, sending up great clouds of dust as they thudded on the sandy floor. The old vessel groaned, admonishing the brawlers who dared to disturb its peaceful slumber. Then a chain as thick as David clinked as it swung mere feet from the Sunbeam's prow, wrapping around a massive I-beam. David looked back at the bow of the old miner and saw the second Prowler hovering in front of the gaping hole. Even as David watched, the miner's ribs and crossbeams snapped as the middle of the ship crumbled upon itself, the collapse working its way toward its outer ends. The Sunbeam had moments before it would join the miner in its final death, sharing in its dusty tomb. They had one chance of escape.

David eyed the rift that split the back of the miner's hull, tilting his head to match its angle. *It just might be big enough.* He slammed the ship's turbofans into high power. The Sunbeam careened toward the crack, the miner's collapsing deck giving chase. He looked at the switches Captain Arold had mentioned earlier, the ones that inflated keel balloons and rolled the Sunbeam. He flicked one on and prayed as the deck shifted and the ship matched the angle of the rift.

"David!" Mercy shouted. "We won't fit—not with the turbofans."

David didn't answer, mostly because he knew she was right. As the stern neared, debris started falling all around them. A metal pole bounced off the Sunbeam's deck, scoring the polymer. The vessel leaned at thirty degrees, which was David's best approximation of the rift in the miner's stern. He waited until the last possible second, until he had squeezed every bit of acceleration out of the remaining distance, before he cut power to the turbofans and initiated the docking sequence. He didn't know how long it took for the fans to fold against the sides of a Sunbeam, so he just based his timing off all he had and prayed it was enough. The ship floated along the same path, speeding toward the rift as the fans folded in at a lazy rate, mocking the impending collision.

Now that the fans were off, David could hear Mercy—and others below—screaming and shouting above the racket of the collapsing miner. He wanted to close his eyes, but he figured that it wouldn't be a good thing for someone to do while piloting. Debris fell all around the ship, each fragment threatening instant death for the Sunbeam and all hands. The air sparkled with dust as the light pouring through the rift clouded.

Then the front of the Sunbeam passed through the rift, the unscathed glass observatory reflecting in the sunlight. David could almost taste the free air, but the turbofans were not quite folded. He decided to join the others and let out a loud shout.

At the last possible second the fans clicked into place and the Sunbeam skidded through the crack, sparks flying as a few jagged scraps of metal scraped the ship's gilded surface. It was not a moment too soon, for as they burst into the sunlight, the last of the mining vessel's skeleton collapsed into the sands behind them, sending up an enormous dust cloud.

David wasted no time. He righted the Sunbeam and superheated the balloon. The ship shot into the sky as its turbofans extended from their cradles and reengaged. He looked back at the miner's wreck. He couldn't see much beneath the cloud of dust; but as he watched, the Prowler with the dual prow rose out of the billowing sands, like a submersible rising out of the ocean. It didn't pursue, not now. The Sunbeam had the advantage of altitude, and the Prowler needed to search for survivors from their unfortunate counterpart.

David slumped against the wheel and wiped the sweat from his brow. He'd had enough excitement for one day. His adrenaline was plummeting, leaving a nauseous feeling in the pit of his stomach.

He looked over at Mercy, who stared at him with wide eyes before asking, "Where in the Fertile Plains did you learn to fly like that?"

Chapter Twelve

ROMANCE OR ESPIONAGE?

David breathed a sigh of relief and rested his head against the wheel. He wanted nothing more than to curl up on the floor and fall asleep. Luckily an engineer came from below deck and relieved him. David hobbled down the stairs, mind in a daze before he collapsed into one of the many sun chairs. He felt hot and cold at the same time, sweating and nauseated. He rested his head in his hands and took long, slow breaths. He jumped when someone touched his back. He looked up as Mercy sat beside him and rubbed his tense shoulders. She knit her eyebrows but didn't say anything.

He closed his eyes and rested his head back in his hands. He heard heavy feet stomping up the stairs. Blythe and Johnson barked out questions, but it sounded far off, like an echo underwater. David looked up and tried to stutter out a reply, but his addled mind only muddied thoughts and slurred words.

That was when something very unexpected happened: Mercy came to his aid. She actually hushed them—two of the most powerful men in Alönia ... and she hushed them. After which, in a far more subdued tone, she explained what happened, how the captain got squeamish and David saved them all. Only the highlights penetrated his mind. He worked his mouth a few times, but gave up and let Mercy explain for him, nodding along.

Blythe and Johnson listened to her story, their expression changing from anger to surprise to shock. Evidently the two men had observed the whole episode from safety restraints in the glass observatory and wanted to know why the blazes David was piloting the ship in the face of such danger.

"But the captain? He actually jumped ship?" Johnson kept asking.

Blythe walked forward and squeezed one of David's shoulders, saying, "Well done, lad. I do believe you saved all our lives. However, in future, let's avoid running into other airships. Now, Mr. Johnson, would you be so good as to lend me a fresh pair of trousers and then direct me to the nearest washroom so I can change into them?"

After the men walked away, David opted to lie down on his back in the sun chair, gazing up at the expanse of clear blue sky. Golden rays of sunshine warmed his face. He never remembered falling asleep.

When he awoke, he wore a blanket. The weather had soured, a sure sign they were nearing the island portion of Alönia. He sat up and looked around. Blythe and Johnson spoke at the front of the airship, Blythe telling some elaborate story while using his hands to form buildings and mountains and airships. Devin hovered behind them, facing Johnson, but all the while looking at David. While David might have been groggy, he still thought that strange. He thought about waving when he discovered Devin wasn't actually looking at him, but rather at something behind him. David shifted on his sun chair and saw Mercy, red hair whipping in the breeze as she walked toward him, a steaming mug of tea in each hand. At some point during the day's adventure, she'd lost her sailor's cap, but he couldn't remember when.

"Feeling better?" Mercy asked as she neared.

"Yes, much." David accepted one of her cups with a smile. "I didn't know I was so tired."

"Everybody was a little drowsy after that episode— everyone except Mr. Blythe and Mr. Johnson. Mr. Johnson even had the chefs prepare a second lunch, and Mr. Blythe hasn't stopped talking since."

David chuckled at that, looking back as Blythe executed the punch line of some exciting tale.

Mercy sat across from him with her own steaming mug and continued, "You probably felt it most of all, given the fact you bore the lives of the whole ship on your shoulders." She took a sip of her tea, eyeing him over the brim of her mug before she said, "You never did tell me where you learned to fly an airship like that."

David looked into his own mug, eyeing the tea as it swirled. "My father taught me. He was an exceptional airship captain himself. His father taught him."

"And they're … gone?"

David nodded. "Dead. My father died saving my mother and me. That's where I got this." David wiggled his metal fingers. "My grandfather died a few weeks later. He was old, and the shock of losing his only son was too much for him. Now it's just my mom and I."

"I'm sorry," Mercy said, and she looked it. She looked in pain, like the conversation hurt her. "Sometimes Jeshua works in ways we do not understand."

David shrugged and searched for something else to talk about. He didn't like talking about Jeshua. He and his parents used to be religious Sanctuary folk, but times had changed for him. Jeshua had turned away, and he had to help himself now. "Perhaps … but it was a long time ago, and, all things considered, life's been good to me. I've got a great job. Mr. Blythe helps me out with my housing costs and my mother's medical expenses. I know I lost a lot, but look how much I have. I look around at everyone else in the Houselands and I think, I've got it pretty good."

Mercy smiled at him. She was gorgeous. David had seen a lot of things this trip. He'd seen the sun rising over Capital Bay. He'd seen the Alönian mountains shrouded in their heavenly mists. He'd seen the rolling House Floyd farmlands and the unruly Desert Maw. But none of it struck him as deeply as that smile. It was more than beautiful; it was pure, heartfelt, intelligent … sincere.

"Nothing dampens your spirits, does it?" Mercy said.

"Would I be any better off if they were?"

"That's a good point. Most Alönians would tell you yes, but it's a lie."

"Everybody has something to complain about, but I think if anyone was to sit down and think about it, they could see how much worse life could be. After my father and grandfather died, the only thing I could think about was how happy I was that I still had my mother."

"Counting your blessings?"

"Yes, I suppose I was."

At that moment the first mate announced over the ship-wide intercom that they were approaching the Landings and would be descending momentarily. By the time David and Mercy finished their tea, airmen had tied the ship off along the sky dock.

"Let me get you a taxi home," Mercy said. "It's the least I could do to thank you. If it weren't for you, I might have been captured by Outlanders and sold into slavery." She put her hand over her mouth in mock surprise.

David smiled and looked down. "Well, all right, but I'm paying you back as soon as I get that raise Mr. Blythe keeps mentioning."

"Of course. I'll add it to the bill."

"David," Blythe said as he and Johnson approached. "How are you feeling? You looked pretty pale earlier."

David blushed at all the attention. "I'm fine, sir. I was just a little tired."

"Good. Well, take a few days off; spend some time with your mother. You've earned them."

"That's not necessary, sir. Really, I'm fine."

"No, I insist." Blythe put a firm hand on his shoulder. "I can't have one of my aides exhausting himself."

"Thank you, sir. I'll see how I feel in the morning and decide if I think I'm up to coming in."

The airmen secured the ship as soon as it bumped along the dock. They extended the gangplank, and the party said their good-byes and went their separate ways. A few moments later David and Mercy stepped off the ship into the muggy Swollock Season climate, and then the temperamental sky frowned, puckered, and cried all over Capital Airship Landings.

David started looking for cover or at least something to use as an umbrella for Mercy, but she shocked him by saying, "What's the matter? Afraid of a little rain?"

Mercy put her arms out and smiled up at the rain, like she wanted to hug the sky, laughing as she spun in a circle. David stammered as she giggled and grabbed his arm, tugging him forward in the warm tropical rain. They walked down the middle of the Landings in defiance of the weather and the people scuttling around for cover. Women held up their bustled skirts, skipping over puddles, squeezing under overhangs and into boutiques. Laborers with crates and hand trucks flipped up their collars around their necks and did their best to ignore the weather as they went about their business. A few window washers walked down the side of a steel-and-glass building in their magnetic boots, calling it a day due to the inclement weather. One of them stopped and gaped at David and Mercy. David supposed he and Mercy did make quite a sight as they smiled and laughed, soaking up the rain and walking down the middle of the street. David heard a few comments from passersby. One elderly lady thought they might catch pneumonia and spend a week in bed. A laborer thought David a lollygagger chasing skirts while the rest of them worked. A little boy asked his mommy if they were sun-crazed. To which his mother replied, "Yes, that's exactly what it is," but then hid a smile behind her hand.

David wondered at Mercy, as she had never acted this way before. Every time he was alone with her, he discovered a new facet of her personality. This must be what she was like when she truly put her hair down, a step further than the time she had taken him to the suit vendor. Or perhaps recent events had made her see him differently, made her see him as more than a fragile political underling. If that was true, the girl must have had a soft spot for a daring airship pilot. No, this was something more complicated. If all it took to win her heart was a reckless man with an airship, she'd have been promised long before now.

Once David and Mercy reached the end of the Landings' docks, they hailed a taxi and climbed into the back, leaving squishy places wherever they paused on the red carpet. They slid onto a bench, squeaking as their wet clothes slid along the leather.

"You know," Mercy said as she snuggled up to David, "typically gentlemen put their arm around a young lady when she's cold." She offered a forced shiver.

David smiled and laid his good arm across her shoulders. She did ask, and it would be rude to refuse. The air-taxi driver looked back, a little annoyed at the wet carpet, but he only rolled his eyes at the couple and asked where they wanted to go.

David opened his mouth to answer, but he wasn't sure what to say. He had no idea where Mercy lived, but he was fairly sure it was in the opposite direction from where he lived.

"The Linden Lodgings of the Third District industrial sector," Mercy said.

The cab driver frowned, clearly taken aback by the length of the trip and perhaps wondering if the young couple could afford the fare.

"For which we are willing to pay handsomely," Mercy added.

The cabbie shrugged and keyed up the airship while muttering something about "crazy kids." David knew he looked a fool, soaking wet with a girl far more beautiful than he deserved embarking on a taxi trip he couldn't hope to afford. On the other hand, he *really* liked it, so he didn't care.

The cabbie flipped on the burner, and the airship rose through the rain until it popped out of the cloud cover into the late-evening sunset. David just stared at it. *You couldn't ask for a more romantic scene.* The taxi's interior glowed with sunrays as it sailed over a golden blanket.

"You never told me about your parents," David said. "I know they're from Armstad, and that they're rich, but do you ever see them? Where do they live?"

Mercy shivered again, but this one also had nothing to do with the cold. It seemed like more of a shudder. She didn't answer, eyes looking at something in the distant past. David inwardly kicked himself for ruining the moment, but after a few seconds she spoke.

"My parents and I are estranged. I haven't seen them since … since I joined Alönian politics. They set up a trust in my name when I was young, so I never want for money, but that's really all I have left from them."

David couldn't think of what to say. Maybe he shouldn't say anything. He wanted to help her, make her feel better, but she hadn't asked for help. He had nosed his way into her business, and she had shown a little piece of her past as a gesture of trust.

"I'm sorry," David said, deciding it to be the best thing to say. "It must be difficult."

He felt Mercy relax a little under his arm. He almost had a heart attack when she rested her head against his chest.

"How about siblings?" he said. "Um, any of those?"

"Three older brothers. But I haven't seen them in a long time either. Ruben is a chemist and an engineer, a real whiz for the Armstad research department, last I heard. Ernst works in counterintelligence. Levi went into the Armstad special forces cycles ago. I don't really know what he does anymore."

"They immigrated back to Armstad?"

"Yes. I was the only one that stayed in Alönia." Mercy wiped some rain off her cheek, as it had now mixed with tears. She sniffled and shook her head, as if clearing unhappy thoughts. "Tell me about your mother. What is she like?"

David had wanted to avoid this. He never told anyone about his mother—not that he was ashamed of her, never that. He just didn't know how people would react, and he loved her too much to let anyone think ill of her. "She's … kind."

"That's it? Just kind?" Mercy sounded a little disappointed, like he was holding out on her.

What was he supposed to say? His mother *was* kind. He remembered that much. But it had been so long since she had said anything to him. He remembered how much she loved him. Time would never allow him to forget that. "She used to be very beautiful, but she got sick … when my father died. She's … never been the same."

Mercy looked up at David before resting her head again. "Well, tell me about your father, then. What was he like?"

David smiled. It was easier to talk about his father; time had healed that wound more so than the situation with his mother. "Tall, sarcastic … he had an easy laugh. Never missed a moment to kiss my mother and tell her she was beautiful. When I say *never*, I mean *never*. Sometimes they were really awkward in public."

Mercy giggled. "They sound like they had a happy life together. You said he taught you to fly. Was he as good as you?"

"Much better. He was the best airship captain in the entire armada."

"And your Grandfather taught him?"

David nodded. "It was the family trade, until … well, until the academy didn't want me after my injuries. They invest a lot into cadets and space is limited. I was more of a liability for the armada than an asset."

"Well, they never saw you fly. I think they'd make room for you if they knew what kind of pilot you are."

David smiled. How little she knew. They had seen him fly. They'd seen him fly like the devil himself, but somehow it had only made things worse.

As they talked, the sun slid beneath the clouds and the moon rose over the frothy clouds. Stars twinkled outside the windows as two friends kindled something deeper than friendship, but not quite love. All too soon the airship bumped and rocked as it docked against a local taxi hub in the middle of the Third's industrial district. David sat up, grudgingly, and unwrapped his arm from Mercy's shoulders. She shivered for real this time.

"Is your apartment far from here?"

"Just down the lane."

"Would you mind terribly if I came with you and borrowed a blanket for the journey home? I can bring it back in the morning."

"Um, well, I ..."

But Mercy didn't let him finish his reply. She dropped a handful of coins in the cabbie's hand, grabbed David's mechanical arm, and towed him out the back of the taxi. After they climbed down the stairs to street level, David was sure to guide them through the most populated areas. Mercy didn't seem to notice the number of vagrants eyeing her as she clung to David and chattered away. Rain still pattered through the muggy evening, but if anything, the rain brought out the worst the industrial district had to offer. Men and women stood beneath every awning, breathing out clouds of pungent vapor and favoring

David and Mercy with false smiles.

Streetlights flickered along the puddled street, a few flashing in time with the garish advertisements along the building walls soliciting dance clubs, illegal surgical upgrades, and free district-issued antipsychotics—as if the people needed any more drugs. David wondered again if having Public Pharmaceuticals would truly benefit the people of the Third or just field more drugs. Users would be so busy escaping their problems they wouldn't be able to take advantage of the new facility's jobs. Then again, having Blythe as speaker was worth the consequences.

David let out a sigh when they stepped into his apartment's shabby steam lift and keyed the top floor. It was only then that Mercy quieted, looking around the steam shaft with wide eyes and a wrinkled nose. The new renovations were coming along nicely. The lift no longer leaked, and the mildew smell was almost gone—almost. Once they reached the top floor and walked down the hall, David fumbled with his keys trying to decide how best to prepare Mercy for what she was about to see.

"Mercy, my mother is perhaps a little more sick than you realize."

"How sick is she?"

"Very. I don't know how much longer I'm going to have her. Doctor says she could leave at any moment."

"Oh." Mercy bit her lip. "Well, it can't be worse than not talking to your parents for the past few cycles, right?"

"No, it can. You'll see."

David found the key and unlocked the door. As he walked through, Mercy let go of his arm and paused at the entrance, one eyebrow raised in question. She walked through the doorway and turned about in the little kitchen, openmouthed.

"I know," David said. "It's a bit snug."

"And it's spotless."

David chuckled. "Ella? I'm home, and I brought a friend."

Ella walked out of his mother's room and smiled at them both. "What are you all soaked for?" she asked.

"Got caught in the rain," David said with a shrug. "This is Mercy, and I'm loaning her a blanket for her ride home. Mercy, this is my mother's nurse, Ella."

Mercy gave Ella a polite nod and smiled.

"Pleased to meet you, Ms. Mercy. I'm sorry, but I have to run. Have some chores that need doing before bed."

"Thank you, Ella. I'm sorry I'm late … again," David said.

"Never you mind. It was nice meeting you, Ms. Mercy," Ella said as she slipped out the door.

"Same," Mercy said as the door clicked shut.

David fidgeted for a moment before walking toward his mother's room. "Mom, I have someone I want you to meet."

His mother was right where she always was. Sitting in the same torn easy chair, wrapped in the same tattered blanket. David kissed her on the cheek and turned back toward Mercy.

She edged into the room, at first wearing a polite smile, but when she saw David's mom, it saddened, looking more forced.

"It's very nice to meet you, Mrs. Ike," Mercy said.

Of course, David's mother didn't say anything. David grabbed Mercy's arm and positioned her in front of his mother's blank gaze, knowing that his mom couldn't turn her head.

"Mom, this is Mercy. She's another one of Mr. Blythe's aides." David leaned a little closer and mock-whispered, "Don't tell her I told you she's smarter than me."

Mercy blushed and looked down, her smile easing a little. David brushed his mother's hair out of her face and kissed her forehead. That's when he saw his mother's eyes. They were twinkling, like they had on so few occasions before. It made him smile and blush ruby red all the way to his earlobes. He knew exactly what his mother was thinking, and the twinkle meant his mother knew exactly what he was thinking as well. David had to stop himself from actually telling his mother to keep it to herself.

"Well, Mercy is here to borrow a blanket. I'll just be a moment, and then I'll brush your hair."

Mercy nodded and presented another smile to his mother before she followed him out the door. Once in the living room, David turned on the light. Mercy's face looked pained, mouth working, but hesitant to ask the question on the tip of her tongue.

He rescued her: "When my father died in the airship accident, he saved my mother and me by tying us both to the only life-balloon on the ship and throwing us overboard. It was a small balloon, and we didn't have enough elevation once I inflated it. We landed poorly. I landed on top of my mother, paralyzing her. She's actually quite lucky to be alive. Really, both my parents gave their bodies to save my life that day."

Mercy nodded. "She can't … speak?"

"Not since the crash."

"I'm sorry. That must be difficult."

"She's alive. It could be worse."

David walked to the couch—also his bed—picking up the only other blanket in the house from where it lay neatly folded on the armrest. He tried to hand it to Mercy, but she was looking at his pinboard, a puzzled look on her face.

"What is all this?" she asked.

"Oh. Well … it's how I keep track of everything—puzzles I'm trying to solve and such."

Mercy looked over the section on Blythe and smiled at the card with her name on it. She read the notes and laughed. "When did you figure out I didn't like sky fish?"

"You nearly spit it out when we had dinner with Johnson."

She turned and eyed him. "I am not infatuated with red."

David shrugged. "You always wear it."

Mercy huffed and looked at the rest of the notes. "The man in the shadows?"

"Oh, that's a bit of a new puzzle."

"Who is he?"

David shook his head. "I don't know yet. It's just, with all the things that have happened the past few weeks, I can't help but wonder if someone is pulling the strings, you know?" He picked up another card and wrote *Prowler Attack* on it, pinning it below the one for the man in the shadows.

"The Prowlers? You think they're connected to him?"

"I can't shake what Captain Arold did with the Sunbeam. It's as if he wanted us to get caught, steering us toward the storm and keeping us at low altitude. And then there's the fact that the Prowlers were waiting for us. They haven't been seen for cycles and then they resurface the moment a ship arrives carrying two of the most powerful men in Alönia? It's too much for coincidence."

Mercy nodded. "It does seem a bit odd." She traced her finger along the string that connected Samantha with the man in the shadows. Mercy looked back at David with an eyebrow raised. "And Samantha?"

David shrugged. "I think she was a pawn. She wasn't intelligent enough to operate alone."

Mercy followed another string from Samantha to Paula and a small cutting from a newspaper obituary. "What does she have to do with Paula?"

"I can't be sure of anything. I'm just matching questions with possible answers, but ... I've always thought Paula's death too horrific and too timely for a simple street murder. A political saboteur filled her position not three days after her death. And then there were the newspapers. That obituary was the only excerpt I could find relating to Paula's death, not even a whisper about her gruesome murder. Yet the *Voxil* had entire pages dedicated to Samantha's scandal, and every other newspaper joined in on the *squandering of public funds* accusation. It's all too convenient and strange. Someone is pulling strings."

"So what do you know about this *man in the shadows* so far? Any leads?" Mercy stepped back from the wall and looked at it as a whole.

David shook his head again. "Someone powerful, someone wealthy, someone who never shows his true face to the world. But I think ... I think I actually saw him."

Mercy looked at David so fast her limp hair spun in an arc, sending drips around the room. "When?"

"After Mr. Blythe gave his speech, there was a man in the gallery, standing in the shadow of the curtains. Everyone was clapping but him. He looked right at me, and then he walked out."

Mercy looked at David with wide eyes before they filled with mirth and she burst out laughing. "Now you're just trying to scare me."

David smiled and looked down, cheeks turning red, but as he did so, the sky flashed and echoed with thunder, and at the exact same time the only working light in the apartment winked out. Mercy shrieked and grabbed David's arm.

"Sorry, sorry. That light is always burning out. Give me just a second and I'll find the candle."

After peeling Mercy's fingernails out of his arm, he rummaged around on his bookshelf. Every few seconds the entire room lit up as lightning flashed across the sky, illuminating the Third's cityscape. Each flash gave him a brief image of the room and Mercy's nervous face. It was then that he realized it wasn't only his unreliable light that failed, but the power across the entire city. He found his candle and a match and struck up the flickering flame. He looked around. Mercy wasn't where he'd left her. She was at the window, looking across the industrial sector. He joined her.

"It's a beautiful view," she said. "Better than the one at my apartment."

"It's the one good thing about this place ... other than the people in it."

Lightning flashed again, giving David a perfect snapshot of a distant skyscraper and some factories before the darkness returned.

"Do ... Do you think Mr. Blythe will be a good Speaker?" Mercy asked.

David looked at her face as it glowed in the dim candlelight. "I know he's been good for my mother and me. If he treats the rest of Alönia like he's treating us, I think he'll be great." He put the candle on a table and draped the blanket around Mercy's shoulders.

She held it around her neck, burying her face up to her eyes in its folds. She looked at David, and he could tell that she was smiling by the crinkle of her eyes.

"Thank you, David. Are you sure you won't be needing it?"

"Not as much as you."

She smiled again, then leaned forward, pulled the blanket down, and kissed him on the cheek before finally walking back toward the apartment door. It was a good thing the power was out so that Mercy couldn't see David's shocked expression. In fact David was so shocked that she was halfway to the door before he reacted. He spun around and walked after her … before tripping on his stool and falling on his face. Then again maybe it wasn't a good thing the power was out.

As David climbed back to his feet, he heard Mercy giggling.

"Are you okay?" she asked.

"Fine, I'm fine."

David grabbed the candle from the table and walked after Mercy. As they passed his mother's room, Mercy stepped inside.

"It was nice to meet you, Mrs. Ike," she said as she bent and hugged his mother. "You should be very proud of your son. He's a good man."

With that Mercy turned and ran out of the room, face flushed, not stopping until she got to the door. "Thanks again for the blanket, David," she said in a rush as she slipped out the door and closed it behind her.

David couldn't help but grin. She'd kissed him. Sure, it was only on the cheek, but a kiss was a kiss.

He turned and walked back into his mother's room, setting the candle down on the little table next to her armchair. He picked the comb up and started combing her hair. Then he stopped and looked at his mom's eyes. They were still twinkling, brighter than he'd seen in a long time.

"What are you looking at?"

Chapter Thirteen

A MEETING OF THE MINDS

Mercy made it all the way to the stairwell before she broke down. She leaned back against the wall and covered her mouth, holding back the nausea. She had to be the most wretched person in all the Fertile Plains. Then the tears came. They flowed freely as she walked down the stairs and exited at the bottom of the apartment. She used the blanket to wipe them, but for some reason that only made it worse. She was abusing one of the kindest individuals she had ever met, not to mention someone who had already been through enough to break the strongest men. But David was not a strong man; he was exceptional—and Mercy would ruin him. What would happen when he found out about her treachery? What would he do? What would he become? He trusted her wholeheartedly. He loved her wholeheartedly, as innocently and ignorantly as a lamb, and she used that against him. Once again she asked herself, *What am I becoming?*

When she exited the stairwell at the base of the apartment—since the steam lift was not functioning in the power outage—she stumbled forward in the pitch black. Her skin prickled as she walked toward a dark alley. She'd been scared to death when she walked toward the apartment with David only half an hour earlier, acting the ditz, yet all the while keeping track of the three vagrants shadowing them. Now she couldn't care less, alone with her tears and her guilt, no comfort to cling to but the blanket she'd swindled from a friend, the only blanket he'd had to keep him company on the dismal couch he used as a bed. It was Swollock Season. What need had she of a blanket in the hot, muggy weather?

And his mother? Poor thing had lost the use of her body, lost the love of her life, only to sit by helplessly as her son struggled through life as an invalid. Mercy wondered when she had gotten into the business of taking advantage of the poor, innocent, disabled, and helpless. It was almost enough to make her run away from her own vile employment … almost. The consequences of her failure were far, far worse. She had more to think about than her own discomfort. She had much more to lose than the respect of one young man.

Mercy turned down a dark street. She couldn't see more than three feet in front of her. Keeping one hand against the wall in case she tripped, she picked her way around street refuse. It smelled like urine and echoed with the scratchings of critters. She hadn't really paid attention to where she was going as she meandered down alley after alley, turn after turn. In truth she didn't care.

"You're awfully pretty to be wandering through some dirty streets with naught but a sundress and a tattered blanket for protection."

Mercy froze. She didn't scream. She knew better than that, but her skin crawled when she heard the voice. It was the sound of a killer—a man accustomed to death … a man who knew his trade well.

"Well, I thought dark alleys were where you went when you wanted to find an assassin."

She couldn't see anything, but she turned and faced the spot where she heard the voice all the same. He was a shadow within a shadow, but she knew he could see her, so she waited. Slowly the shadow moved, extricating itself from the corner where it stood, walking forward until it was only a few feet from Mercy.

"I trust you had an eventful night?" Francisco asked, mechanical eye swiveling to the right and peering through the darkness as easily as a voxil.

"If by *eventful* you mean I lied, seduced, and cajoled a poor, lovesick boy into spilling secrets, then yes. It was extremely eventful."

Francisco snorted as he raised a hand and pointed it down the alley. A bolt of electricity shot out, illuminating the alley for a brief second—and the two vagrants who had been trailing Mercy. One of them yelped and then there was the sound of scuffling as several pairs of feet retreated out of the alley.

"Is it hurting your feelings? Does it make you sad that the poor boy is in love with you and you don't even care?" Francisco asked in a mocking tone.

"Don't, Francisco, just don't." Mercy pulled the blanket tighter around her neck and glared at the assassin.

He sniffed. "Touchy, aren't we. If I didn't know better, I'd think the boy's lovesick heart was warming your own? But then again you're a hardened aide, here to sabotage a campaign from the inside out, the most brilliant political strategist of our time. Or do I have the wrong girl?"

Mercy clenched her jaw and looked at the ground. She wanted to scratch his eyes out. "I'm not as hardened to the underworld as you," she said. "I still respect character, purity, and goodness. David is every one of those and more. He hasn't warmed my heart; he's pricked my conscience. He's not the enemy I expected to fight—just more collateral damage."

Francisco said nothing to this, not even offering a grunt.

"Anyway, take me to him," Mercy said after she wiped the last of the tears away with the blanket. "We have much to discuss."

Francisco took her arm and guided her down the alley until they turned into an even darker lane that ended in a brick wall behind a construction facility. Francisco pulled a lever and the wall folded away.

"He's in the Third?" Mercy asked.

Francisco grunted as he steered her into the opening and down a set of stairs. The air tasted of chalk. They walked past a few hundred feet of scaffolding, electric trolleys, and steel beams. Rocks chattered as their feet kicked them across a metal floor. Francisco tugged Mercy to a halt and lifted a tarp, revealing a wooden door so new it hadn't even been sealed yet.

He opened it, and she stepped through the threshold. The room she stepped into was similar to their last meeting place. They always were: one central light above one central table, an assortment of seats, a substantial amount of dust, and a man waiting in the shadows. This time, however, the man was not sitting relaxed with his feet up, as he usually did. He paced back and forth, each turn twirling his knee-length coat. He repeatedly clasped and unclasped his hands.

Mercy sat on a stool at the edge of the light's halo, crossing her legs and pulling the blanket around her shoulders. While she had never actually seen his face, she could tell the man was furious. In previous meetings he had always been casual, yet stern. But now he looked like a caged animal waiting to pounce on the first unfortunate thing to cross its path.

Finally he stopped, his back to Mercy. "That boy is becoming an annoyance. This is the third time he interfered with my plans, and each time he displays some unusual brilliance that thwarts hours of preparation by the smartest minds in two countries with a simple wave of his hand. How?" He turned and slammed his fists down on the table, top hat still shadowing his face.

Mercy jumped and wondered, not for the first time, how well she really knew this man.

But then the man let out a deep breath and continued in a more controlled manner, "Why didn't you tell me he was an expert pilot?"

She shook her head. "I didn't know. I had no idea until tonight. He never told me his past. Everything I knew I told you."

"Well, enlighten me, then. How did a boy with absolutely no previous record take command of an airship for the first time and outfly two captains with decades of experience?" The man resumed his pacing, but more controlled now.

Mercy didn't bother pulling out her little booklet from its hidden pocket, even though it contained all her notes. She doubted she would be able to forget recent events, even if she wanted to. "His father had him flying airships since he was eight cycles old, and he taught him everything he knew until he was fourteen. His father was a captain or admiral or something in the armada."

"Which is it—a captain or an admiral? There are so many blasted Captain Ikes, but only a few admirals."

"I'm not sure. He didn't say. … Captain, I think."

"Pity. What else?"

"Well, supposedly he was one of the best captains of his time, and he learned everything from his father."

"Whose father? The grandfather?"

"Yes, David learned from his father, who learned from the grandfather."

"What was the grandfather's name?"

"He didn't say."

"Well, what did he say?"

"Piloting has been in the family for three generations. Even though David hasn't flown since the airship accident when he lost his father, it's still second nature to him."

"His father died in an airship accident? When?"

"Four cycles ago."

"Four cycles ago?" The man stopped pacing and peered out of the shadows at Mercy.

"Yes," she said.

"You're telling me that four cycles ago a man named Captain Ike died in an airship accident?"

She nodded. "Yes, and the grandfather died soon after. David and his mother—"

"Mercy," the man interrupted, holding his fingers to his temples. "This is very important. Captain Ike, David's father, died four cycles ago, and then his father, David's grandfather, died three weeks later?"

Mercy looked at the man. He had never called her by name before. "I don't know if it was three weeks later, but, yes, that's what he said."

She paused, waiting to see how the man reacted to this. He straightened and paced a few more times, rubbing a shadowed jaw. Mercy could hear a few days' growth of facial hair prickle against a calloused hand.

After a few moments she continued, "The crash that killed his father maimed David and his mother."

The man stopped and turned toward Mercy again. "Mother? He has a mother?"

"Yes." The topic made Mercy's nauseous feelings return. "I met her tonight. She's completely paralyzed. It looks like David feeds her with a tube and has a nurse take care of all her other needs. How he managed to survive on his own as a fourteen-cycle-old cripple and care for his paralyzed mother ..." Mercy shook her head as her eyes misted over.

"What did she look like?"

"I couldn't look at her. Every time I did, I felt guilty enough to vomit."

Mercy heard Francisco grunt a little laugh at that.

But the man just said, "Think, Mercy." He gripped the edge of the table, catching her off guard. "What color was her hair?"

He seemed so intense. Mercy could see a prominent nose and frantic eyes through the shadows.

"It was very gray, but there were still traces of brown."

The man nodded and retreated back to his shadows, finally sitting in the chair at the back of the dusty room.

"That's how Blythe won his loyalty," Mercy went on. "He negotiated to have David's rent reduced and set up a nonprofit on Mrs. Ike's behalf. After seeing David's apartment, I think it's probably the first financial assistance anyone has given him in four cycles. By caring for his mother, Blythe gained an ally in David for life."

The man nodded again.

"There's more, though," Mercy said. "He knows about you."

She expected this to spark another reaction, but the man just kept nodding. Had he heard her?

"He knows you exist, and he has already attributed the Prowler attack to you."

"That figures. It wouldn't take anyone very long after that fool Arold jumped ship."

"He also attributes Samantha's work to you. He thinks she was a pawn."

Now she heard Francisco shuffle his feet behind her.

"Anything else?" the man asked from the shadows.

"He saw you."

"You mean he *thinks* he saw me?"

"No, you were at the grand speech, weren't you—in the gallery? I know because your message ordering me to switch districts arrived only moments after the speech. David looked in the gallery and saw a tall man wearing a long coat and a top hat, standing in the shadows. He's convinced it was you. Don't ask me how, but he's convinced."

"Hmm. Clever lad. I knew I shouldn't have looked at him, but I wanted to see who it was that had foiled my ten-cycle plan. That's when I saw him looking around while everyone else applauded, then he scribbled something down on a notepad." The man let out a long, slow breath. "So you're telling me there is no chance that we could bribe David away from Blythe."

"No, sir."

"Could you seduce him away?"

Mercy thought about that for a moment before finally shaking her head. "Most of the reason he likes me is because he thinks I'm sincere. As soon as I ask him to betray his conscience, my spell over him will break."

A pause, then the man asked, "What if we help his mother?"

"He would appreciate it, but once we start asking him to betray Blythe as payment, he'll see through the ruse.

David will never willingly betray Blythe, no matter what we do for him."

"Yes ... yes, he is his father's son."

"Sir, you knew his father?"

"I knew *of* him. He was a legend in his day. Patrolled the Maw for a tour and singlehandedly removed the Outlander overlord. They say he was as brilliant as his old man, though he never got the chance to prove it. You should feel proud, Mercy. The last living heir of the Ike legend is in love with you. I'm sure of it now. Only an Ike could fly like—"

"What?" Mercy said, gaping at the man.

"David Ike III, the son of David Ike II, the son of Admiral David Ike, hero of the Protectorate War, finds you to be quite the dish. You do know who Admiral David—"

"Yes, I know who the legend is. You're telling me that he was David's grandfather?"

The man nodded. "His father was as loyal as they came, as was his grandfather, the legend himself. Did you know that the Alönian houses offered him an estate in the farmlands as a reward for his services when the old goat finally retired? He turned it down. Lived in moderation to his dying breath, as did the son. I heard about the accident that killed David's father, but the family didn't live in the public eye, so it passed through the news without much notice. While they lived, the Ikes avoided all news agents, keeping to themselves. After the incident it seems David and his mother disappeared from society altogether. Few enough people knew about them anyway." He rubbed his jaw again.

"Sir, David is not our enemy. He's only being used by Blythe."

"Perhaps that would have been true before his father died. But now? David is more dangerous than I ever could have imagined. His name has more esteem than Blythe's could ever have. Whether he is being used or not does not diminish his potency. The question is: Why hasn't Blythe revealed that heritage yet? What is he saving it for?"

Mercy snorted. "He doesn't know!" It was more of a comment to herself, but she spoke it aloud.

"What? Why would David keep his name a secret? A heritage like that would have helped him out of the sludge. How else do you think he got where he is?"

Mercy shook her head. "From my observation Blythe thinks of David as any other David Ike named after the legend. Besides, you don't know him, sir. You don't know his work ethic. I have no doubt that he worked for every bit of his aideship. I don't know why he's keeping his heritage quiet, but if he was in the habit of using it to get places, don't you think he would have told me? How better to impress a girl? I asked him directly about his family, and he still concealed it."

The man shook his head. "An Ike through and through. If that's true, then we dare not reveal it ourselves. Who knows what kind of publicity Blythe would get if he announced that the grandson of the famous Admiral Ike worked for him?" The man resumed his pacing in the shadows. "Time is limited, Mercy. If we are to pull this off, we can't afford any loose ends. That is exactly what David is: a very famous, intelligent, capable loose end."

Mercy pursed her lips, then said, "But he's not the enemy."

"You just told me that he was loyal to Blythe and that there was no way to bribe or seduce him away. Not to mention he believes in Blythe's cause *wholeheartedly*. What else would you describe him as if not our enemy?"

Mercy shifted on her stool and buried her nose in the blanket—David's blanket. There had to be another way, one in which David didn't get destroyed in the crossfire. But how? How could anyone turn a sincere young man? Then Mercy had a thought and said, "He would never willingly betray the man he knows, but if he were to suddenly believe that Blythe was a villain, perhaps he would. David operates off conscience. If serving Blythe suddenly bothers his conscience, he would switch sides."

"Mmm … perhaps. But why do we have to have the boy on our side? True, he would be a grand ally, but destroying Blythe is the victory we need, and right now we are losing. We need to take what we can get."

"Because every time we try to destroy Blythe, David foils us. You said so yourself. I've watched David make Blythe, and he is the only one who can bring him down."

"Possibly, but even if that is true, we've already dragged Blythe's name through the dirt and David remained loyal."

"Not *we*—you. You have yet to allow me to soil the good Blythe's reputation. If I do it, David will turn. I promise. And once he turns, he will tear Blythe's campaign to the ground."

"We are running out of time on this one, Mercy. We have half a season before the census. If you fail, we won't have any other chances."

"If I fail, there is always Plan B."

The man in the shadows steepled his fingers at that. "Francisco, are you prepared to step in if politics fail us?"

Francisco broke his silent vigil and grunted.

The man in the shadows looked back at Mercy. "What did you have in mind?"

Mercy folded her arms beneath the blanket and started speaking. The man in the shadows rose and at first paced his usual route, but as she continued, he slowed and then stopped, facing her with his hands on his hips.

Once she'd finished, he nodded. "You have a devious mind, Ms. Lorraine."

Chapter Fourteen

BORN HERO

"Are you nervous?"

David tried to relax as he tightened his gloves. He wasn't about to turn around, not in his present state. Nervous was an understatement; he was terrified.

"I'm fine," he said before clearing his dry throat.

He fumbled with the strap on his helmet, as the snaps were elusive to his gloved fingers. He really should have put his gloves on last. He felt a steady hand on his shoulder squeezing through his flight suit. David clenched his shaking hands at his sides and put his head back as he let out an unsteady breath. The Taumore Season air might have been crisp, but all he felt was sweat pouring down his brow. It was a sunny, brisk day, the first of the Golden Days. He looked over the top of his skiff at the fifty identical ones beside him.

"Father, I ... I'm scared. I can't stop shaking. How am I supposed to fly if I can't even hold my hands steady?

How did you and Grandfather do it?"

David envied the other boys' laughter as they squeezed into flight suits, strapped on helmets, and checked over their skiffs. They seemed excited while he felt terrified. Every other cadet participating in the race was at least three cycles older than David—older, bigger, and smarter—and every one of them had an entourage of well-wishers. As he watched them, one of the older cadets, David Harris Ike, nudged some of his friends, Jerome and Conroy, and pointed at David with a sneer. David Harris was the academy favorite. Before David had arrived, he'd convinced a good many people that he was the grandson of the famed Admiral Ike. He was quite humiliated when the true heir of the Ike legend enrolled in the academy this season.

David—younger, smaller, and … less intelligent—only had his father with him at the starting line, no friends. His mother couldn't watch such "reckless endeavors," as she called them. Even now she hid behind the stands, praying for the race's cancellation. His grandfather was too old to meander among the skiffs at the start line, so he waited in the stands for David's father to return. Of course it took longer than half a season to make friends, and he was the only freshman cadet daring enough to participate in the annual academy skiff race. Most boys waited until their sophomore or junior cycle before entering. It was no wonder why the other racers had friends and well-wishers.

David's father turned him around and stared through his visor into his eyes, squeezing both of his shoulders as he did. His father's brow furrowed as he reached for words.

"Don't think about the finish line. Don't think about the victory. Stop thinking about the end of the race and start thinking about right now." He pulled David's helmet straps down and snapped them beneath his jaw, tightening it to his head. "Think about how much you love to fly. Think about the wind in your hair and the tingle in your stomach. Think about your skiff as it glides through the air. If you think about those things, you have nothing to be nervous about, but if you divide your mind between the technicality of flying a skiff and the glory of victory, you'll only fly half as well as you could."

David nodded. "I want to win so bad, though. You won your first academy skiff race, and so did Grandfather. I'd be ashamed to break the tradition."

"We were two cycles your senior. Never you mind about that. No matter what happens today, your mother and I and your grandfather couldn't be any prouder. Understand?"

"Yes, Father," David said, lowering his head.

"Good. Now let's do one final check. Hop in."

David climbed over one of the low-profile pontoons and slipped into the confining cockpit in the middle of the racing skiff. It was the school's skiff, all blue with a single engine and a polymer frame—older but light, agile, and quick as lightning. David shifted in the cockpit. The designers had sacrificed many of the common comforts, such as pad seating, in favor of a utilitarian design. The burner was only a few inches behind his head, and at full burn it rattled his seat something fierce. At least he didn't have to worry about getting cold. The skiff looked a bit like a dinghy, except for an air intake where the nose would be. The sleek pontoons followed the curvature of the slim cockpit, pointing out the back on either side of the single turbine.

David's father began calling out the preflight check: "Tail. ... Flaps. ... Burner. ... Thrust nozzle. ... Good. Good." They continued like that, checking and rechecking the machinery until the academy administrator called for noncompeting personnel to clear the starting line. David's father reached over the right pontoon and gripped David's shoulder through the small window in the side of the cockpit.

"Remember the family motto: *Look where no one else is.* Do that and nothing will ever surprise you."

David nodded, faced the signal steam, and focused his mind.

"Jeshua be with you, my son," his father said with one final squeeze, and then he was gone.

The rest of the boys cleared the start line, patting their fellows on the back with whoops and hollers. The crowd cheered so loud from the stands, David could hardly hear the hum of his skiff's burner.

Each cycle the academy selected a random location within the Houselands and constructed a skiff-racing course. Each cycle presented a different type of course with different types of challenges. Last cycle's was on the Alönian coastlands, where cadets battled against strong ocean winds; the cycle before that, the marshlands of

House Franklyn. This cycle the academy outdid themselves. It was as if they knew David was competing, and they wanted to test his mettle at the House Hancock canyons. All the school skiffs were affixed with altitude governors, forcing them to stay within the confines of the canyons.

The race constructors marked out the raceway with green and red smokers—green meaning the correct direction and red meaning … death. It was a good thing too, because the redstone cliffs and caves were a maze of different paths. No one knew the exact path the constructors plotted through the canyons because the academy commandant concealed the raceway and allowed no practice runs. This forced the cadets to balance speed with caution. While no one had died during the academy skiff race in a while, it had been known to happen in the past.

David wasn't concerned about the canyon path, or the caves. He knew how to handle a skiff. What bothered him were the geysers. He'd read about the Hancock canyons and how many of them boasted powerful geysers that rocketed spurts of steam hundreds of fathoms into the air. If a blast hit his skiff, it could superheat his pontoons and send him soaring out of the canyon.

"Cadets, take your marks," a race official announced over a loudspeaker.

David and fifty other pilots heated their pontoons and in moments rose ten feet into the air at the starting line. A few overeager lads heated their pontoons too much and the official had to wait for the cadets to level off their airships before he could start the race. David eyed the signal steam. It flashed red for now, but as soon as it flashed green, the race would begin. From his ten-foot vantage point, he could see the entire plateau that held the start line and the stands of onlookers, as well as the edge of the canyon and the drop-off beyond. All vegetation ceased at the top of the canyon walls, and only a few vines dangled beyond. From there smooth, stratified walls disappeared into endless canyon depths. The Alönian rains had washed out these canyons thousands of cycles before. Any vegetation unfortunate enough to take root along the canyon floor during Taumore Season either drowned or washed away beneath fathoms of raging water during Úoi, Swollock, Prumuveour, and Derecho Seasons. This left smooth, redstone walls that flowed and rolled like ocean waves throughout the canyon.

"Steady, lads, steady," the race administrator called from his loudspeaker. "We will only begin this race once. All false starts will be immediately disqualified."

David blocked out everything around him, save for the flickering red puff of steam.

"On your marks. Get set."

The announcer paused for a dramatic moment, a moment that felt like an eternity. A moment in which a twigjumper decided to land on David's windscreen and crawl around in random circles. David pursed his lips and looked around the annoying bug at the steam signal beyond. Four cadets panicked in that moment and powered their skiffs past the start line. Some of the observers moaned or gasped. A few snickered.

"Well, at least I can't take last place anymore," David mumbled to himself.

He ignored the twitchy cadets and kept his eye on the flashing red steam. It flashed green at the exact moment the announcer shouted, "GO!"

David slammed the throttle down as fast as he could, along with forty-six other skiff pilots. He rocketed forward a few feet in front of the others thanks to quick reflexes. The unwelcome twigjumper blew to the edge of his windscreen, where it clung for a few heartbeats before the wind tugged it free.

David knew that there were two schools of thought about beginning a skiff race. Elevation presented a unique advantage. Gliding above competitors could make the difference between winning and losing when the race got tight. At the same time, pushing a skiff to higher elevation would cost speed. Most competitors balanced between the two, racing forward at best possible speed while nudging the burner and gaining precious fathoms along the way. David chose the more reckless school of thought, directing all power to his single engine. He inched farther and farther ahead of his competitors as he approached the edge of the plateau. To all observers it appeared a foolish move. This racecourse demanded elevation for victory, as the bottom of the canyon was narrow. Let them think him a fool. He knew what he was doing.

He angled his skiff toward the giant steam signal, glowing green into its vaporous heights. David checked above him, where a few other skiffs glided a fathom or so behind. It would be tight. He pushed so hard on the thrust control that he thought it might break off, but he needed every last possible fathom if this was going to work. Then he raced over the steam signal only a few inches above the disk-shaped unit that dispersed the steam and projected the light. The light winked out as his skiff covered the projector, but then he felt his craft buck as the steam's updraft pushed his little airship up, giving him another twenty feet of elevation and matching him with the other racers.

One skiff bumped into his rear as he ascended in front of it. The crowd roared, some cheering, some booing. Strictly speaking, this was a no-contact race, but accidents did happen, and technically he bumped into David. For a moment he thought he could hear his father bellowing "That's my boy!" but then his skiff shot off the edge of the plateau and he felt gravity tugging him into the canyon as the governor engaged and the burner shut off.

David's skiff plunged forward, leading the pack as they dove into the chasm. The smoothed redstone walls rose hundreds of fathoms into the air, and David had a slight bout of vertigo as his ship tilted forward and he looked the entire distance to the rugged canyon floor. Lines representing thousands of cycles of rock strata shifted like pink waves of water as he soared past them. David laughed as the wind howled over his skiff and the cockpit hummed: a sure sign of terminal velocity.

As he neared the canyon floor, the governor disengaged, and David turned his burner to full power, heating his pontoons as much as the altitude governor would allow. He leveled off about twenty fathoms from the canyon floor—not a lot of room to work with. He could almost feel the other skiffs rumbling behind him. He wanted to look back, but the canyon narrowed ahead and he needed all his concentration forward. David leaned left and right inside his cockpit, anticipating each turn as he guided the skiff between the close walls. Two skiffs could barely fit abreast. One skiff edged up beside David, but he nudged it back at the next turn. All was going well … until the canyon opened up. A skiff bumped David on his starboard pontoon. As David scowled over at the other pilot, he saw a distinct red stripe on the skiff and realized it was David Harris. The older cadet backed his skiff off, cocking his helmeted head as if to taunt David. At that very moment another skiff crashed into his port pontoon, knocking him toward the canyon wall. David had two choices: slam into the smooth rock wall or cut thrust. He cut thrust, and David Harris and two other skiffs, clearly Jerome and Conroy, shot over him.

A dozen other skiffs zoomed past as David struggled to get his airship under control. Once he leveled off and re-engaged his thruster, he was somewhere in the middle of the pack. He could still see David Harris' skiff where it flew in a V formation with Jerome and Conroy, barring anyone else from passing him. David cursed himself for falling for the oldest trick in the book. If he'd kept his mind on the race, he probably would have seen through that. But at the same time, David remembered his father's advice: *Don't think about the victory; think about now.*

David watched the racers in front of him turn to the left and drop into a cave at the base of the canyon wall marked with green smoke. He held his breath as he banked his skiff and charged into darkness. It took a moment for his eyes to adjust as the cave ceiling blocked out the sun. But once the darkness swallowed the sun, glowcrystals illuminated the cave walls, casting a dim light. He rounded corner after corner, each one reflecting a faint green light. The cave opened into a giant chamber, the entire floor covered with spiky green glowcrystals. If he'd had the time, David might have admired the scenery. As it was, he heard a few skiffs impact against the cave wall at the opposite end of the chamber and knew he was in for some sort of challenge. He saw why as soon as he turned out of the underground cavity and into a tunnel. Several skiffs collided with each other as the chasm narrowed into a skiff-wide passage. David guided his skiff over the others, following the glowcrystals along the narrow passage until he saw a sparkle of sunlight in the distance. He aimed his skiff at that point and increased to full thrust. The sparkle grew, and after a few moments his skiff shot through the cave opening, kicking up a dust trail at the low altitude.

The cave spat David's skiff out into a giant redstone basin, with grandfathom-high canyon walls encircling the depression. David looked across the basin and saw a dozen skiffs racing toward the opposite side where the bowl split into three caverns, the center one marked with green smoke. Even as David watched, leaning forward and focusing on the other skiffs like a voxil stalking prey, a geyser exploded a hundred fathoms ahead of him, giving him a start as rocketing steam and sulfur erupted into the sky, carrying an unfortunate skiff with it. The skiff shot into the air and spun as the pilot cut thrust and guided it back to the ground. The other skiffs veered around the geyser. David almost followed suit, but then he had a thought. He angled his skiff right over the place where the geyser exploded and prayed he was right. David figured that a geyser only erupted when the pressure beneath the ground built to a crescendo. That meant he had at least a few minutes, probably, before the next explosion. Not steering around the geyser would let him pass at least two more cadets, so it was worth the risk. As David passed over the place, he smelled the distinct scent of rotten eggs. He held his breath and chanced a glance down at the bubbling crater. The center was already bulging in anticipation of another eruption. He breathed a sigh of relief once he passed over the crater's other side, but stiffened when the geyser burst only seconds after his crossing. It was probably best not to tell his mother about that part of the race, if he ever wanted to race again.

Only eight skiffs remained in front of him as David soared to the other side of the basin and angled into the cavern on the opposite side. As he entered it, he saw the leading skiffs: David Harris and his two cohorts still flying the V formation.

The cavern wound through the redstone canyon, a little stream trickling along the base. David cut every corner, banked every turn, and squeezed out every bit of thrust he could during the straightaways. He passed another two skiffs in the cavern, outmaneuvering them in the tight confines, leaving only half a dozen in front of him. As they exited the cavern, green smoke directed the racers toward a winding canyon. David couldn't be sure, but he suspected this was probably the final portion of the race, though it seemed a bit mundane. Even as he had the thought, a geyser exploded a few feet to his right. The wave from the blast rocked his airship, but nothing more. If it had been bigger … Well, it hadn't been, so what did it matter?

He realized the uneven ground along the canyon floor was actually thousands of geysers, each one bubbling and bulging. As he sped through the canyon, geyser after geyser burst along the stone floor, knocking three additional skiffs behind him. It was down to him and the triad of frontrunners.

He tried to pass them by cutting the canyon corner, but each time one of the trailing skiffs would cut off his advance. If he was going to pass any of them, he'd have to pass all of them at the same time. Flying over was impossible, and under would be suicide. As they rounded the next corner and raced down a straightaway, he drafted behind David Harris until his skiff was only a few fathoms behind. If he could squeeze into their formation, he might be able to pinch off the two rear skiffs in the next turn. Then it would only be him and David Harris. Unfortunately, just before they reached the next turn, one of David Harris's partners bumped David and knocked him back again. He was in the middle of planning his next attack when he felt his skiff buck so hard that he thought he'd collided with the canyon wall. His head rattled inside his helmet as he slammed into the hard seat backing. He gasped and tried to regain his bearings, only to choke and cough as his lungs filled with an acrid taste of rotten eggs. He looked out his windscreen, but it had fogged over. He cut thrust on instinct—an instinct that told him flying at full throttle in an unknown direction was a bad idea. All at once, he felt himself give way to weightlessness. Then he figured it out.

He rubbed his windscreen and cleared just enough of the fog to realize he was half a grandfathom in the air. A geyser must have caught him from beneath and superheated his pontoons. His governor automatically shut off his burner, sending him into a free fall, the canyon floor approaching far sooner than he preferred. The same geyser blast caught one of David Harris's companions—David couldn't tell which—and his skiff floundered a few fathoms beside him in uncontrolled circles. The pilot's governor would turn on before he smashed against the canyon floor, but if he didn't get his glide under control, he might impact against one of the redstone walls. David looked around, trying to see over his pontoons at what lay beneath him. That was when he saw it: the end of the raceway. From this vantage point he could see the stands, the finish line, everything. Before the geyser had caught him, he was about to round a knob of the canyon, the last U-turn of the race. That was it, then; he'd lost. The Ike legend would end with him.

He sighed as he angled his skiff forward and toward the raceway. If he was lucky, he might still come in fourth, and that was worth something. But David paused, and without thinking he angled his skiff over the canyon knob rather than back down toward the raceway. If he could glide over the knob, he might have a chance at cutting in front of David Harris. He could still win this race.

David clenched his jaw and slammed down the throttle. It was going to be tight. If he could get enough forward thrust, his skiff would glide over the canyon wall, cut off the final turn of the race, and maybe, just maybe, pass in front of David Harris. If he couldn't get enough forward thrust, well, David just hoped his mother was praying at that moment.

His skiff seemed to be moving forward at a painfully slow rate while falling at an excessive speed. As David glided over the canyon knob's front edge, he checked his altimeter: *A hundred fathoms*. This would be very tight. As he passed over the knob's midpoint, it read fifty fathoms. David squeezed the wheel and yelled as his skiff dove toward the raceway. As David crossed the canyon wall's back edge, his altimeter read zero fathoms. He felt the bottom of his skiff scrape rock and vegetation before he plunged back into the canyon. He had made it—sort of. Hopefully the academy wouldn't charge for the dent in the skiff's hull.

David roared down the canyon wall at the same time that David Harris came around the last turn in the race. They were on a collision course. David opted for speed over elevation, pouring every bit of power into the thruster. After he got in front of David Harris, then he could work out the altitude discrepancy. David angled his skiff a little so that he could turn back onto the raceway before smashing into the canyon wall opposite him. David Harris appeared to be pushing his skiff for every bit of speed it had, but he couldn't compete with good old-fashioned gravity. David left a trail of dust down the side of the canyon as he shot in front of David Harris and turned down the raceway toward the hill that led to the finish line. David Harris and his remaining cohort drafted him, but there simply wasn't enough race left for tricks. David sped up the hill, then roared through the stands of onlookers and across the finish line.

The people thundered with delight. No doubt they'd witnessed his stunt of jumping the canyon wall. David coasted to a stop and released his grip on the controls. His hands ached. He leaned back in his ill-padded seat and took a long, slow breath of the acrid, still air. What had just happened? The people continued to cheer, loud enough to echo inside his helmet. He had a funny feeling—part shock, part disbelief, and part delight. He'd done it! He'd actually won! He could join with the Ike legend now, not just ride in its wake. He didn't know what to do with himself. Should he shout in delight and run around his skiff, or just smile and take a bow? He'd never been in a situation like this before. In the end he just started laughing. He popped his canopy, climbed out of the skiff, and looked around at the cheering people and their smiling faces. It took him a moment to find the place where he had left his father and grandfather, as there were at least twenty thousand people in attendance. But he saw them now, their arms raised and their faces beaming. His mother was with them. She looked … more relieved than ecstatic. David laughed and waved back.

As he watched, David Harris climbed out of his skiff, along with Jerome. Conroy followed a moment later after he'd coasted to a stop; his skiff listed and rattled something awful. They didn't say anything as they walked by him toward the stage where the judges sat. It was then that David saw the smoke rising from the back of his own skiff. Evidently his little *scrape* had done more than just dent the hull. No matter—it was worth it. As he checked over the rest of his skiff, more contestants glided in and parked their skiffs behind his. A few congratulated him when they learned he'd won. A group of them hoisted David up on their shoulders. In time all the other cadets flew in and each pilot collected around the judge's stage. The students holding David on their shoulders tossed him up onto the stage. He was red from his nose to his toes. For once, he was thankful for the flight suit. The academy's commander, Commandant Cripton, motioned the crowd to silence, and David shuffled over to where David Harris and his cronies stood. Why Conroy was there, David didn't know, as he had taken fourth place and wouldn't receive any special accommodation. They were just then talking with the judges, but before David was close enough to hear what they were saying, Commandant Cripton started speaking:

"Congratulations, cadets. You have finished a

challenging course, and finishing this race is an accomplishment in and of itself." He allowed the crowd to cheer again before he continued, "Skiff racing is the pride of Alönian culture. We are unique in the Fertile Plains for requiring all military airship officers to first pilot a skiff before receiving any kind of command in a man-of-war. The skiff races are a way for our cadets to prove themselves, and participating in a skiff race is required to graduate from our military academy. The majority of the racers here today are seniors, and this race signifies for many of them the first step toward graduating this cycle."

The crowd cheered again as the commandant paused. David heard one or two enthusiastic families yell embarrassing things to their blushing sons.

"Now," the commandant said as he turned toward David and the other frontrunners. "On top of race completion certificates, we also hand out special accommodation for those pilots who place first, second, and third."

The crowd interrupted with another outburst of delight.

"Yes, yes," Cripton said, "I understand we are all very excited. However, before I issue those awards, I'm afraid that I must deal with some rather unpleasant business. Cadet David Ike. Not David Harris Ike—just David Ike."

David stepped up to the commandant and stood at attention. He did his best not to smile, as he supposed he was about to be the object of some practical joke. Another fun thing about being the youngest cadet in history and the son of a legendary family was the endless hazing he had to deal with, but it was all in good fun.

"Mr. Ike," Cripton went on, "while you did arrive in first place, you only did so by cheating. You cut off the final turn of the race by riding a geyser over the canyon wall. You may, if you choose, receive an academy skiff race completion certificate, but only if you take your skiff back and complete the final turn of the course." The commandant looked past David and continued with hardly a nod. "For that reason Cadet David Harris Ike will receive first place, Cadet Jerome Whitely will receive second place, and Cadet Conroy Franklyn will receive third place. My congratulations to each of you; it is a fine achievement."

David stood for a moment in the center of the stage waiting for the commandant to turn around and wink, or laugh, or slap him on the back, or something, but he didn't. It was when the commandant started handing out the awards and David found himself in the way of the pictures that he realized it was not a practical joke. Cripton had been serious.

The audience didn't seem to care one way of the other. They cheered just as hard for David Harris as they had for him, except now the sound gave David the chills. Each whistle made him jump, and all the pairs of eyes gazing at the stage made him want to run and hide. He did his best to slip off the stage, escaping with only one snort from David Harris. He picked his way through the other cadets, unable to look any of them in the eyes. Luckily he still had his helmet on, so he didn't have to. As he reached the back of the crowd, he went to the only place he could think of: his skiff. Once there, he leaned against the pontoon and took deep, soothing breaths.

David might have been the youngest cadet in history, but fourteen was still far too old for tears. He grunted and cleared his throat and started looking over his skiff by habit. There was a slimy residue smeared across the bottom of his pontoons, the same sludge smelling of rotten eggs. When he bent to look at the burner, wondering if that was where the smoke wafted from, he felt a firm grip on his shoulder. He knew the grip in an instant. It was his father.

Before the race he couldn't look at the man because he was afraid to show his nervousness. Now he didn't want to turn around for fear he might show his distress.

"David? Are you okay?"

"Um … yeah, I'm fine. That last geyser shook me up, but I'm okay."

"That's not what I meant."

David closed his eyes and sighed. He turned and looked up at his father. He saw the same compassionate man he'd seen at the beginning of the race. Everything was the same, save the fire behind his eyes, the fire of a father concealing righteous anger.

David took off his helmet and let his head slump against his father's chest.

"Why did he do that, Father? He called me a cheater in front of everyone. I … I was just making the best out of the geyser. I didn't mean … I didn't know that it was cheating. I … I'm sorry. I'm sorry I embarrassed you and

Grandfather."

"You did nothing of the sort! You didn't cheat, and you didn't lose. That was some of the best skiff flying I've ever seen. This ... This has to do with something else."

David rubbed his eyes and frowned at his father. "Something else? But I lost."

"You used the circumstances you were given and made the best of them. You used the terrain to your advantage, as any good airman should. Look, David, there are two things that come with a famous heritage. Sure, you get instant recognition, easy popularity, and sometimes the things you work for will come just a little bit quicker. But there are downsides too. People will hate you just as easily as they'll love you. They want to see you fail just as much as they want you to succeed. Your friends will never be anything more than shallow, yet your enemies will always be malicious. Things have happened recently. Your grandfather and I took steps that many in the armada disapprove of. For that reason we are seeing some backlash. I just never imagined they would stoop as low as to attack my son. Do you understand what I'm trying to tell you?"

"I think so," David said as he wiped his face and started peeling off his flight suit. He wore his academy uniform beneath. "A lot of the things that come my way, whether good or bad, will be because of who I am, not what I've done."

His father nodded. "Some, but not all. You found a place in this academy through a blind application. Neither your grandfather nor I had anything to do with it. But, yes, because of what your grandfather and I are doing in the Houselands, your name and heritage will probably start to bring you more problems than opportunities."

"What are you and Grandfather up to?"

David's father smiled. "Something during my last tour, but don't you worry about that. You get through this academy, and then we can talk military politics."

David realized that his mother and grandfather were standing behind them. He dropped his flight suit on his skiff and gave them a half smile. His mother looked miffed—probably something to do with the smoke coming out of the back of his skiff. His grandfather leaned on his cane, a smile beneath his bristling white mustache.

"Well, we might as well get a picture of the three of you in your uniforms while you're all still living," David's mother said with a huff as she lifted the insta-camera that David's father had bought her for her last birthday. "If David pulls any more stunts like that, it will be a miracle if he outlives Grandfather."

David smiled as he walked over with his father to pose beside his grandfather.

As they walked, his father said, "Yes, and after this we will wait here while David takes his skiff down to finish that last turn."

David scowled. "I'd rather kiss the commandant's boots."

His father snorted and smacked him across the back of the head. "Don't be a cur. I didn't tell you the things I did so you could hold a grudge. You will finish the race, and you will collect your skiff race competition certificate."

David nodded sheepishly and posed next to his grandfather.

"Yes," his grandfather said. "Do collect that certificate." But as David's mother lifted the camera and told them all to smile, he added under his breath, "So I can shove it up the commandant's ass."

It was an excellent photograph—three brilliant smiles.

Chapter Fifteen

SNOOPING

This was perhaps the most stupid thing he had ever done, and that was saying a lot. David pondered his current predicament as he leaned against a stone wall in Speaker Walker's courtyard, straining to hear a whispered conversation. If he got caught spying on the speaker, he could kiss any future in politics good-bye. Why did he put himself in these situations?

It had been a few weeks since the Prowler attack, and David had adopted a more aggressive method of gathering information: espionage. In reality he was really just snooping around, but *espionage* sounded so much more important. The airship transportation facility was mere days from completion, as well as Public Pharmaceuticals—and the census still loomed. There was no way the enemy would give up so soon. David arranged with Ella to look after his mother for a few nights while he went on a *business trip*. At least that's what he'd told her.

The Prowler attack had escalated events. David needed answers, and he needed them soon. So he'd come up with a brilliant and also idiotic plan. He made a list of all the individuals who either had ties to the speaker or who David suspected of political foul play. It was a short list of four names, as most of the people he suspected had done nothing more than give him a sour look. The list might have contained all thirteen remaining Pragmatics, but time was short and most of them ran farming, logging, or fishing districts, all of little threat. However, the four names that made the list were all high-profile political officials. Speaker Walker was chief among the suspects, along with two of his closest allies: Representative Donald Evanson of House Thornton's First and Andrew J. Bolten of Stone's Third. They all stood the most to lose if Blythe succeeded in his bid for the speakership. Each of them had built their futures around a Pragmatic speakership. Losing it would mean financial and political devastation. The last person on the list was a wild card: Representative Herald of House Livingston, Mercy's former boss. Before Blythe, Herald had been the frontrunner for the Equalist party. However unlikely it was, Blythe had demolished Herald's bid for power. The chances of him holding a grudge were enough for David to add him to the list.

For the past three days David had dressed as a beggar—something he'd had quite a bit of practice doing over the past few cycles—and spent one night waiting outside each representative's home: Evanson, Bolten, and

Herald, respectively. David didn't know why he did it, as there was slim chance his spying on these men's homes would produce any real information. Perhaps he just wanted to see them in their element, see them in a place where they weren't wearing the political mask. Perhaps he was getting desperate and losing his touch.

Evanson and Bolten had both been a complete waste of sleep. Each man kept a modest yet comfortable home on the outskirts of Capital City while the Assembly remained in session. Both had families, and both spent the entire evening with their family. The only thing it revealed to David was his own longing for a family and the hope that he might have one again someday—not the most productive credentials for espionage.

Representative Herald was the complete opposite. He arrived at his home after dark, shared a few harsh words with his wife, left the house not ten minutes after arriving, and walked to the nearest dance club. David decided against following the representative inside, as he had no interest in the kind of activities that occurred in such establishments and likely couldn't get in looking the way he did. Perhaps he was a poor spy if he couldn't do what was necessary to gather intelligence. On the other hand, a man who drowned his sorrows in dance clubs was probably not a man who could orchestrate and command a complicated, underground organization.

Tonight, however, proved an entirely different matter. David had saved Speaker Walker for last partially because he hoped he'd find a lead from at least one of the other three men before he risked spying on the speaker, as spying on an Alönian speaker was something of a crime. David gaped when the air-taxi dropped him off in front of the speaker's mansion. His beggar garb was perhaps not an appropriate disguise for snooping in the Victorian Quarter of Capital Island.

Every major city in the Houselands had a wealthy residential district, but there was only one Victorian Quarter. It lay along the far eastern coastlands of Capital Island, facing the waterway that divided the Houses of Alönia from the City of Armstad. There the breadth of the Alönian Island sheltered the waves of the water, the most peaceful bit of ocean in the known plains. They had flown over it in the Sunbeam before the Prowler attack not three weeks back. No apartment towers graced the Victorian Quarter, as the houses there were apartment towers in most respects, with every single one standing several stories tall—mansions of gargantuan proportions. Strange and exotic species of shrubs and trees filled the entire quarter, creating a sort of giant park that wound between the residences. Gravel and cobbled paths connected and segmented the estates, lit by gilded lamps. There were no streets here, as it had been nearly half a century since steam cars graced the Victorian cobbles.

David paid the airfare and smiled at the taxi driver in a way he hoped was confident. However, the driver moved the coins around in his hand before looking back at David with a raised eyebrow. David rolled his eyes and handed over one more coin with a groan. Why was it air-taxis always wanted more than their advertised fee? David hoped he'd find some useful information tonight. If he did, Blythe would probably reimburse him for the whole foolish escapade.

After the taxi left, David looked up and down the scenic path, trying to decide if he'd be better off hiding in the bushes, hoping no one spotted him, or loitering as a beggar on the path, hoping nobody cared. One look at the manicured park, and he opted for the bushes. It would be dark soon, and chances were slight that anyone would see him. David dove under a shrub with wide, rubbery leaves and peeked between some spiky plants that made up a low hedge. Within moments insects were burrowing beneath his clothes and crawling along his skin. They were small, determined beasts, nibbling on his back. But he endured, keeping his vigil on the speaker's mansion.

A perimeter fence of stone and twisted iron surrounded the speaker's estate. Behind that David could just make out lush gardens, sprawling trees, and a tall stone house with elegant windows and a copper roof. Speaker Walker arrived at his estate at exactly six o'clock, riding in a Windward VX2—the latest luxury skiff, large as a gunship and known for its posh interior and comfortable ride. His driver dropped him off at the dock on the top of the mansion and then glided over to the skiff-house. David watched as the skiff disappeared behind a tree and wondered what he should do next. From his vantage point he couldn't even see shadows in the windows. It was past dusk now, the last light of the day shooed away by darkness. As the temperature shifted, the soggy ground gave up its moisture and evening mists mixed with the night, covering the Victorian Quarter in a dense, low-hanging fog.

David decided to take a little more risk; after all, he'd come this far. He got up and crossed the park walkway under the cover of the fog. He perspired in the humidity of Swollock Season's last day, causing his cheeks to redden. The winds were shifting, and in a couple of days it would be all thunderstorms for an entire season. David didn't mind the storms; it was the resulting vomit in the public airships he dreaded.

As he ran across the stretch of ground, each footfall crushing a trimmed plant, he shook his ragged shirt out to extricate the bugs. Once across the path, he slipped into the undergrowth that fronted the estate wall. The wall seemed smaller from across the path. However, now that he stood next to it, he realized it was a good three fathoms tall and topped with curled iron spikes. He looked down the length of smooth stone and saw a vine growing up its side a few paces farther. If he climbed the vine, he could peek into the estate. *Why not?*

David ducked down beneath the fog and crawled along the wall until he reached the vine. He paused at a patch of trimmed grass, a good spot to post up without stickers or insects to worry about. Hooking his fingers into the lattice of the vine, he lifted himself off the ground. The vine held his weight, so he climbed. On his third reach he heard the most peculiar sound. It vibrated the air around him like an angry beehive. He looked through the darkness, but he couldn't tell where the sound came from—until a shadowy shape passed over and into the lights of the mansion. It was an airship unlike any he had ever seen. He barely heard it even though it flew right over the top of him. In fact, if it wasn't for the tree beside him and its umbrella of foliage, it might have spotted him clinging on the side of the wall.

From his place on the vine, David could just see over the wall. The airship turned 180 degrees and landed on the patio in front of the mansion, squeezing between a fountain and a stone bench with hardly a foot on either side. Angular and aerodynamic, as well as aggressive and agile, it was shaped like a small catamaran: two long pontoons bridged together by a single-man cockpit. Two engines dangled below the cockpit, but they were unlike any engine David knew of. They looked more like rocket carousels. David gawked at the ship. Everything about it was wrong: pontoons too small, engines too exposed, and a hull that didn't have enough room for both man and machinery.

As David marveled at the ship, the windscreen opened with a hiss and a lithe man slipped out and walked across the patio toward the main entrance. He walked with his hands clasped behind his back, his step light and deliberate. The front door opened before the man reached it, and Speaker Walker stepped out and clasped hands in a curt but familiar fashion. After the two exchanged what were likely the usual formalities, Speaker Walker motioned toward a path leading to the gardens around the side of the house, and the pair disappeared.

David bit his lip when he lost sight of the men around the side of the mansion. He looked around the yard, spotting two guards on the far side patrolling the main gate of the estate. His mind itched to know who the stranger was. He might not be able to overhear the conversation he and the speaker were having, but maybe he could get a closer look at the skiff. It was no ordinary person's skiff. It had a military look about it, a minimalistic design with a deadly purpose. A closer look could reveal volumes.

Clinging to the vine, David waited a few more seconds until the evening fog billowed along the ground on the opposite side of the wall. Then he lifted himself onto the crest, squeezed between the iron frills, and dropped into the fog with a thud. It was a bit farther down than he'd anticipated and his breath rushed out in a hiss. Peeking between some succulent bushes with yellow fruit, he spied the guards. One of them looked toward David's hiding place, but after a moment he returned to the conversation with his fellow. From there David crawled on his hands and knees across a bed of turquoise moonflowers. He held his breath, knowing that the flowers' lusty scent was a powerful sedative. *Who puts moonflowers in their garden?* The guards rambled on in the background as David squeezed under benches and caught different articles of clothing in a whole variety of thorny bushes, all the while keeping below the level of the fog. He had almost reached the patio and the curious airship, crawling around one last manicured hedge, when he came nose to nose with an enormous voxil hound. David held his breath, waiting for the inevitable, but the dog did nothing but twitch its nose in the air and give him a bored look. After a moment David's head throbbed, reminding him to breathe. He let out his air with a rush right into the dog's face. It sneezed twice before it looked at him again. Then its tail started wagging.

David realized that this was not a guard dog—much the opposite. Everything about the dog drooped: droopy eyes, droopy jowls, and droopy ears. David tried to crawl past it, but the beast was almost as big as he was. It crouched on its front legs and nuzzled him back into the bush. David shoved the animal aside, but it shoved him back like some strange game. There was only one thing for it. David lay on his belly and slid through the grass toward the patio as the dog nuzzled his side. But once he reached the steps, the enormous beast stepped on his back, pinning him to the ground as it licked his neck. David grunted beneath the monstrous paw and tried to crawl up the stairs, but the hound must have weighed ninety kilos. Finally the animal sat up and ran toward the gardens on the other side of the patio.

David looked around to make sure no one had spotted him while he frolicked in the grass, but the guards were still engrossed in their chat and everything else about the estate looked quiet. David scrambled up the patio steps, keeping the airship between him and the guards. The only risk was the main door, as it was directly behind him. Hopefully nobody in the house planned on an evening stroll that night. David crept up to the airship, growing more fascinated the closer he got. Chain-guns poked out of the front of the pontoons, confirming David's suspicion about it being a military vessel. But something else about the pontoons puzzled him as he rubbed a hand along their surface. Small, sterling-sized bumps pocked the entire surface of each. David wanted a closer look, but time was not his ally, so he moved on to the airship's fuselage, which bridged between the pontoons. It was tiny, barely big enough for a man. Certainly not big enough for a burner ... and that's when the whole conundrum clicked in his mind. He knew exactly what this ship was.

A few cycles back the Armstad military had experimented with the idea of electronically regulated balloons, eliminating the necessity of a burner. Rather than heat the gas within the balloons, the Armstad scientists floated particulates within the gas and affixed diodes around the balloons. With the flick of a switch the pilot could electronically manipulate the lift of his balloon, eliminating any delay and allowing the ship to fly in near silence. No wonder he hadn't spotted it until it was only a few fathoms above his head. The question being: Why was an experimental Armstad stealth vessel sitting on Speaker Walker's patio? The visitor had to be Armstadi as well.

And that's when David had another terrible idea, the stupidest one in his whole life. He looked down the path where the speaker and the Armstad stranger had disappeared. He fidgeted for a moment as he considered the foolish thing he wanted to do. There really wasn't any choice here. This was no social call, and he needed answers; but as he turned toward the path around the mansion, he almost fell on his head when he stepped on something round and squishy. That same dumb voxil hound had apparently brought its ball out and sat patiently while he inspected the airship. David groaned and stepped around the dog even as it looked at him with large droopy eyes. Then it whimpered. David jumped back behind the airship and peeked through the windscreen at the guards on the far end of the estate. He sighed in relief and rested his head against the ship. The men hadn't stirred. He whirled around and glared at the dog, but when it cowered beneath his stare, he lost his resolve.

He picked up the ball, to the apparent delight of the dog, and tossed it in the opposite direction of the speaker and the Armstad visitor. The dog ran after the ball and disappeared into the hedge maze. As the guards looked at the bounding dog, David slipped out from behind the airship and slunk around the side of the mansion. He avoided any landscape lighting, clinging to the shadows as much as they clung to him. He had been halfway around the mansion when he heard voices up ahead. He dropped to his hands and knees and crawled through a flower bed along the side of the house, fog wisping around each of his movements. When he'd reached the edge of the flower bed, he stood up and leaned against the stone wall of the house, straining to hear the conversation between Speaker Walker and the stranger.

And that's where he found himself now, pondering how he'd gotten here and wondering if he'd ever done anything so stupid in his entire life. He had to ask himself why he did these things. Why did he have to go above and beyond the job description every single time? When would he learn to just do what he was asked and nothing more?

He slowed his breathing and tried to bring his mind back to the present. It was a little late to be scolding himself. That could wait until after he'd safely left the estate. He was only twenty feet away now, and he could just make out what they were saying. The stranger spoke with clipped syllables, a telltale sign of an Armstadi accent.

"... and the census?" the stranger said. "What result?"

"We have some people working behind the scenes," came the speaker's voice, "but I am becoming increasingly concerned that power will shift in the next term."

"Your district, it is the most populated, no?"

"Yes, but something is stirring among the districts. A previously unknown representative named Blythe hijacked one of our companies using an old method we didn't foresee."

"This is not good. We do not need any more wasted time. We need results."

"It's not so bad. We need only wait a census, maybe two, before the population will shift back to my district. Blythe's policies are too unstable. His popularity will crumble the moment his funds run out."

"The situation is not what you think. We do not have one census to wait. Our timetable has accelerated."

David heard a rustle of clothing, and he peeked around the corner to see the Armstad man pull a letter from his coat pocket and hand it to the speaker.

"We intercept letter last week from the Berg czar to the Viörn emperor. There is to be union by marriage."

"A union? Who?" Speaker Walker looked shocked as he tore the letter open and scanned its contents. "The Berg prince and the Viörn princess. But this means—"

The stranger nodded. "Yes. It means the countries officially close hostilities between each other. But not between us, we suspect."

"No. One does tend to hold a grudge after you demolish their armadas in a single engagement. When's the marriage?"

"That we still don't know. Soon."

"What about their warships? Any change?"

"They still mass-produce. Berg is stocking airship at a mountain village called Serov. It's along Rorand Mountains. We have lost track of the Viörn fleet. Our spies say they spread out."

"So Berg masses in the north and Viörn in the south, and this marriage means they don't intend to fight each other."

"You see my point, I think. We don't have time to waste."

"No, we don't. ... Damn you, Blythe! You had to have your moment in the sun right before a storm."

"You want I should kill him?"

"No. I don't think we've reached that point yet."

"You haven't reached point. My people are buffer between you and combined forces of two realms. I reach point already."

"The moment we start assassinating our own is the moment when the Alönian political system fails. Who would be left to help you after we finished our own civil war? Corvin, you must give me time."

The Armstadi nodded. "How much you need?"

"All of it."

The stranger, Corvin, sniffed at that. "Just remember, when guns start firing, my brothers and sisters and cousins will be spilling blood so you can work out your petty power struggles."

"Do you think I don't know that? I'm doing my best, but we are not the same Houselands that we were sixty cycles ago. Last time we fought the war on principle, and we won it on cunning. This time when the call comes, I'm not sure we will have what it takes to answer. We don't have an Admiral Ike, and our armada is weak."

"How about tunnel? When will it be completed?"

"Impossible to say. Nobody knows how to drill a tunnel better than our friends in the north, but they don't exactly maintain progress reports."

David patted down his beggar rags, searching for the notepad and pencil he'd brought along. He found it and was scribbling down the pertinent information as fast as he could when he felt a nudge in his side. He raised his hands and turned very slowly, expecting to see a guard with a pistol pressed against his side. What he found was the same droopy-eyed voxil hound sitting on its haunches and nuzzling him, ball in mouth. David dropped his hands and breathed a quiet sigh, holding his chest as his heart pounded. He peeked one eye around the corner at the speaker and his guest just as the blasted hound whimpered. In the middle of exchanging good-byes, the pair looked his way. Corvin whipped out a pair of gas-pistols so fast that David could have sworn they were attached to his hands. David's mind worked furiously as he slowly pulled the side of his face back into the shadows, something made difficult as the dog continued to nudge his side with the ball. Then he had a thought. He plucked the ball from the dog's mouth and tossed it into the neighboring bush. He heard Corvin leap over a hedge and take up a gunning stance on the other side of the corner where David hid. The droopy dog bounded after the ball, climbing through the bushes in hot pursuit. David stood as still as possible. He could hear Corvin breathing on the other side of the wall.

"Not to worry, Corvin," the speaker called out. "It's just Rupert."

David heard Corvin holster his pistols, and he took the opportunity to crouch down behind some bushes. Not a second later Corvin rounded the corner of the house and stepped in front of the bushes where David crouched.

"I nearly put hole in your canine. Perhaps you should use leash."

"That docile beast couldn't hurt a child if it were pulling its tail. All size and no bite, I'm afraid. Come, Rupert, let's see Corvin to his ship."

David watched through his bushes as the dog pranced by, ball in mouth, beside the pair of men. David didn't stir until he heard the odd buzzing of the Armstad stealth vessel dissipate into the distance. Only then did he emerge from his hiding place and scuttle across the estate. Speaker Walker had long since retired in his mansion, and the guards were still conversing at the estate's front gate. He crawled on his belly all the way back to the place where he had dropped over the wall, only to realize he couldn't leave the way he'd come. No vine clung to this side of the wall. He'd have to find another way out of the estate.

He breathed a few times, reminding himself not to panic. He looked around the perimeter of the wall until he saw a viable option. A tallish orchid tree stood a few fathoms down from where he sat, and it had branches that extended over the wall—the only problem being that it stood in the middle of a lawn. If he crouched, he could hide in the evening fog as it churned a few feet off the ground, but once he started climbing, he'd be exposed. David army-crawled across a garden, squishing perennials as he went. He wondered which guard would be reprimanded for trampling the cutting bed. When David reached the lawn, he slid on his belly across the grass, using the fog as a blanket. He arrived at the tree a few moments later. Its many roots sprouted from the trunk and wormed their way across the grass in a chaotic pattern, growing with unparalleled patience. He popped his head through the fog, eyeing the guards. Both were distracted by their discussion, but one would be able to see him climbing if he happened to look in the right direction. David decided he'd have to risk it.

Taking hold of the lowest branch and stepping on a root, he hoisted himself up into the foliage, trying his best to stay on the side of the tree opposite the guards. The orchid tree was in bloom, and its dinner-plate-sized blossoms wafted fragrance around him as he climbed through its bowers. He grimaced with each step along the branches as the supple tree shuddered and shook. He shimmied down the branch that extended to the outside of the estate, metal fingers scoring the wood. It bent at a precarious angle as he slid to the end and dropped over the other side of the perimeter wall. The last thing he saw before the wall obstructed his view was a puzzled guard observing the quivering orchid tree.

David broke into a sprint the moment his feet felt the ground. He didn't stop until the mansion was long out of sight, and even then only because his lungs were burning and his gimpy leg ached. He made his way to the boutique shopping center in the middle of the park and was lucky enough to catch an air-taxi. Its pilot was making one last round before calling it an evening. David jumped into the taxi and stretched out on one of the benches to catch his breath.

During the ride he pondered what he'd overheard, especially the part about a marriage between the royalty of Berg and Viörn. That was impossible, wasn't it? They'd been enemies for more than a hundred cycles. It was just another ploy by Speaker Walker to cement his position. But the Armstad messenger, Corvin—if that was indeed his identity—he was real enough, and he seemed to believe what he was saying, even if he looked and acted like an assassin. Why would he lie? Armstad was still Alönia's greatest ally. Unless he didn't represent Armstad?

He might be a lone faction.

Perhaps David was viewing this whole incident from the wrong angle. What if Speaker Walker and the Armstad assassin weren't spewing false facts, but rather their perception of the facts was built off a false premise. Perhaps they were so ingrained in their political ideology that they couldn't see the truth of the matter.

David cradled his head in his real hand as he pondered on. Speaker Walker and the rest of the Pragmatics complained of Alönia's weakened military state and had been for cycles. Perhaps that was a valid concern once—thirty cycles ago, yes, but now? The Outlanders were all but gone, minus a few Prowlers working as mercenaries obviously. The Bergs and Viörns had been peaceable for the past sixty cycles without a single act of aggression. If they were massing ships near the Armstad border, perhaps they themselves felt threatened. Armstad was the most sophisticated country in all the Fertile Plains, and they boasted a sizeable standing army for their small population. Maybe Berg and Viörn perceived Armstad might as backed by Alönian power. The point was that a Pragmatic would assume the worst when faced with such facts and jump to the conclusion of imminent danger. An Equalist assumed the best in people. An Equalist believed that people's intentions were basically good, even if sometimes misguided. To an Equalist these facts were nothing more than Viörn and Berg making an effort to heal old wounds and rebuild the armadas they'd once boasted.

David sighed. He liked that perspective much better.

The common decency of humanity gave him more comfort than the depraved nature. On the other hand, he wondered how his father and grandfather would view these facts. Speaker Walker's comment about David's grandfather did not go unnoticed. What would the hero of the Protectorate War do in this situation? David knew the answer to that question; he'd heard it a million times while growing up: *Look where no one else is, and you will never be surprised.*

So where was no one else looking?

Chapter Sixteen

MOVEMENT IN THE SHADOWS

It was finished—finally finished. No more trains to the Seventh or expensive taxies to and from Capital Orbital. David had his very own airship transportation facility boasting a nonstop flight from the Third straight to the orbital.

He felt giddy despite the raging Prumuveour Season wind that blasted him as he stepped out of his apartment's steam shaft and into the bustling morning street a full hour later than usual. The new direct flight cut his commute time in half, allowing sixty extra, beautiful minutes of sleep. The prospect was even more welcome considering the past week's all-night antics. As David rounded a corner, he pushed through a crowd of workers walking in the opposite direction—workers, in the Third ... all of them commuting in for their first day at Public Pharmaceuticals. There were thousands of them, all holding their coats closed as the wind ripped at their clothing, and they were only a small percentage of the facility's workforce, the rest being brand-new citizens of Braxton's Third District. The facility itself looked spectacular, not a spot of dust left from the old airsail company. The remodeled factory had a modern twist, with its glass-and-steel dome surrounded by the original structure's brick walls, all washed and sparkling after its facelift. Everything was coming together perfectly.

As David pushed his way past the crowd of workers, he looked up and saw half a dozen shiny, new airships fighting the wind as they soared to and from a couple of glass spires that poked up over the top of the industrial district's decrepit old buildings. When he stepped around the next street corner, he saw it: the transportation facility. It was a crystal palace, all steel and glass. The circular structure had four train lines leading up from four different directions, servicing travelers twenty-four hours a day from all corners of the Third. Each train rolled into a glass station extending off the side of the main airship facility, providing cover for the passengers as they walked to and from airships. The airships docked at one of the thirteen spires poking up from the circular facility. Each tower represented a different house destination, all listed on the great steam projector in the facility's foyer.

David crossed the street to the transportation facility and walked through the gleaming metal doors. While the outside of the place was sparkling steel and glass, the inside featured copper stairs and arches leading to dozens of different steam lifts, each rocketing travelers to the tops of the towers, where they would await airships. The polished metal floor bore David's reflection when he looked at it. He almost felt guilty as he walked on it for fear his shoes were dirty. He scanned the steam projector's daily flight schedule where it sat in the middle of a fountain that he could just hear bubbling over the sound of the busy station. Today, Capital Orbital's *direct* flight left from Tower 4.

David climbed the stairs, running his hand along the cold metal railing. He reached his steam lift and stepped into the glass cylinder alone, having the entire lift to himself. Evidently not many people commuted from the Third to the Capital Orbital—big surprise there. As the glass cylinder rose in its glass tube, he could see the entire inside of the transportation facility before his lift passed through the ceiling, and then he saw the whole industrial district sprawling out in front of him. As he watched, raindrops tapped at the glass with a persistent rattle. It started slow, but this was Prumuveour Season. In no time the large drops seemed to reproduce and multiply into a torrential downpour, washing down the glass steam lift in a consistent stream. David smiled. It was almost like a christening for the new facility.

He walked into the office an hour and a half later, a broad smile on his face. He was so thrilled that he failed to notice the commotion around him until after he'd gulped down a cup of tea and settled into his chair. Mercy caught his eye as she ran back and forth from her desk to the file room, arms full of accounting papers and ledgers. David shook his head and looked around the rest of the office. Bethany sat at her secretarial desk next to Blythe's double doors, matching one list of documents to another. Francisco pushed a dolly bearing boxes of documents out of deep storage, lining them up by date across the carpet.

David wrinkled his nose and asked, "What's all this about? You all look as if we're under investigation."

"Nearly so," Mercy said as she tossed David the morning paper from her desk. "You really should get in the habit of reading the paper if you want to become an expert aide."

David caught the paper and flipped to the front page. His elated mind had a hard time comprehending the grandeur of the main article, but upon the third time reading the title, he understood the general commotion in the office.

CENSUS FRAUD

Citizens of neighboring districts report offers of monetary compensation to register at the Third District in next week's census.

So that was their latest ploy. Only thirteen days until the census and the opposition had apparently decided on one last-ditch effort to thwart Blythe.

David looked back at Mercy, who was just then sifting through another box of documents. "What's being done?" he asked.

"The Census Oversight Committee has ordered us to present our financial records for the past five cycles. They also asked for a list of our primary benefactors and donors, but Blythe is disputing the legality of that request."

"Is that where he is now?"

Mercy nodded as she flipped through an armload of documents and checked them against a list.

David rubbed his face with his palms, stamping down his excitement and preparing himself for a long day's work. "Okay," he said. "Give me the most recent financials. You work from the past forward, and I'll work backward."

"Agreed," Mercy said as she looked up from her ledger.

"Here, pass me that box, Francisco," David said.

Mercy looked relieved as she let out a sigh and put a hand on her chest before she went back to her documents. She appeared unusual this morning, unnerved in the extreme. Evidently this audit was more threatening than David thought.

The work was slow, tedious, and more boring than a conversation with Francisco. In two hours' time David had worked through three boxes, and he was still searching records that he had signed less than two months earlier. However, all work halted when the main office door flew open and then slammed shut. Bethany squeaked as she sat bolt upright, the noise pulling her from her afternoon nap.

Blythe entered the office wringing his hands and growling something under his breath about a "two-faced Oversight Committee" and "soft-handed sops." He paced back and forth, venting steam, until he dropped out of exasperation into an armchair in the middle of the boxes of records.

"How long will these people accuse me of villainy?" Blythe said. "When will I be able to help the needy, feed the hungry, and heal the sick? I've just about had enough of these power-mongering overlords." He leaned back in his chair and closed his eyes, breath whistling between his lips.

"The donors?" Mercy asked.

"We are ordered to produce all political donation records along with names. It's an unquestionably illegal directive, but what can I do? The more I fight it, the more I'm perceived as having something to hide. And in the end disclosing my supporters won't really harm anyone."

"But why would the Oversight Committee want donor records?" Mercy asked. "The campaign office was accused of census fraud, not the donors."

Blythe shook his head. "Only a fool would bribe the populace with his own campaign funds. The committee intends to search the financial records of every one of my donors. Oh, that will include employees. All of your financials will be searched as well."

Mercy stiffened at that, and David knew why. A search of her personal life inevitably meant a search of her parents' lives as well. That was a thread she hadn't tugged in a few cycles. The financial inspection didn't bother David much. It would only take five minutes to sift through a cycle's worth of rent and Charra gruel receipts.

"How long do we have to present the records?" David asked.

"The committee is sending a team down at close of

office tomorrow. We have until then." Blythe sighed again. "Well, we have a long few hours ahead of us. I will start collecting all my personal records. You all should finish with the campaign finances and then begin on our donor lists." He stood and straightened his jacket before walking into his office.

David watched Blythe disappear behind the door before he turned back to his records. Everyone else was already sifting through documents. Even Bethany busied herself turning pages in a folder, though anyone who watched her could tell she wasn't reading a word of them. He made a mental note to check over all the material Bethany reviewed. As the hours flew by, so did the pages of financial records. David worked tirelessly until midday. Blythe was kind enough to order lunch for them all. But after the short respite they were back at it. The only transaction that surprised David was the cost of office supplies. He was shocked how many reams of paper their little office could go through in one month. As the day came to a close, he looked around and saw that only two boxes remained. That meant they would probably finish the campaign transactions today, leaving the donor lists for tomorrow. The knowledge gave him new vigor, and he pulled open a box and began sifting through the files as fast as he could. In thirty minutes he and Mercy had finished, everyone else having retired for the evening.

He slumped down into his chair, knocking his arm against the desk. He watched a few sections of newspaper flutter off the side with dazed eyes. "I'm going to think twice from now on before I make any office transactions," David said with a groan as he bent over to pick up the newspaper pages that had fallen.

Mercy laughed. "Well, maybe you should stop writing everything down and then we wouldn't have nearly as many records." She sat on the edge of her desk and crossed her legs beneath her billowing white dress covered in red flowers.

"Ha-ha," David said in a mocking tone as he glanced through the newspapers he'd knocked off the desk. "At least half of those transactions were ..." But he trailed off as he read the page in his hand.

"Were ... what?" Mercy asked.

But it didn't penetrate his focused mind as he read a short notice. It was out of the same newspaper Mercy had tossed him that very morning, only this notice was in the obituary section, buried behind the countless stories on Blythe and other political or sexual scandals. His jaw hung open and his eyes went wide.

"Hello? ... David, what is it?"

He didn't answer. He re-read the notice and then turned the page to see if there was any more. "Mercy, did you see this?"

"See what? What are you looking at?" Mercy hopped off her desk and walked toward him.

"It's Samantha Samille. ... She's dead."

Mercy froze in place. "What?" She ran the last few paces and leaned over David's chair to read the notice.

David silently read the short notice again, hoping it would penetrate his dulled wits this time:

Ms. Samantha Tori Samille
Lived 3221-3241
Beloved Daughter of Richard and Angelica Samille
May She Rest in Peace

"You're sure that's the same Samantha?" Mercy asked.

"Positive. The first time we met, she filled in her date of birth as this cycle. Never forgot her file after that. I wonder how she died. I'll bet she was murdered."

"David! How can your mind arrive at such vulgar results so quickly?"

"Just think about it. Our last secretary was—"

Mercy held up a hand to cut him off. "I don't want to think about it. I want to go home and soak in a hot bath. I want to unwind after a difficult day. I don't need any more horrifying thoughts to think about right now." She stalked away from David's desk. Her voice sounded choked and her faced looked pained.

"Right. I'm … I'm sorry, Mercy. I just never stop thinking, and this obituary raises too many questions."

Mercy turned away from him as she nodded and collected her coat. "Well, you think on it, then. I'm going home like a normal human being and resting."

She offered him a forced smile before she slipped out of the office, but she didn't fool him. This news was as troubling to her as it was to him. Murder was the only possible reason behind Samantha's death. Two of their secretaries dead within a few months of each other? David fidgeted for a moment before he got up, walked over to Bethany's desk, and keyed up the phonograph. As he dialed the operator, he realized that this was Samantha's old desk. A shudder ran through his spine.

David jumped when the operator spoke and a cheerful woman's voice chirped through the speaker: "How may I direct your call?"

"Yes, could you connect me with Inspector Winston of the Capital City Police?"

"Do you have a first name?"

"Um … yes … it's …" David shuffled through some papers on the desk as he racked his brain. "Um … Kenneth … Inspector Kenneth Winston of the Capital City Police."

"One moment please."

After a few moments the steam projector switched on and the inspector's face shimmered into shape.

"Yes, this is Inspector Winston."

"Inspector, this is David Ike of House Braxton's Third District. I didn't expect to get ahold of you so late."

"Comes with the job, my boy, comes with the job. What can I do for you?"

"I'm calling about a death notice I saw in the newspaper. It reminded me of Paula Carbone's case. Have you had any luck on Paula's murder?"

Winston shook his head. "Not a single lead. I actually filed it away with the cold cases a few days ago while I wait for new evidence."

"I might have just that. Have there been any reports made on behalf of the late Samantha Tori Samille?"

"Um …" Winston moved out of the projection and David heard him shuffle some papers. "I don't have any reports in my office, but it could have been filed with one of the other inspectors. Hold a moment. I'll check with the records office."

The steam image froze as Inspector Winston placed the call on hold. David tapped his fingers on the desk and listened to his stomach growl. He hoped his hunch was wrong, but a feeling told him otherwise. Five minutes later Inspector Winston's image shifted.

"Hello, Mr. Ike?"

"Yes, sir, I'm here."

"You're right. We do have a report on Ms. Samantha Samille."

"What kind of report?"

"A murder report. I'm not sure on the details. Why is it you ask?"

David squeezed his eyes shut as he felt his pulse quicken. "Inspector, she was our secretary after Paula."

"Blessed Maker. I have no note of that here. The investigative team must have missed it. Morons! Information like that could be a breakthrough."

"It actually doesn't surprise me. Samantha only worked here for a few weeks, and she did not leave on the best of terms. As it turns out, she was a political spy. No idea who she was working for, but it makes sense that she would bury any connection to her secretarial position after the scandal."

"Well, I will certainly have a look at the evidence. I appreciate the tip." The inspector looked as though he were about to cut off the call as he looked away.

David stopped him. "Inspector, if I came down there,

might I have a look at the evidence?"

"Oh … well, I don't see why not. Now that there is a viable connection between my case and this one, there shouldn't be any trouble transferring the evidence to me, as my case has seniority. An extra pair of knowledgeable eyes might make a difference." The inspector rubbed his jaw.

"Excellent. I'll be there as soon as I can."

"What, tonight?"

"Sir, the census is less than two weeks away. If there is a connection between the two cases as we suspect, we might not have much time before the killer strikes again. I'm convinced it's a political rival. I just can't figure out who."

"True. I guess that won't be a problem. I didn't plan on going home tonight anyway. I'll have the evidence transferred, and we can look at it together. Ask for my office when you get here."

David ended the call and raced out of the office. He ran straight for the taxi dock and didn't stop to think until he was soaring through the air toward Capital City. If he spent much more money on air-taxies, he wasn't going to have enough for rent. The taxi rustled through the air as wind battered its progress. Prumuveour Season rain tinkled as it struck the airship windscreen. Fifteen minutes later the taxi glided to a stop and docked against an old stone tower. The Capital City Police Department was one of the oldest towers in the city, as demonstrated by its solid-stone core and narrow windows. David paid the pilot and stepped out of the taxi into the pelting rain.

He hurried across the dock—which more resembled a rampart than a skiff dock—and toward the police entrance. Once inside, David shook his head and mopped some of the rain out of his hair. He stepped up to a window and smiled at the receptionist. The room around him was little more than a hall with a door at the end, with one wall a long window looking into a receptionist office. The rotund secretary frowned at David from behind the iron bars and her thick glasses. Her look bespoke a person who, while at work, didn't want to be bothered with any activity that involved the same. David knew her type, as he had met many similar people in the past three months of politics.

"Excuse me," David said, "I'm here to see Inspector Winston."

"Is he expecting you?"

"I believe so."

"Unless he is expecting you, I can't let you back after hours."

"No, he is expecting me. I spoke with him not thirty minutes ago." David kicked himself for his answer. If one were polite in the world of house workers, one would never achieve anything.

The woman sighed and swiveled her chair around to a registrar's switchboard. She keyed in a code and David heard a man's voice answer.

"Were you expecting a visitor? Very well."

She pulled a lever without even looking at David or giving him instruction. One of the doors at the end of the hall clicked, and he had to run to open it before it automatically locked again. He stepped through the door and found a wide stone landing with four circular stone staircases leading up and down from the dim room. He looked around with some confusion, clueless as to which stairway or which direction led to Inspector Winston. He walked up to the first staircase on the right and looked up and down the dusky steps. David was about to explore that set of stairs when he heard the scuff of feet behind him. He turned and saw Inspector Winston walking down the second staircase on the right.

"Ah, Mr. Ike. Good to see you. I see Miranda failed to instruct you. Don't worry, it's not you; she's just like that. On her bad days she gives visitors direction to the prison ward. If you'll follow me, I have all Ms. Samille's evidence waiting for us."

David hobbled after the inspector, shivering as the cold, dreary air blew across his damp clothes. As it happened, they walked down the same stairway that he had considered after entering the foyer. He put his metal hand against the wall of the circular staircase, as there was no handrail. He followed after Inspector Winston, each of their steps echoing around the stone confines even as David's metal fingers scraped along the granite blocks.

They passed three floors before David spoke up. "Isn't there a steam lift?"

"No. This old fortress predates the steam shaft. The police chiefs have always been something of traditionalists and resist any attempts to update. On the one hand, no prisoner has ever escaped this facility, so I can see the reasoning. On the other, all these steps do tend to wear out the knees."

"I see," David said.

He pondered the structure. It seemed the entire tower was constructed of carved stone, an impressive feat to be sure. Later, perhaps far later, someone had added electric lighting, yet only sparingly. As they passed floor after floor, he noticed that the staircase itself had no lights, which meant it was darkest at the middle of their descent between floors and then grew lighter as they approached the next floor. Finally Inspector Winston stepped out of the staircase and into a long stone hallway lined with doors. It was good that he did, as David's weak leg ached from the exertion. They walked down the hall, passing door after door, each bearing a number along the top. They passed number *30* as they rounded a corner and David saw that the hallway extended at least a hundred fathoms into the distance.

David said, "We must be—"

"Underground, yes," Winston said. "The police tower extends much farther down than it does up. Capital Island is an old volcano. Didn't you know? Many of the old buildings were built into the stone crater cycles later, with all the modern edifices covering up the old-world structures. Century upon century of foundations gave the island a flat appearance, though it's rumored that the ancient lava tubes still connect the entire city, but no one has ever proven it. Time does create the best secrets."

David swallowed and looked at the floor's flagstones as they walked down the hallway. "Volcano, huh?"

"Aye … and here we are."

Inspector Winston stopped in front of door *82* and unlocked it. The first thing David noticed was the room's bright light contrasting with the dingy hall. As he stepped inside, he shielded his eyes against the four lights that illuminated the small square room. Not only that, but it was a cold room—very cold. Once his eyes adjusted, he chanced a glance around and froze when he saw the table in the middle of the room. On it lay a woman, every part of her body covered by a white sheet, save her pale face.

"Oh, I guess that would be what the evidence is," David said as he stared at the body.

"Messy business. Poor girl looks like she used to be a beauty." Winston stepped up to the body without a hint of hesitation. He pulled a file from a neighboring desk and ran a finger down the page.

David inched closer to the table and looked at the pasty face poking out of the white sheet. He couldn't see any of the former beauty there, despite what the inspector said. Lifeless eyes peered out of a ghoulish face, bearing no resemblance to the former seductress. Plump lips that were once ruby red looked stiff and blue, her upper one split. Her skin looked odd, blotchy, and pale.

"Well, well. It looks like we have a match," Winston said as he turned a page in the file.

"A match?" David asked.

"Yes, same manner of death as your previous secretary, Ms. Carbone."

"You mean Samantha was … tortured as well?"

Winston gave a short nod. "I'm afraid so … and in the same manner. See these lines." He pointed to some stripes along Samantha's neck. "Strangulation marks. Ms. Carbone had them too, as well as the extensive bludgeoning along the torso."

Winston reached for the white sheet, but David stayed his hand and said, "I'll take the medical examiner's word for it, if it's all the same to you."

"Right. Apologies."

"Which injury was the cause of death?"

Winston puffed out his cheeks as he turned another few pages. "Unknown. It would seem all the injuries contributed."

"So … she was beaten to death?" David grimaced even as he said it. He was no fan of Samantha, but no one deserved to die like that, especially not a woman. Something about it prodded his inner manhood.

Winston replied, "That is the consensus of the examiner."

David tore his eyes away from the face. "Where did they find her?"

"In an alley, much like the alley where they found Ms. Carbone." Winston nodded as he turned pages. "Definitely the same killer."

"Did she have any personal effects with her when they found her?"

"No … just a body in an alley."

David gritted his teeth. What good did it do to know that the same person had killed both women if they weren't any closer to knowing the identity of that person? What did they have to do? Wait until the killer struck again so they could collect more evidence? David felt sure it was the man in the shadows, the same man who had ordered the Prowler attack. However, earlier he had suspected that man in the shadows had also ordered Samantha to seduce Blythe. Had he then ordered her death to tie off loose ends? And what about Paula? Why did he have her killed?

David rested his chin in a hand and thought for a moment. "Does torture mean the killer was trying to get information out of them?"

"Not always, but as a general rule, yes."

"So our political rival theory is still sound. Somebody wants to know what goes on in our office. I wish they'd just walk in and ask. It's all pretty general stuff." David folded his arms and sighed. "How much evidence is there on Paula?"

"A little more, some personal effects, but I inventoried her entire apartment a few weeks back. Even then the evidence was scant. The woman lived a simple life."

"I'd like to see that evidence if I might. It seems to me that if they were tortured ... and if they were tortured in order to gather information ... and if both of them were in a position to know information on the Third, it would follow that there should be some sort of political evidence these women had in their possession. Perhaps I'll see something in the evidence associated with the political office that might not mean anything to you."

"Of course. I'm all ears on this one, but you'll have to give me until at least tomorrow to pull Paula's records from the cold cases."

"Excellent. Give me a call when you have them

available."

The inspector nodded, then gave David a tight smile and shut the file. "Agreed. Anything else while you're here?"

David shook his head, eager to be away from the dead body. Even looking toward the sheet made him feel dirty.

"Very well, then. I'll see you to the door."

David nodded, sparing one last look at Samantha's ruined face before he turned and followed the inspector out the door. It was a somber walk back down the hall and up the stone stairs in the dingy lighting. Inspector Winston held the door for David as he stepped into the harsh rain and ran toward a waiting air-taxi. The evening sky was black as ebony iron, and the thick raindrops made even the closest lights appear as twinkling stars.

"Mr. Ike!" Inspector Winston called from the door just before David entered the back of the taxi. He stepped into the rain and walked up to David, ignoring the drops as they splashed off his shoulders. He looked uneasy as he opened and closed his mouth before he spoke. "It … It might be a good idea to tell the rest of your office staff to be careful until we can sort this out. Two identical murders usually means there'll be a third."

David managed a nod, but as the air-taxi door shut, he felt uneasiness creep across his skin like a shiver. Who would be next? Bethany? Francisco? Maybe Blythe himself. Not Mercy. Absolutely not Mercy. *Merciful Jeshua, please not Mercy.*

Chapter Seventeen

THE BUTCHER'S BILL

"Tortured?" Mercy said in a hushed whisper as she and David stood in the corner of the office at the refreshment station.

"Same as Paula," David said, nodding as he handed her a cup of tea. "They were ... beaten to death."

Mercy set her tea down and stared at David for a long moment. Then she looked away, putting one hand over her mouth and stirring her tea with the other.

"Mercy, listen to me," David said, daring to put a hand on her shoulder. "They tortured them because they wanted information from them—information from this political office. I know you think my *man in the shadows* is a crazy fantasy, but these murders aren't. Someone is killing our office staff, and they will continue to do so until they get what they want. Why they chose our secretaries, I don't know, but they will only get more brash as the census approaches. Do you understand what I'm saying?

You need to be careful."

Mercy didn't look up from her tea. She continued to stir long after what was necessary. "I understand," she said, still not looking up. "Thank you for telling me."

"Good. Will you warn Francisco? I need to tell Bethany, but I'm not sure how. I feel like whatever I tell her falls out of her head."

Mercy nodded with a snort. "I'll tell them both. Francisco is my assistant, and I think Bethany might take it better from another woman."

"True. And what about Mr. Blythe? Should I tell him?"

Mercy picked up her tea with both hands, probably for fear that her nervousness would make her spill. She took a sip as she watched Blythe's door. "No. There are already some security measures in place to keep him safe. Telling him will only make him worry, especially since he and Samantha were … involved with each other. He doesn't need that right now."

David nodded, also looking toward the crack under Blythe's office door. Even now he could see the shadow of the man pacing across the room. A lot rested on the representative's shoulders, the future of Braxton House for starters. Even a strong man could only take so much.

"Well," Mercy said with a huff. "As if we didn't have enough to worry about this morning. How about those political contribution records? Are you ready to dive in?"

"Absolutely. I love a good audit."

They walked back across the office toward their desks. Francisco had already moved a good portion of the records from storage into the middle of the room—business donations on the right and nonprofit on the left. Bethany sat at her desk, hard at work on some daydream as her head moved back and forth following Blythe's shadow.

"How about I take the nonprofits and you take the businesses?" Mercy said. "We can record the names and donations in two lists. No need to give the auditors any more information than that. This order is illegal enough as it is."

"Sounds good to me." David grabbed the top box from the business stacks and sat down at his desk, ready for another long day. But before he could start, a deep sigh from across the room interrupted him.

Bethany looked up from her doodling and groaned. "This is so boring," she said.

Everyone in the room paused what they were doing and looked up. David bit his lip to hold back a laugh.

"Bethany, why don't you see about ordering us all lunch?" Mercy said in a motherly tone. "We will probably be at this all day."

Bethany rolled her head around like she was stretching and then flopped down on her desk. She spoke from beneath a mess of hair, asking, "What do we want to eat?"

David worked through the boxes at a good pace, though he was a little distracted waiting for Inspector Winston's call to tell him Paula's evidence was in, but as time wore on, he fell into a rhythm. He'd open a box, pull out a file, write the business name from the file on a ledger, and move on to the next file. This same repetitive procedure continued for hours, but just before lunch a name passed David's desk that he recognized. David had just opened a business file titled *Braxton Industrial Investments*. He penned the name in his ledger and was about to move on to the next file when he saw the name of the business manager: Lloyd Bentsen. David paused in his work. He knew that name, but where had he heard it before? Then it hit him: Lloyd Bentsen had a card on David's wall at home. That was the first man Blythe had introduced David to on his first day of work. It was the man Blythe had been speaking with in his office when Paula gave David a tour. The business gave a sizeable donation—twenty thousand sterling—and right about the time that the construction of Public Pharmaceuticals and the transportation facility was announced.

David puzzled over the information. The Third's industrial sector was not exactly the most profitable area. Where did Bentsen get twenty thousand sterling to blow on a campaign donation? However, it might not have been Bentsen who donated the money. He was the manager of Braxton Industrial Investments, but that didn't necessarily mean he was the owner of the company. David wrote the information down on a scrap of paper and was just about to call Braxton's office of business organizations when a knock came at the office door and then a deliveryman entered with everyone's lunch.

David was famished and decided to leave the question until later. He put the scrap of paper in his top drawer and walked over to collect his lunch. Bethany had of course confused everyone's orders and each sandwich was a hodgepodge. David got Mercy's bread with Francisco's meat and Blythe's tubers. Nobody said anything. It wouldn't do any good.

After lunch the group, minus Bethany, was back at it. They worked for another few hours, finally finishing at a few minutes before close of business. It was well that they did, for the audit team arrived not five minutes later. David and Mercy presented the donor lists: businesses in one, nonprofits in the other, and individuals in a third.

After the audit team left, everyone was too tired to celebrate a job well done. Blythe left the moment the team did. He hadn't been very talkative since the last accusation. Francisco escorted Bethany home at Mercy's request—per David's instructions—and then it was just David and Mercy left in the office.

"Can I escort you home?" David asked.

"Is that concern I hear, David?" Mercy said as she slipped her red coat on and pulled her flowing hair from the folds in the fabric. She turned around and gave David a mischievous smile.

David blushed and looked down. "Maybe a little. I'd hate to see anything happen to you."

Mercy's smile softened into an expression David had never seen before, or at least not for a long time. It was the same expression his mother used to wear whenever his father paid her a compliment, or helped her with her coat, or took her hand when she stepped out of an airship. David didn't quite know what it meant, but seeing it on Mercy made him feel warm inside, like he'd just drank an entire bottle of spiced wine.

Mercy said, "I'm walking straight to the air-taxi dock, flying directly to my apartment, taking a hot bath, and then going to bed. Now tell me, apart from staying with me, which I will not allow, what could you do but sleep on my porch in the rain?"

David blushed even more as he walked to the door of the office and opened it for her. "I'd do it if it meant you were safe."

Mercy smiled. She walked right up to David and gave him a peck on his cheek. "I'll be fine, David. You should get some sleep. All this work will get you sick if you're not keeping up on your rest. Good night. I'll see you in the morning."

She walked out the office door. David watched the way she went long after she had disappeared around the corner. Finally he shut the door and walked over to get his coat. For a moment he considered waiting a few more minutes in case Inspector Winston called about Paula's evidence, but in the end he decided to take Mercy's advice and catch up on some sleep. With the new airship facility he was able to get home in half the usual time and was in bed only a few minutes after dark.

The next morning, he walked into the office feeling more rested than he had in weeks. He was the first one there, so he set about making a pot of tea. Twenty minutes later he heard the door open and turned with a smile, expecting to see Mercy. It was Francisco, and David felt very silly as he stood there grinning at the stoic man.

"Um, fancy a cup of tea?" he asked as Francisco held the door for Bethany.

"Yes please," Bethany said as she walked by Francisco and sat at her desk.

David made them each a cup of tea and then took up residence at his desk, reading the morning newspaper he'd picked up on the way to work. He'd been caught off guard twice now because he hadn't kept a careful watch on the news, particularly the *Voxil Tribunal*. He wasn't going to let that happen again.

An hour later, after Blythe arrived, David put down his paper and wondered why Mercy hadn't arrived yet. He checked the clock. She was forty minutes late, far past due for a girl who was always early. He drummed his fingers on his desk. Why did she have to be late the day after he'd told her to be careful and basically to not get murdered? He sighed and resolved that she must be taking a little extra time this morning due to the past few days of hard work, that was all. She couldn't be early every day, after all. She deserved a late start.

David meandered over to the refreshment station and poured himself another cup of tea. He sipped it, too preoccupied to care that it had gone cold. Walking back toward his desk, he put a hand in his pocket. Bethany still sat at her desk, sound asleep with her head down and hair sprawled out on the desk. Francisco read his newspaper with his good eye, his mechanical one following David as he moved across the room. David grimaced and walked a little quicker. He paused at his desk and idly pushed some papers around.

"Odd, don't you think—Mercy being late?" David asked Francisco.

The man only grunted in reply.

"I mean, in all the months we've worked here, has she ever been late?"

Francisco sighed and let his paper fall to the desk. He stared at David with both of his eyes before making an eloquent reply: "No."

David ignored Francisco's apathetic manner and started to pace back and forth across the office. Images of Mercy lying on a table in a cold room came unbidden to his mind. He shook them from his head. He was being paranoid. She was fine. She was perfectly fine. He paced for another thirty minutes before he had a thought.

"Bethany? ... Bethany!" David said, louder the second time.

The girl shot up in bewilderment, her light blonde hair a mess of static and loose strands.

"Yes? Who—I mean, what do you want?"

"I need Mercy's file. It should be in your desk."

Bethany huffed and pulled open her drawers one at a time, far too slowly for David's mood.

"Top left drawer, Bethany. No, your other left—the top one. Oh, let me do it!"

David scooted Bethany's chair away from the desk, along with the girl on it, and pulled open the correct drawer. He slid out a stack of files and dropped them on the desk, sifting through them and knocking several of them onto the floor. He found Mercy's file and flipped it open to the contact information she had filled out along with her application. David grabbed Bethany's phonograph and slid it across the files, but as he prepared to key up the operator, he realized that Mercy had left the phonograph section blank.

David gritted his teeth and resumed his pacing, ignoring the pouting look Bethany was sending him. No matter what he did, images of Mercy pale and lifeless returned to his mind and the pacing only made it worse. He couldn't take it anymore. What if she needed help? What if they were torturing her this very moment? He turned and ran to Bethany's desk, snatching up Mercy's file. Ripping her address page from the folder, he let the rest fall to the floor as he ran from the office without even shutting the main door.

When he arrived at the orbital taxi station, he didn't bother waiting in the line. David pushed and shoved to the front, knocking a lad down as the glass doors opened. David heard some commotion behind him, but he didn't care as he hopped into the first taxi he saw. He read off the address from the scrap of paper he still held in his hand and told the taxi driver it was an emergency.

The driver placated David with a vigorous nod and then proceeded to fly at the same pace as every other pilot. David tapped his foot the entire flight, clenching and unclenching his fists. By the time the taxi bumped to a halt as it docked, the piece of paper bearing Mercy's contact information was nothing more than a crinkled wad. David hopped out of the taxi and threw a handful of coins at the driver. The driver yelled a few expletives as

David raced across the balcony. Only then did David realize where he was: Château Fleur, the nicest apartment tower in Capital City. It stood at the very center of the residential district, with gardens built into the side of the structure, dangling down to the levels below like a hanging paradise. This was the top apartment in the tower, the most expensive of the lot, arguably the most expensive in the city.

David skidded to a stop in the middle of the porch and checked his raging emotions. Was he overreacting? He was about to barge into Mercy's apartment uninvited. If anyone saw him doing it, he'd be arrested before he could jump off the balcony. But the image of Mercy lying on a table still hovered at the back of his mind, and he pressed forward. David stepped around lush greenery and fragrant orchids, picking his way toward a brass door with frosted glass. When he reached it, David lifted his hand and knocked, but before he could knock again, the door swung open. It had already been unlatched.

David stood for a moment at the doorway, hand still raised mid-knock, gazing into the dark apartment. He called for Mercy, but no reply came. The scoring along the doorframe did not escape his notice. He stepped into the apartment and gaped at the white marble floors and plush rugs. The white walls reached eight fathoms high before they curved into coffered ceilings. Gold-and-crystal chandeliers reached down and sent their sparkles around the room, reflecting the light coming through the open door. A sickly sweet smell hung in the air, and the scent of it made David's heart race. He walked farther into the glamorous abode, looking around at furniture that appeared unused. The marble countertops still had the manufactured sheen. He followed a dark hallway with doors on either side. A broken vase lay on the floor beside a crooked console table. The door across from the broken vase stood open. He inched forward. He called Mercy's name again, to no avail. The apartment was so quiet that he could hear himself breathing. He reached the open door and looked in. The room held a sprawling bed, but the bedclothes were in a heap on one side. The rest of the room décor lay strewn about, some of it broken. However, that wasn't what brought tears to his eyes.

Blood coated the bed and the carpet, even some of the walls. It looked like someone had handed a toddler a bucket of red paint and sent him in to play. David stumbled into the room, throwing caution to the wind. He shouted Mercy's name as he spun around searching. He ran into the conjoining closet—nothing. He ran back, knocking dresses off hangers in his haste, and threw open the bathroom door. There he froze in place, choking off a sob. On the floor, wrapped in a bloody nightgown, lay a body with flowing auburn hair arrayed in a tangled mess. David dropped to his knees and rolled the body over.

It was Mercy.

David gasped for breath as he clutched the body—his eyes disbelieving what he saw, but his hands forcing the truth into his mind as they held the bloody figure. He called her name a few more times, but it was a different kind of call, more of a keening. He sobbed into her silky red hair. It still smelled of her floral perfume. He buried his face in her neck as he held her close. She couldn't be dead. He had seen her just yesterday. She was fine. She was alive and beautiful, full of life and intelligence. But as his face rested against her neck, her cold, pallid skin told him the truth. There was no life here, no more laughter or sarcasm, no more sweet words or small kisses—only cold, unfeeling flesh.

It was some time before the sobs stopped, before his eyes dried out and the tears stopped flowing. He laid the limp body back onto the floor and arranged the limbs in a proper fashion. Then he sat back against the washroom vanity and stared at the body. Fresh bruises puckered the face and strangulation marks striped the neck. The part that David found strange—at least the portion of his mind that wasn't filled with grief—was the bloody stab wound along the torso. That was something new.

David sat there for a long time, or perhaps it was only a minute or two. He couldn't tell, but his senses returned when he vaguely heard some commotion somewhere in the apartment. A moment later a man in a dark suit spun around the corner into the washroom and pointed a pistol at David.

"Show me your hands, lad," the man said.

David turned his head slowly toward the man, tears staining his cheeks. He lifted his hands in a gesture of surrender. A moment later two other men in dark suits entered the washroom and hauled David to his feet. David let them drag him into the hallway, where they laid him down on his face and cuffed his hands behind his back. He didn't care that the blood on his clothes soaked into the thick white carpet. One of the men searched him, but all he came up with was a crumpled wad of paper bearing Mercy's address.

After a few moments a team of men entered the apartment. Unlike the first men, they wore white lab coats and walked straight back into the bedroom. A few minutes later they scooted across the floor as they carried out a long bag—a body bag ... Mercy's body bag.

"Is this the man?" someone asked.

"Yes, sir. I flew him here not thirty minutes ago. He told me it was an emergency. Didn't think much of it at the time, but now ..."

"Right. You may go."

After a moment someone grasped David's hands and uncuffed them. Then two men lifted him to his feet and led him to the living room he'd passed on his way back to the bedroom. A man sat there, penciling down some notes on a pad, and David assumed him to be a police inspector.

He looked up at David and offered a sympathizing smile. "Have a seat, son. If you're feeling up to it, I'd like to ask you some questions."

David sat on the couch across from the inspector. He sank several more inches into the cushion than he had anticipated. It made him feel uneasy and trapped, so he scooted forward and perched on the edge of the cushion.

"You knew Ms. Lorraine?" the inspector asked.

"Yes, sir."

"How?"

His questions were quick, but not insensitive. He spoke in a manner that made it clear he wanted to get this over with as fast as possible, yet still emphasizing significance.

"We were both aides for House Braxton's Third District."

"You arrived here this morning in a rush. Were you concerned for Ms. Lorraine?"

"Yes. There have been two other murders of our office staff, and when she didn't arrive at the office this morning, I presumed the worst."

"And when you arrived, you found the … scene … as it was when I entered."

"The door was already open when I got here. I rolled the body over, but that was it."

"I'm guessing you held it for a while as well." The inspector pointed with his pencil at the red stains on David's coat.

David looked down at his clothes for a moment, and then he realized the implications of the questions. "Yes—yes, but I didn't kill her, if that's what you mean. We were … close."

"I know you didn't kill her."

David frowned. "But …"

"I just wanted to hear you say it. That body has been dead for at least a couple of hours. The taxi pilot said he brought you here less than an hour ago. Unless you were here last night as well …" The inspector paused and gave David a look. "… then you did not kill Ms. Lorraine."

David shook his head. "I didn't even know where she

lived until I looked it up in her file this morning."

The inspector nodded and made a note. "You mentioned other murders?"

"Paula Carbone and Samantha Samille, previous secretaries for the political office. Inspector Winston is on those cases, and I've talked to him about them. I'm sure he will want to see the evidence of this case as well, given that Mercy was … killed in mostly the same fashion." David swallowed hard.

The inspector opened his mouth to ask another question, but shut it again and made a note.

"How did you get here so fast?" David asked, just now realizing the strangeness of the circumstances. "Did someone from our office call?"

"No." The inspector paused for a moment as he took a breath and held his mouth open, poised to speak. "I am not an inspector with the Homicide Division. I'm not even with the Capital City Police. I'm the inspector dispatched by the Census Oversight Committee."

"What? Why would that bring you here?"

"The committee did an audit on Ms. Lorraine's finances. Several thousand sterling were transferred from her accounts to a shell company in the Third. That money was then doled out to bribe citizens outside the Third into registering inside the Third in next week's census."

David stared at the inspector for a long moment, a thousand thoughts spinning in his addled mind, but one forced itself into words: "And then she was murdered."

The inspector looked at David before nodding. David leaned over, rested his head in his hands, and let out a long, shaking breath. It made sense in a way. Mercy had said many times before that she would do anything to unseat Speaker Walker. Evidently that included committing a house crime. But she wasn't an idiot. If she were going to commit a crime, she wouldn't be so obvious about it.

"Officer, why don't you see this lad home?" David heard the inspector say.

Someone rested a hand on David's shoulder, and David stood and followed after a police officer. He felt unusually tired, like he had just run a ten-grandfathom race … and lost. He hardly remembered the ride back to the Third in the orbital gunship, a ride he would have otherwise enjoyed. All David could think about was Mercy's bloody, ruined body. He had fretted over this possibility for days, and yet he had still let it happen.

Chapter Eighteen

WHERE NOBODY ELSE LOOKED

Observing the death of a close acquaintance would affect different people in different ways: pain, fatigue, emptiness, longing, even guilt. Observing multiple deaths of loved ones would only compound those emotions with each additional loss. Losing a father, a grandfather, and 90 percent of a mother in the space of a month would crush most people, no matter their strength. To add the death of the woman you loved on top of the original loss would leave a man, any man, in emotional tatters. That's how David felt. Every good person in his life had died a tragic death or wasted away in silence. First his father, then his grandfather, and his mother would join them soon. Now Mercy. Was he so lethal? It seemed just being near him caused death.

How high and mighty he had been when he told Mercy all about his manner of dealing with grief. Counting blessings had worked before, but there was something different about this death. He'd known it was coming. It was within his power to prevent. Why didn't he go with Mercy that night? He would have gladly slept on her balcony in the rain for the rest of his life if it meant he'd get to see her alive each morning.

Why hadn't he been able to solve this ludicrous mystery and find this man in the shadows? The answers were there; he just couldn't see them. These and other thoughts flowed through David's head as he sat in his apartment facing his wall of questions. Mercy's death had broken him. He'd seen a glimmer of hope in her, a type of hope he had not felt in a long time, and to have it snuffed out before his very eyes had crushed him. He sat for days in front of that wall, wondering, wishing, yet always, always thinking. On the one hand, he wanted desperately to find Mercy's killer. He wanted to inflict pain—torturous pain. But on the other hand, would it bring her back? Why continue to slave away at a job other people were actually paid to do? He was not an inspector. He was an aide … a lowly, underpaid aide. But the question mark on his wall would not go away, and if there was something David couldn't leave alone, it was unanswered questions. The question gnawed at his mind—an itch he couldn't scratch. He'd spoken it out loud so many times, it rang in his ears: Who was the man in the shadows?

David had a vague impression that today was important. Yes, today was census day. At sundown tonight the Houselands would confirm a speaker for the next three cycles. More than likely, according to David's math, it would be Blythe. It should be cause for celebration, but the moment was not all he'd imagined it to be. At some point in the last few months, David's hopes and desires had altered. His future projection of himself had shifted. While before he hoped to someday be a powerful aide or even a representative himself, meeting Mercy had changed all that. Family—he wanted family now more than anything else.

But as he sat, desperate for the strength to go on yet incapable of summoning it, something happened—something powerful, something that happened every day in Alönia, but only seen on the rare occasions when the rain clouds parted. The sun rose. Golden rays stabbed through the storm clouds and filled David's apartment with glorious light. It tugged on him, calling him, driving him away from his sullen mood and toward the window. David placed a hand against the glass and closed his eyes as the sunshine bathed his face. It wasn't a normal kind of light. Normal light couldn't melt a heart of stone, warm the chill of sadness, or soothe the sting of loss. It was a deep kind of light—the kind of light that made someone realize how big the Fertile Plains were … the kind of light that made problems seem small and possibilities endless. This light always left David feeling the exact same way, and thinking the exact same thing: *Jeshua is real and working.*

David leaned his head against the window, leftover rain sliding down one side and his tears the other. In the distance he could hear bells calling the people to Sanctuary, bells that he had ignored for a long time. He'd have to reconcile that void in his life, and soon. But for now, he was still alive, and regardless of how he felt, there was work for him to do yet. He took a deep breath and prepared himself to face the day—just today. He'd worry about tomorrow when it arrived. After a quick bite to eat, he washed, dressed in his tattered suit, kissed his mother good-bye, and walked to the airship transportation facility. An hour and a half later, he stepped into the Third District office, which was completely empty.

David turned a few times in the middle of the room, looking at the empty desks. He even checked Blythe's office—after knocking, obviously. He was a full hour late and still the first one to arrive? Not likely. Evidently census day didn't pose many duties and Blythe had closed the office. David considered leaving right then, but something stopped him. He'd avoided looking at it since he'd entered, but no longer. David walked over to Mercy's desk, and after a moment's hesitation he sat in her chair. He pushed past the thoughts of never seeing her again and asked himself a question that had been bothering him for some time: *Why had the killer chosen her?* If it was a political rival and they wanted information, why hadn't they chosen him? Paula he could understand; she was the most senior employee at the office. Samantha also made sense as a target, as it was public knowledge that she and Blythe were having an affair. Pillow talk had a way of transferring *delicate* information. But the next obvious target was him, not Mercy. He had the mastermind behind Blythe's interception of Public Pharmaceuticals. He had been there during Blythe's grand speech—he and nobody else. So why Mercy?

As much as it felt wrong, David started rummaging around in Mercy's desk. Somehow she had discovered something. Somehow she had positioned herself as a prime target. David opened the drawers on the right and found several months' worth of newspapers all categorized in chronological order. A few of them had markings and comments, but nothing of particular note. He sniffed away some tears as he remembered her advice about newspapers. The drawers on the left contained nothing more than office supplies and a few articles of makeup. David shut the drawers, doing his best to leave everything exactly the way he'd found it.

He eyed the top of the desk and found only a few things: a couple of ledgers from the audit and a few loose folders. The ledgers left a sour taste in David's mouth. Two straight days of counting donors was enough for a lifetime. He made a cursory scan of the documents, rifling through them like somebody's trash. There was nothing there, just a list of nonprofit organizations. David dropped them on the desk and slouched in the chair, breathing a long, slow breath. His eyes fell into a blank stare, taking in the desk as a whole. What was it that Mercy had discovered? David just had to be missing something.

He frowned. One of the ledgers he'd dropped back on the desk had some markings on it. Mercy had circled one of the names: AIR Fund. The circle didn't mean much to him, as he often circled names to mark his spot, but perhaps this was something more. He scanned the rest of the document and saw plenty of checkmarks but no other circles.

AIR Fund? What in the Fertile Plains is that? … And they donated almost a hundred thousand sterling? That was the largest donation he had ever seen—a fortune. No wonder she had circled it.

He stood and walked back into the file room to look for the corresponding box Mercy had listed on the ledger. He switched the light on since the door had a nasty habit of shutting by itself. He picked through the files until he found the nonprofit. Opening the file, he began to read silently:

AIR Fund: Airship Injury Recovery Fund
Establishment: Swollock Season, 3241
Stated Purpose: To assist those injured in airship accidents
Designated Beneficiaries: Those injured by airships
Manager: Lloyd Bentsen

"Lloyd Bentsen again?" David said, his words dampened by the stuffy file room. First Braxton Industrial Investments and now the AIR Fund.

He scanned the rest of the folder, but there was nothing else of note. He shut the file and slid the box back onto the shelf with a thud. He turned to walk out of the file room, but as he did so, the door swung open and an enormous man pointed a hand cannon at him, a revolver so large that any other man would need to hold it with two hands. David froze and looked at the man—his black eyes and scruffy face … and his coat could probably fit three of David.

On instinct David put his hands up. This was it; they'd finally come for him. The man backed out of the doorway and waved the massive barrel of his revolver out into the room, directing David to follow suit. David walked slow but thought fast. The others had been tortured first. If it were up to David, he'd rather be shot than beaten to death. Perhaps if he lunged at the man right as he passed him, he might be able to grab the gun. He'd have to be very fast. He felt a bead of sweat roll down his back as his heart rate increased. Another three steps and he'd tackle the brute.

"David? What on earth are you doing in there?"

David looked up from the thug with the hand cannon and saw a very perplexed Blythe standing in the middle of the office with another enormous man beside him, this one shouldering a compact gas rifle, though other weapons were clearly visible on his person.

"Mr. Blythe? ... I ... I was just looking up some records, sir." David looked back at the man with the gun and raised his eyebrows. "These friends of yours?"

"Oh for goodness' sake, put the gun down, Gerald," Blythe said, waving a hand in frustration. "Come on out of there, David. Where on earth have you been? We've been worried sick."

"I needed a little time for ... you know, to recover," David said, looking at his shoes.

Blythe nodded. "Mercy's death was a shock to us all. After we found out, I gave the rest of the staff—rather, *what's left* of the staff, time off until the census was over."

David nodded and moved to the middle of the room,

still eyeing the two giant men. "And your companions?"

"Oh, well, matters being what they are, I decided a little extra security wouldn't go amiss."

David nodded, only now feeling comfortable enough to relax. "I'm sorry I was away so long. I was the one that … found Mercy. It was quite messy. I just … needed …"

"David, it's quite alright. You've been working like a dog these past few months. Even if Mercy hadn't passed on, I would have told you to take the time off regardless." Blythe put a hand on David's shoulder. "I'm where I am now because of you. The cost along the way has been greater than expected, but our victory today will set many wrongs right."

David nodded and wiped away an unbidden tear. "I know."

Blythe clapped David on the shoulder. "Good man. You should go home, son. We aren't doing anything today."

"What? And miss your appointment as speaker? I wouldn't miss that for the world."

Blythe smiled. "Well then, I guess I'll see you at tonight's Assembly," he said as he turned and walked toward his office. "No sense in being here, though. I just came by to collect my wallet."

"I won't stay long," David called after Blythe as the representative rummaged around in his office. "I'm just checking Mercy's desk to see if I can find out why they killed her."

"Oh?" Blythe said, returning from his office. "I'm not sure if you've heard or not, but as it turns out, Mercy was the one who funded the census fraud. The Oversight Committee told me the day after she died."

"Yes, I was there when the Oversight Committee arrived at her place."

"Well, given that, isn't it obvious why they killed her?"

David shook his head. "I just can't help but think it's more complicated than that."

Blythe nodded as he put on his coat. "Well, don't stress yourself over it too much. Remember, nothing you do will bring her back. Speaking of stress, how is your mother doing?"

"Fine. Same as always."

"Good, I hope those checks are helping. I wish there were more, but times being as they are, people just aren't interested in giving to the poor." Blythe sighed. "Well, I'm off. See you tonight."

"Oh, before you leave, there's something I wanted to ask you about. On my first day at the Third, you were meeting with a man—a Bentsen," David said.

"Yes, Lloyd ... wonderful fellow. What about him?"

"I was wondering what exactly it is he does. During the donor audit I found his name associated with both a nonprofit and an investment company. Between the two he donated almost 120,000 sterling."

"Well, he's a businessman ... a damned good one too. Probably one of the wealthiest men I know."

"I see. Thanks," David said as Blythe walked toward the door with his two oversized bodyguards.

"Don't mention it. Until tonight."

The door shut, and David walked back to his desk,

puzzling over Mercy's circling of the nonprofit and wondering if it was just chance that her circle coincided with his own notation on Bentsen. As David shouldered his coat on, Bethany's phonograph whistled, pulling David out of his reveries.

Technically the office was closed and he didn't have to answer the phonograph. But as it continued to whistle, David gave in. He walked over to the device and keyed it on. After a moment the steam projector formed into Inspector Winston.

"Mr. Ike? Finally! I've been trying to reach you for over a week. What happened? Did the whole office go on holiday at the same time?"

"No, um … I'm so sorry, Inspector. I've been unwell, and the office shut down after last week's murder."

"What murder?"

"Well, I assumed you knew about it. One of our aides was killed last week. You actually met her the day you came into the office—the girl with the auburn hair."

"Half-witted records office! Another murder associated with my case and I'm the last person to hear about it. Well, maybe I can order that evidence while you go through Paula's evidence." Winston's face moved out of the projection as he mumbled to himself.

"Actually, Inspector, if it's all the same to you, I'll just review Paula's evidence. You see, I was the one who found Mercy's body."

"Oh. Never mind, then. You still want to see the other evidence, though?"

"Yes. Is it available? I can leave right now."

"Had it drug up from cold cases a few days ago," Winston said. "I'll wait for you here, then."

The steam projector dissipated. Evidently Inspector Winston wasn't in a chatty mood. David walked through the orbital toward the air-taxi landing. The whole orbital was abuzz with news agencies and reporters in anticipation of the census, and David had to squeeze through more than one crowd of people. After an uneventful taxi ride, David walked into the Capital City Police Department foyer. Miranda was not at her seat, and David knocked on the glass for a full five minutes before the portly woman waddled into her reception room. After an additional few minutes of cajoling and insisting he had an appointment, Miranda finally let David inside.

Moments later Inspector Winston was leading him down the cold stone stairway, through considerably more people than he'd seen the last time, and toward an evidence room. This room was different than the one David had visited before. For one, there was no dead body … and the room was a decent temperature. Stone walls enclosed a moderate but not well-lit room. It was small, with only two chairs and a table. Half a dozen boxes lay to one side. Inspector Winston motioned to one of the chairs and David had a seat.

"You go ahead and work through the evidence," Winston said. "I'm having a spot of bad luck locating that most recent murder you mentioned. Mercy, wasn't it?"

"Mercy Lorraine—um, Mercedes Eleanor Alexandra Lorraine, actually. Everyone called her Mercy."

Winston touched his head where a hat would be and walked back out of the room. David lifted the first box and removed the lid. One glance at the titles on the folders inside, and the lid was back on. He didn't need to see any autopsy photographs. However, before he slid the box off the desk, he decided the medical examiner's report couldn't hurt. He slipped that folder out and perused it. It was Samantha all over again, and Mercy too. Strangulation marks around the neck, blunt force trauma to face, head, and torso. However, Mercy was the only one who had a stab wound. David shut the file as images of Mercy's mutilated body flashed back into his mind. He slid the folder to the end of the desk and lifted another box onto the table.

This box contained numbered photographs detailing Paula's apartment. The only thing it told David was that Paula must have made considerably more sterling than he did. Blush carpets matched soft couches in an artistic color scheme. As he closed up that box and slid it aside, Inspector Winston returned.

"Nope. No entries under that name either. I swear, sometimes I think they do this on purpose."

"Strange," David said, "I even told the other inspector you were investigating a series of murders associated with Mercy's. Would it make a difference if he was an inspector with the Census Oversight Committee?"

Winston frowned and gave a short nod. "Some. That might explain why the evidence is late in arriving, but still—a whole bloody week? Incompetence. You see anything interesting?"

"No. Well, actually, I did notice that Paula and Samantha didn't have any stab wounds. Mercy did."

"You're sure?"

David looked down. "Positive."

"Hm. Well, that can mean a variety of things. Usually it means the murderer got what he wanted and ended the … inquiry, as it were."

"Maybe," David said, gritting his teeth. "I wish I knew what it was he wanted to know from Mercy. I knew more than she did about the campaign. Why didn't they come after me?"

"Who knows? Could have been something she discovered recently."

"Exactly …" David said, a thought dawning on him. "You don't happen to have any business records here, do you? Or nonprofit?"

"No. Civil records are kept in the building across the street. We do have a direct line there, though, and they answer all our questions."

"Would it be too much trouble to do a record search on a name?"

"Not at all. What's the name?"

"Lloyd Bentsen. I know he has some affiliation with the AIR Fund and Braxton Industrial Investments."

"A-I-R?" Winston asked as he jotted the name down on a notepad.

"That's right."

"Shouldn't be any trouble. I'll just be a moment while you look through those other boxes."

As the door rattled shut, David slid another box onto

the table. It contained every book and scrap of paper with any sort of writing on it from Paula's apartment. David spent some extra time on this box. He read everything—every grocery list, every budget ledger, everything. One thing that struck him as odd was the amount and regularity of her grocery lists. What it must be like to live with plenty. Toward the end of the box he found a little notebook, no larger than a wallet. Most pages contained addresses, but one held some interesting figures:

Site Property: 40,000 Sterling—2,000,000 Sterling
Industrial Dance Club: 18,000 Sterling—90,000 Sterling
Lousy Lodgings: 700,000 Sterling—1,400,000 Sterling
Industrial Power Station: 45,000 Sterling—250,000 Sterling
6 x Vacant Buildings: 35,000 Sterling Each—200,000 Sterling Each

David stared at the list. Why was Linden Lodgings on some booklet in Paula's apartment? And the numbers? Those could only mean property values. Had they really increased that much? How had Paula known that? More importantly, why would she want to know that? David set the booklet aside, intending to come back to it. He rifled through the rest of the papers, only finding one other scrap of any curiosity, a small note bearing no address or greeting:

A divorce would ruin me, and you cannot offer me enough to justify the loss. Are you not happy with what we have?

Perhaps that was the reason for the extra food: Paula

had a lover. David put the note back in the box and slid it aside, moving on to the last two boxes. They bore a collection of all of Paula's personal effects. She didn't have much: a few articles of jewelry, some perfume, and a few purses with their contents. He rifled through the items without much confidence, but then he noticed a silver broach Paula had worn. Actually she'd always worn it; he'd never seen her wear anything else. It was a simple spiral of silver, identical on both sides. David leaned back in his chair and twirled the broach in his fingers. If she always wore the broach, it evidently had some meaning. Yet she possessed other articles of jewelry that were prettier and more expensive. Why the broach? A gift, perhaps?

But as he thought about it, Inspector Winston pushed the door open and walked in with a large notepad containing a lot of scribbles. David realized he'd been in there for hours and not even noticed.

"Any luck?" the inspector asked as he handed David a cup of tea.

"There are some interesting figures in the back of that address book. If I'm right, they represent the increased value of the Third's industrial district before and after the announced move of Public Pharmaceuticals."

"Now how did you figure they are all buildings from the Third? Those names could be anywhere."

"Not Lousy Lodgings. That's where I live. Its real name is Linden Lodgings, but everyone calls it Lousy. This was pretty interesting too," David said as he took a sip of his tea and held up the note about the divorce. "It seems Paula had a lover."

"Ah, that's what I thought too. The problem is, there is absolutely no record of him anywhere. Not the faintest idea who he is."

"I think this broach will tell us that." David held up the silver spiral.

Winston blanched. "What's so special about that?"

"Nothing, and that's just the point. She always wore it. Clearly it meant something to her. Could be a gift from a lover, don't you think?"

"Possibly. Still, not a lot to go on."

David nodded. "I'll have to think on it. What about our Mr. Bentsen?"

"Ah yes," Winston said as he held up his notepad. "Sorry it took so long. The records were privatized, and it took some doing. Made a few calls on him, though, and this is what I got. He isn't an investor at all, or a businessman—not even that wealthy. He's Blythe's manager."

David furrowed his brow and shook his head. "Manager?"

"That's right. Blythe is actually a well-to-do businessman as well as a successful representative—quite a man. All those donations were actually donations from Blythe to his own campaign."

"What? No … not all of them. What about the hundred thousand sterling from AIR Fund?"

Winston looked down at his notes. "Let's see. Blythe is the sole board member of AIR, which is also managed by Bentsen."

David paused, trying to process this strange twist. "That's odd. I read the bio of that nonprofit, and it said it was for victims of airship crashes."

"I think I have that here too. ... Yes. Established on the twenty-sixth day of Swollock Season for the support of victims of airship crashes."

David choked on some of his tea and looked at Winston. "What? Did you say the twenty-sixth day of Swollock Season?"

"That's right."

David's mouth fell open. That was the very same day he had received a letter from Linden Lodgings, increasing rent. That was the same day Blythe had established a nonprofit for his mother's benefit, a nonprofit for others similarly situated.

He blinked and tried to think of what this meant, then asked, "How much money has AIR received since its inception?"

"Um ... just over a hundred thousand sterling."

"And all of that was donated to the campaign?"

"All but five hundred sterling, yes."

David looked at the inspector before putting his head in his hands. "No. No, no, no, no."

"That's not uncommon," Winston said as David moaned. "Nonprofits donate funds to other nonprofits all the time. The campaign office is a nonprofit itself."

David shook his head. "You don't understand. My mother and I were injured in an airship accident," he said, head still in his hands. "My mother more so than me. She's fully paralyzed. Blythe established that nonprofit for the benefit of my mother and others like her. To date we've only seen enough sterling to pay a nurse part-time, but not enough for any treatment. Now I find out he's been using the nonprofit to fund his own campaign. He's using my mother." David rested his hands on the table and looked at Winston. "He's using me."

"Oh dear. That would chill the working relationship."

"I want to see the rest of his properties. What else does Blythe own?"

"I have the addresses here." Winston turned a few pages on his notepad and handed it to David.

After looking at the pad for a moment, David pointed to one of the addresses and said, "That's Linden Lodgings! He owns that? You're sure?"

Winston shrugged. "That's what the records office told me. Copied it down myself."

David clenched his teeth, then grunted. "That greedy bastard! He doubled rent, knowing I lived there, and then swooped in to save the day. He probably had the entire thing planned. Called up his own manager and chewed him out about rent he himself RAISED!" He slammed a fist down on the table.

"Beg pardon?" Winston said, looking a little uncomfortable as a silence drew out. "I'm not sure I follow."

David gazed down at the desk and took a long breath. His eyes focused on Paula's booklet. "Wait! Wait a minute." He fumbled for the booklet and turned to the rest of properties she'd listed. He lifted Inspector Winston's list of addresses and compared the two. "I need a map, Inspector—a map of the Third's industrial district."

A few minutes later and both of them were hunched over a map of the Third District.

"There—110 Industrial Road. That's Linden Lodgings," David said. He marked the map with a pen and checked the address off on both the inspector's list and Paula's list. "... and 111 Industrial Road is the power plant. It's right next door. Let's see now—55 Braxton Boulevard." David marked another place on the map. "That's the local dance club." David checked the buildings off the two lists and looked at the others. "These six addresses here must be the *Vacant Buildings* on Paula's list. I know where this one is. It's right next to the train station." David put a mark at the corner of 23rd Street and Grand Road as well as the other five addresses.

"But what about the *Site Property?*" David said as he tapped the pen to his lips while scanning the map. "Oh blessed Maker." He stabbed the pen down onto a point in the map. "That's the new transportation facility! That must be the site property. Blythe owns that? ... If so, then he owns most of the industrial district. Paula didn't know the half of it."

David threw down his pen and looked at the rest of the addresses on Inspector Winston's list. There were three times as many as Paula had in her booklet. "He condemned Linden Airsail so he wouldn't have to sacrifice any of his own property, and now he's increased his own net worth tenfold."

David stood up, shoving his chair back, and then

paced in the cramped room. A sick feeling welled up inside him—the feeling that a selfish monster had used him to do his dirty work … and now he was going to be speaker! David felt his face heat with anger as he clenched his fists, but he grunted with pain when something bit into his palm. He was still holding the silver broach in his hand and he'd squeezed so hard that it left a spiral print in his skin. David held it up by the chain to his eye, examining it closer. He saw a uniform seam around the outside of the spiral—a locket, then. David pulled on either side, but the small knot of metal wouldn't budge. He looked at the locket again, eyeing the spiral pattern and wondering if it was really that easy. He grasped either side of the seam and turned counterclockwise. The spiral broach swiveled and clicked. He pulled the two sides of the locket open and held them up to the light. Both sides bore engravings. On the left was *WJB,* and on the right, *IV.*

David stared at the engraving, knowing what it meant but disbelieving what it entailed. He'd been fooled. He'd been completely fooled by a mastermind: William Jefferson Blythe IV.

Chapter Nineteen

THE MATTER OF THE SPEAKERSHIP

"I'm an idiot!" David said as he whirled around and grabbed his coat from the back of the chair. He was so furious that his arm missed the sleeve three times.

"What? What did you find?" Inspector Winston asked.

David held up the open locket and said, "*WJB IV*— William Jefferson Blythe IV."

He stomped across the small room, threw open the door, and ran as best he could for the stairs.

"Wait!" the inspector called from behind David. "Where are you going?"

"What time is it?"

Winston checked his pocket watch as he hurried after David. "A few ticks before five. Why?"

"I lost track of time. Hopefully I can still make it," David said as he climbed the stairs as fast as he dared.

"Make it where?" Winston said, following him up.

341

David stopped on the landing outside the department foyer and turned to face Inspector Winston. "To Capital Orbital. Someone needs to warn the Assembly that they are about to nominate a murderer to the speakership."

David pulled the door open and ran out of the department, leaving Inspector Winston gaping after him.

As he sat in an air-taxi, bobbing along in the fierce wind, David cursed himself. There was unusual air traffic clogging the skies in anticipation of the census. More than a few airships collided in the congestion, and everyone now flew with an abundance of caution. David tapped his foot in agitation. How could he have been so stupid? It was so obvious now; he'd just been looking the wrong way. He'd been looking for a man in the shadows when the true enemy—the common factor among the murders and the beneficiary of mass financial fraud—was right in front of him.

He'd helped this man! No, he'd *made* this man! He'd swallowed the caring politician routine like a sky fish with a lure.

Lowering my rent when he himself had raised it! Setting up a nonprofit on behalf of my mother and only distributing half a percent of the funds, absorbing the rest into his campaign. Condemning land from an honest businessman in the name of a public purpose. David shook his head. *The bastard only wanted to raise the value of his own property! What's worse, he owned vacant property. What was wrong with using those buildings for Public Pharmaceuticals?*

But all this paled in comparison to murder …

Blythe and Paula had been lovers, probably for cycles

prior to David's aideship. The locket proved that. She knew more about Blythe than anyone else, perhaps even his own wife. She knew her position was tenuous, so she recorded all of Blythe's dirty secrets in her little book. Then Blythe had an unexpected rise to power after his grand speech, and she wanted marriage. She knew grandeur was coming, and she was tired of being the mistress. She wanted a position of prominence, not one of shame. He refused her, and then she died. Now that David thought about it, it was obvious why: she'd tried to blackmail him. She'd told him what she knew and her willingness to take it to his rivals. That's when he had her killed … but why the torture? David pursed his lips. Perhaps Blythe wanted to know if she'd already sold the information? Or maybe he wanted to know who her buyers were. Either way, he'd killed her, and to all the Fertile Plains their secret relationship never even existed, save for the locket.

But a man with a thirst for lust couldn't long avoid the vice. He turned to Samantha, trading Paula for the newer, younger model. Samantha proved unfaithful from the beginning. She had ulterior motives, even more so than Paula. She was a spy. David pounded a fist against his forehead, realizing that when he'd exposed her motives, he'd all but sentenced her to death. After the news agencies cooled off, Blythe had tracked her down and beaten her for information about her backers—beaten her to death just as he'd done with Paula. David wondered if Blythe had paid someone to do the dirty deeds or if he'd done them himself.

David sighed. That left Mercy.

He gripped the taxi's leather bench so hard that his metal fingers ripped through the leather. Heat flushed his cheeks as he ground his teeth. Mercy must have uncovered the truth about Blythe's financial dealings, and he tried to drown the truth in a river of her blood. Blythe didn't need information from her; he'd killed her and then disguised the stabbing by mutilating her body, hoping to cast all three murders as torture by a political rival. It was Blythe who had paid for the census fraud through Mercy's accounts ... all to make it look like a violent political rivalry!

David felt sick with fury. He'd elevated Blythe with careful political strategy to the highest position in the Houselands. He should have let the *Voxil Tribunal* destroy him. He should have let the Prowlers capture him. He should ...

David paused in his own personal tirade. He was still missing something. Blythe was certainly the monster in the closet, but he wasn't the man in the shadows. Someone had still ordered the other events, the Prowler attack, the newspaper stories, Samille. Perhaps Speaker Walker, but that was too obvious a choice. There was someone in the background fighting against Blythe. Someone, it seemed, that Blythe knew about ... and was willing to kill to discover the identity of. If the man in the shadows did indeed exist, and he stood opposed to Blythe, then David still needed to find him, but for completely different reasons. He might not wholly agree with the man in the shadows, but he couldn't be any worse than Blythe.

David roused from his reflections as the air-taxi bumped into the orbital dock. He paid the pilot with his last few sterlings and ran for the orbital entrance. The halls were even more packed than when he'd left, as this census marked the first credible threat to Speaker Walker in many cycles. Clearly the Assembly gallery had overflowed into the halls. Even as David pushed his way through the people, he heard the final tally echo through the megaphones along the hallway:

"The census ranks House Braxton's Third District as the most populous district in the Houselands. This census calls for a new speaker."

The people in the hallway cheered so loudly that David had to cover his ears.

"Will Representative Blythe please approach the speaker's dais and accept the speaker's oath."

David broke into a run, disregarding decorum and shoving people out of his way. He heard several curses as he knocked men and women to the floor, but he didn't care. He had to stop that oath. As he ran, he heard the Assembly's cheering crackle through the megaphones. That was good. The longer they cheered, the longer he had. He pushed his way up to the second level of the orbital and toward the Assembly foyer. The closer he got, the thicker the crowd—and the more obstinate. David yelled for people to move, but they hardly noticed him. He squeezed between them, but these were people who still thought they had a chance at entering the gallery. As he pushed, they pushed back, eager to hold their places in line. He was in danger of starting a riot. David switched tactics.

He held up his aide ID and called for people to move. "I'm Mr. Blythe's aide and this is an emergency."

It helped, but only a little. As he reached the foyer, he noticed an additional security checkpoint. He pushed ahead the last few fathoms and held his ID up to a guard, panting as he did so. Then he heard it, the beginning of the oath: *"I, William Jefferson Blythe IV ..."*

The security guard squinted at the ID and scowled. "David Ike, huh? I've let thousands of you in. How do I know this ain't a fake? If you were really an aide for Representative Blythe, you would have been here hours ago."

David paused and heard, *"... swear to faithfully fulfill the role of house speaker."*

"Uh," David said, "I had pressing business in the city for Mr. Blythe. Please, sir! The orbital guard stamped my ID. What more do you need?"

"... to guard the sanctity of the Houselands from acts both foreign and domestic."

The guard smiled at David. "I'll bet you'll be in a world of trouble for being late." He handed the ID badge back to David and opened the temporary gate.

"... to provide for the needs of the people by moderating the will of the Assembly."

As David ran across the foyer, he heard the sound of the oath morph into the actual sound of Blythe's voice. The first time David had run across this foyer, the sun illuminated the entire room, filling David with hope. That was the first time he'd met Mercy—the first time he'd felt hopeful in four long cycles. Now darkness reclaimed the expanse as night settled over Alönia. No moon glimmered in the sky—no reminder of the sun that would rise the next morning.

"... *to uphold the House Rules in accordance with magistrate opinion, I do so swear.*"

David ran down the dark hall and burst into the Assembly to the railing that overlooked the egg-shaped room. He arrived at the very moment Blythe spoke the last word of the oath. David opened his mouth to stop the proceeding, but as he filled his lungs with breath, the auditorium erupted into a thunderous applause and his shout dissipated into the din as if he hadn't said anything at all. He yelled a few more times, but to anyone around him he looked like every other ecstatic bystander. He looked up at the speaker's dais and saw Blythe take the podium. He was too late. Blythe was speaker, and any accusation against him had to be filed through the appropriate channels in accordance with House Rules. David clamped his fists, still holding Paula's locket. He wasn't sure what to do. By habit he walked up the stairs and sat in his seat in the Third District balcony even as the rest of the auditorium quieted down in anticipation of Blythe's acceptance speech.

"My fellow Alönians," Blythe began, "today's census has marked a new beginning. With high hopes and brave hearts, the Alönian people have made their will known by packing up and moving to a place of change."

The crowd cut Blythe off with more thunderous

applause, only quieting when he patted the air in exasperation.

"This census is a clarion call for the Houselands. A call for change from the ways of fear and defense. A call from the peoples of Alönia to view the Fertile Plains as they are: peaceful and friendly. A call to restore balance to our Houselands and opportunity to our people, to empower the poor with the means to live a normal life. For too long we have ignored these problems. We must convert our economy from one of hoarding to one of giving. And perhaps most importantly of all, we must bring our people together like never before. We must create a place where everyone counts equally. Are we not Equalists?"

Blythe lifted his hands in the air, and the auditorium thundered again.

"I want to begin this speakership by thanking the people who made it what it is. First, my friends. I need not list you all one by one; you know who you are. You have supported me all the way. I want to thank my staff. Francisco and Bethany—they came to the Third in our time of need and have been invaluable in their efforts. I also want to take this time to remember those who gave their lives along the way."

The auditorium gasped at that.

"Paula Carbone was murdered a few months back, and Ms. Mercy Lorraine, who died just last week, also murdered."

A murmur arose around the room as Blythe paused to wipe away some tears. David frowned, noting that he skipped mention of Samantha Samille.

"I know not who took their lives, but I make a vow here and now that I will find their murderers and make them pay for their horrific crimes." Blythe punctuated this last sentence by jabbing his finger toward the crowd.

David restrained himself from jumping up and calling Blythe a liar. The depravity of it all was a disgrace of the highest order. As Blythe continued with his speech, David festered and fumed. He had to do something, but what was there to do? Blythe was now the most powerful man in the Houselands, lacking both morals and conscience. What good would an inquiry do? David's mind drifted to his father's old revolver. He could do it. He could smuggle the pistol past the guards and pull the trigger before anyone was the wiser.

"I want to thank the people of the Third District. You stood by me in the hard times. You believed in me even when we were failing. Our time has come. Our suffering has ended and our hope finds rest today!"

It was a long time before the crowd stilled and allowed Blythe to continue, the echo of their cheering in time with the throb of David's heart.

"There is one more person I want to thank," Blythe went on. "He is the real person you should be celebrating tonight … a man born and raised in the Third. He lived among us for cycles, yet none of us knew his worth. He scrounged and worked in poverty until he broke free of society's shackles and earned an aideship."

David felt silent screams gnawing at the back of his throat. His stomach churned with anger and regret, forging into solid lumps of guilt.

"I saw potential when I met him, and he did not prove me wrong. I saw his heart, and I knew he was a man in line with my own interests. He reminded me of why I fight for the Third and the prosperity of Alönia's forgotten. Within a week he had shocked this entire Assembly and orchestrated the first steps that led to my rise. I stand here because of this man. I stand here because of the tireless efforts of my aide, David Ike."

Blythe stopped and pointed a finger up at David as he sat in the balcony—and it felt like a knife in his heart, every word an accusation.

"David, stand and be recognized."

The auditorium rumbled its approval and every eye looked toward David as he stood. He gritted his teeth and put on his best smile, waving as though he enjoyed the attention. For the first time David felt like a real politician: fake. All these people, all these sycophants ... if only they knew the truth. How many of them already did? He looked around at all the representatives and aides, but the gallery drew his attention.

He was up there somewhere—the man in the shadows ... once David's enemy but now the only hope for Alönia. At last the applause died down, and David seated himself as Blythe resumed his speech.

David had a thought then. Every eye in the Assembly was on Blythe, but David was willing to bet there was one exception. Blythe had just named David as the mastermind behind his sudden rise. If the man in the shadows was in the gallery, and if he was as much of an enemy of Blythe as David suspected, then David figured he was at this very moment watching David, not Blythe. There were a lot of *ifs* in his line of reasoning, but at the moment a slim chance was all he had.

David pulled a pen and scrap of paper from a cupboard in front of his chair. He made a note on the paper and opened the copy of *House Law* on the desk in front of him. He slid the note inside the pages and pushed the book into the middle of the desk. It was a risk. If anyone else found that note, he might find himself the victim of some very gruesome torture. As casually as he could, David looked around his box as Blythe reached the crescendo of his acceptance speech. Everyone looked ecstatic, eyes forward and smiles broad. None of them seemed to have taken notice of his little note.

"I accept tonight the responsibility that you have given me to be the leader of these fine Houselands. I accept it with a full heart and a joyous spirit. But I ask you to be Alönians again, to be willing to give your share, to start assuming responsibility beyond the finances of your own home, not only in looking out for yourselves, but in looking out for all Alönians. We need a new spirit of community in the Houselands, a sense of equality and balance. If we have no sense of equality, the Alönian dream will wither away in war and quarrelling. Our destiny is bound up in the happiness of every Alönian. We rise or fall together. That is my message. Join me in the new utopia. Join me in the end of poverty and the beginning of prosperity. Follow me into the next era of peace."

Blythe raised his hands with the final words of his

speech as if reaching for the stars. David covered his ears as the Assembly Room shook with exultation, but Blythe only smiled as he basked in his newfound power.

That was the trouble: the people loved him. David had spent most of the last three seasons making it so. Removing the man would mean riots. Accusing him of murder would mean riots. Opposing him would mean riots. David grimaced.

How much of the populace still even recognized what it meant to be Alönian? How many still remembered David's grandfather and all the things he'd stood for? What percentage were wholly deceived? Until very recently David was among that group—ignorant, oblivious, and happy for it. How easily he had believed the monologue of *share and share alike*. What it really meant was: *Share with me, and I will bleed you dry of your hard-earned wealth and syphon it into my own pockets. And when I'm done, everyone will be equally poor—save me.*

The people continued to cheer as Blythe left the speaker's dais and joined David back at the Third's booth. Tonight would be the last time Blythe would grace it for at least three cycles. David smiled at Blythe and shook his hand, doing his best not to think about Mercy's bloody body as he did so. He would maintain the status quo … for now. But as soon as he got his chance, David would tear the man down from his pedestal of lies.

Blythe smiled back at David and waved to the people as they continued to cheer and then come and greet Blythe and David personally. It continued like that for another forty minutes before all the people, hoarse-voiced, found their way out of the auditorium. A great many of the representatives had even stopped by the Third's booth to shake hands with the new speaker and tell him they'd *always* supported him. David had to bite his lip to keep from laughing at the spectacle: one liar lying to another.

After everyone had left, Blythe leaned against the booth's desk and said, "David, we did a good thing today. I feel hope again, more so than ever before."

David smiled. "I think a lot of people believe in you. Evidently they feel hope as well."

"Ah yes, my boy!" Blythe said.

He wrapped an arm around David's shoulders and led him out of the box and down the stairs to the foyer. The great window there looked blacker than ever to David. He wondered if it might suck him out into the expanse with the rest of the light.

"Great things are coming, David. Did you hear them in there? I could hardly finish my speech. There is a movement, and I am at the forefront. Make no mistake: I will change the Fertile Plains." He sighed and gave David's shoulders one last squeeze. "Well, I best let you go. I know you have a mother who needs you. But tell me, how is she, really?"

David bit his lip, hoping it concealed his fury in an expression of concern. *She's the same she has been for the past four cycles. The doctors say she will not recover. She will die. I just don't know when.* But he said none of that: "She's the same, sir."

"I'm going to take a personal interest in your mother,

David. I've helped as much as I could in the past few months, but now that I'm speaker, I'm going to give her the attention she deserves. Trust me, she will lack nothing in my hands."

David swallowed hard. He wondered exactly what Blythe meant by those words. Every time before when Blythe had asked, it felt hopeful and loving. Now it felt like blackmail, a prison he couldn't escape. Was it a threat, or was David overreacting? Did Blythe know what he had been up to these past few hours? The truth was, David could not survive without Blythe. His mother would die in an instant unless he could find help somewhere else. If Blythe did know of David's secret investigation, then David was dead and his mother not long after. If he didn't know, then David had to keep it that way.

David put on an emotional face, looking up at Blythe with admiration and respect. "You are too kind, *Speaker* Blythe."

EPILOGUE

It wasn't terrible; it just wasn't what it once was. Blonde was so different, striking in another kind of way. It shimmered in sunbeams and sparkled in moonlight. It certainly demanded attention, not because it was any prettier, simply because others couldn't ignore it—like a black spot on a white sheet. And blue eyes ... silver-blue eyes the color of the sky on a clear sunlit morning. Blue eyes looked deceptive and untrustworthy. That would make things more difficult. Perhaps the hair would compensate.

She tossed her hair as she looked at her reflection in the polished metal door, combing it with her hands, first pulling it back and then forward, trying to see if there was anything familiar about it. It was so very odd to look at herself and see a stranger. She sighed and replaced the golden hairpin. Drawing up her shoulders, she summoned all the elegance she possessed and knocked on the door. It swung open an instant later and she strode in, her royal-blue dress swishing across the floor with each step.

Light poured in from three sides of the square room through tasteful, old-fashioned windows. Clouds drifted by at a lazy pace, curling and churning into indifferent shapes, uncaring of the storm approaching. The man himself stood at the far end of the room, looking out the window of his magnificent airship at the city below. A few others sat at the carved table in the room—all familiar faces to her.

The man turned and looked at her, his eyebrows furrowed. "Back from the dead, I see. Blonde suits you well. Your brother is a good teacher." He nodded to himself as he appraised her new look. "I'll miss the red, though. It brought out the fire in your personality. ... Have a seat."

He gestured to a leather armchair on the far end of the table, and she sat there.

The man walked back to the window and observed the clouds for a long time before he spoke again. "It was a cunning plan, a grand effort, but I'm afraid we were too late. We now find ourselves in a precarious position. We burned one of our most valuable assets—an asset two cycles in the making. Blythe now sits in the highest seat in the Houselands, and he has the popular support of the masses. We can't even assassinate him, not with his new security measures—and not without a riot. It will take turmoil to remove him, and given the current state of the Fertile Plains, that is something Alönia cannot afford." He sighed. "David failed us."

"David did not fail us," she said from her seat.

He looked at her. "You saw him. He sucked up that

applause like a sea sponge, smiling and waving like a good little aide."

She shook her head. "I saw so much more than that. I saw a man in turmoil … a man conflicted. And while the rest of you were glued to Blythe and his utopian speech, I watched David." She pulled a small scrap of parchment from a fold in her skirts and held it up for all to see. "He wrote this right after Blythe recognized him during the acceptance speech, then slipped it into a copy of *House Law* and left it on the desk." She smoothed the paper and read the message aloud: *"I know the truth now, and I'm ready to meet."*

She looked up from the parchment at the various people around the table. "He knew we would be watching. Luckily I was."

"Mm, that's all well and good, but perhaps you should look around," the man said. "You are fixated on this boy, but we have a war on our hands. We are mere seasons away from the greatest threat Alönia has ever seen and you want to put your hope in a lowly aide?"

She let out a clipped sigh. "Don't you see? He is so much more than that. He's Speaker Blythe's aide, and he has his absolute trust."

The man shook his head and turned back to his window, but she continued, "He knows the truth now—maybe not all of it, but enough to see Blythe for what he really is. You burned an asset, true, but you gained a better one. Mercy was only ever a pretty face to Blythe—a woman he hoped might one day be persuaded to join his entourage. David is ten times more than that. You heard

Blythe's speech. He believes David to be a mastermind, and now we know he is willing to be *our* mastermind."

"But it doesn't matter anymore. Blythe is speaker for the next three cycles, and by the end of that time there won't be enough Alönia left to muster against our enemies."

"Three seasons ago, would you have believed that a no-name—Representative William Blythe—could rise up and steal the speakership from right beneath our noses? David did that in his first week as an aide. How much do you think he is capable of if we give him our support?"

The man didn't answer as he looked out his window, but she could tell he was thinking on it, so she pressed on, "The people longed for a hero, and right now they think that hero is Blythe. If you take away their hero, they will rip the Houselands apart. But if you tear down their hero and show them a better one, you will win their loyalty forever. Right now they have hope in the wrong man. You can't win them over by fighting against their hope. Their hope must fail, and when it does, we must be ready to replace it with real hope."

"And you think David is their hope?" The man frowned. "You think this lad is a hero?"

She nodded. "I know he is. You said it yourself: as the last living heir of the Ike legend, he is capable of unifying the people like no one else. He is a born hero."

The man continued to look out the window, his hands fidgeting behind his back. Another airship drifted by—a warship bristling with armaments.

She knew that he was on the edge. He wanted to

believe, so she brought her case to a close: "It's time to bring him in. It's our only play left."

The man turned away from the window and looked at her, his eyes focused, peering straight through her latest façade and into her soul.

"You'd better be right, Mercy."

THE END

FROM THE AUTHOR

I love writing fiction, but more than that, I want you to love my fiction. Write a review and help me improve my craft. If you are looking for updates on future books or just want to chat, contact me through my website at

sashaffer.com

S.A. Shaffer

Made in the USA
Middletown, DE
06 November 2023

42070358R00217